SOPHIE'S SUMMER KISS

Debbie Viggiano

This one is for the children, Rob, Ellie and Rianna,

with much love.

Chapter One

I stared in disbelief at the private Instagram message.

Congratulations on your engagement. Clearly you are unaware that your fiancé is a cheater! From a well-wisher.

What on earth?

I sat down heavily on the edge of my bed and, for a moment, stared blankly at the carpet. The sender of that message couldn't possibly be talking about George. Not *my* George. Not George with the waistline that bore testament to his love of steak-and-kidney puddings. Not George who had recently taken to doing a comb-over to hide his ever-expanding bald patch. I mean, well, George was George. George Baker. Not George Clooney.

My fiancé wasn't around to see the message, having left for work five minutes earlier. My immediate instinct was to search George's belongings for clues but, unfortunately, I was sitting on the bed at my house, not his. Nor were there any of George's belongings under my roof. Not even a toothbrush. He always came to my place fully prepared, having previously neatly packed his stuff in an overnight bag. His holdall arrived with him, and it left with him.

Neither of us had ever got around to giving each other a key to our respective homes and, in truth, I was secretly pleased about that. I told myself that it kept things fresh between us. That it was more fun to have the anticipation of George staying in my bed once or twice a week or, alternatively, me going over to his place to snuggle up in his vast custom-made bed. However, after we were married, the plan was for me to permanently move in with George, and for my place to be rented out.

I tried not to think about making the transition to George's modern detached house in nearby Kings Hill. It had been tastefully decorated throughout in white and dove grey but – if truth be told – I found it a little cold and depressing. I much preferred the rather hectic colour scheme at Catkin Cottage with its multi-jewelled rugs and bright throws. However, right now, our spare key situation meant I was unable to let myself into George's place for a sneaky look around.

I tore my gaze away from the Axminster and gazed once again at the phone in my hand. The mystery messenger was called *Thomas*. A tabby cat featured as the profile picture. Neither meant anything to me.

I clicked on the name. Immediately, a notification flashed up. *This account is private*. A quick look at Thomas's posts revealed nothing had ever been uploaded, and he – or she – had no followers. Also, Thomas was following just one person. Presumably me.

I took a deep breath, then exhaled gustily, aware that my stomach muscles felt tense and knotted. A sane, sensible part of my brain clamoured to be heard.

This message is nonsense. Utter rubbish. Click off it now!

2

Shakily, I swiped my mobile's screen, then went straight to my list of contacts. I should've known my best friend's number off by heart considering how often we spoke to each other, but thanks to digital life this wasn't the case. My bestie answered on the third ring.

'Sue!' I gasped.

'Soph,' she chirped. 'You sound tense. Surely half past seven on a Thursday morning is a little early to be so fraught. What's up?'

'Sorry, but' – I stood up and began pacing the bedroom – 'I've received a weird message via social media, and it's unsettled me.'

'Don't tell me' – I sensed Sue at the other end of the connection, blue eyes narrowing as she concentrated, one hand raking her blonde hair – 'a rich overseas prince wants to deposit a billion pounds in your bank account, then pay you a vast sum of cash by way of reward but only if you help with his money laundering.'

'Nothing like that,' I said, pausing by the window.

I yanked the catch and pushed against the wooden frame, savouring the rush of sweet air as I gazed at the fields beyond the garden hedge. The pasture was full of cows. Oh, look! Overnight, another calf had been born. I gazed at the tiny creature in awe. Another miracle of Mother Nature in this new month of June. Despite the early hour, cornflower-blue skies were promising a day of warm sunshine. The heady scent of honeysuckle wafted through the open window, tickling my nostrils.

'How many guesses do I get?' Sue prompted.

I turned my back on the bucolic scene and resumed my pacing.

'None,' I said, chewing my lip, willing the anxiety to go away.

'Then spill the beans and make it quick, or Charlie will be after me. He'll want to know why I'm still starkers in the bathroom and not downstairs frying his eggs and bacon. Bloody man. All he thinks about is his belly. When it comes to food, he's more insatiable than–'

There was the sound of a door opening. In the background I heard Sue's husband asking if she'd finished with the shower.

'Oh, er, yes, darling. You go ahead. I'm just on the phone to Sophie.'

'Morning, Sophie,' Charlie called.

'Tell him I said hi,' I said to Sue.

'Sophie says hello too,' Sue repeated.

'Tell her I don't know what you girlies find to talk about so early in the morning.'

'Did you hear that?' said Sue, a grin in her voice.

'I did, and give him my love.'

'Sophie sends her love,' Sue told Charlie.

'And tell her I send all love back but now' – there was a shooing sound – 'I'd like the smallest room in the house to myself, without Sophie overhearing any rampant trumpeting. A man likes to oversee his ablutions without being overheard, so out you go, dear wife. Be off with you. Go cook my breakfast.'

'I'm going, I'm going,' Sue assured. A second later came

4

the sound of a door closing and a bolt being drawn. My bestie tutted theatrically. 'Talk to me while I throw on my dressing gown and get myself downstairs. I'll have my shower after Charlie has left for work and the house is quiet. So, come on, Soph. What's this message all about?'

I glanced at the bedside clock. The big hand seemed to be galloping through its upward sweep reminding that I, too, should be getting ready for work, not gassing to my mate.

'The message said that George is playing away.'

There was a pause at the other end of the line, and I could almost visualise Sue doing some rapid blinking.

'*What* did you just say?'

'You heard. Someone called Thomas – with a profile picture of a tabby cat – messaged me to inform I was betrothed to a cheater.'

'That's insane. Find the message and read it to me properly.'

'Just a minute.' I swiped the screen, then tapped the Instagram icon. 'Oh, I don't believe it.'

'What now?'

'It's gone.'

'The message?'

'Yes, it's disappeared.'

'The author must have unsent it. Tell me exactly what it said.'

'I can't remember now. Not precisely. But the gist was' – I screwed up my face trying to recall the words – 'congratulations on my upcoming nuptials, and was I aware that George was an unfaithful bastard?' My voice rose an

5

octave as I said those last two words.

'Calm down, Soph. Look, listen to me. This is George we're talking about, right?'

'Obviously.'

'Exactly, and George wouldn't do that.'

'How do you know?' I wailed.

'Now, don't be offended. I know George is your fiancé and you think the sun shines out of his briefcase, and that he runs a thriving stationery company that recently flogged a trillion paperclips to WH Smith–'

'Are you insinuating that George is boring?' I interrupted.

'I asked you not to be offended.'

Now it was my turn to rake a hand through my hair.

'Okay, no offence taken.'

'I mean, who, in their right mind, wants to have a fling with George?' Sue asked.

My jaw dropped.

'Well *I'm* having a flipping fling with George,' I said indignantly.

'No, you're not,' said Sue quickly. 'You're having a *relationship* with him. That's totally different. A fling is' – she paused to consider, no doubt her thought processes swiftly back-peddling – 'something tacky. And George isn't tacky,' she added loyally.

'No, he's not tacky, just boring,' I said sarcastically.

'I thought you said you weren't offended? Listen to me, Soph. Let's start again. George is reliable. Okay? *Reliable.*'

'Do you think?' I whispered, collapsing down on the bed

again. 'Oh God, Sue. What if Thomas Tabby Cat is telling the truth?'

A background clattering momentarily had me holding the phone away from my ear. Sue was banging pans about as she set to work cooking Charlie's breakfast.

'I think you're getting worked up over nothing,' she said staunchly.

'I'm not so sure. Wouldn't you be unnerved by such a message? After all, I'm marrying George this Saturday. That's forty-eight hours away.'

'Don't you see what this is?' said Sue in exasperation. 'It's a troll. Some jealous saddo with nothing better to do than pour a bucket of cold water on a betrothed woman's happiness. Like many people who use social media, you wanted to share your joy with a pic of your beautiful engagement ring, and some nasty little prat has zoomed in on you, hoping to spoil things.'

I fiddled with a hole in my dressing gown. Sue's words held some truth.

Here I was. Fifty-year-old Sophie Fairfax. One failed marriage already behind her. Then finally – *finally* – I'd found a guy who'd asked me to marry him, who'd sealed the deal by whisking me off to Hatton Garden for a ring. I'd been so delighted. So ecstatic.

Once home, I'd snapped away with my mobile's camera. There had been one of me beaming away, long dark hair falling in waves, brown eyes sparkling with excitement as I'd presented my third finger to camera. I'd then zoomed in on the diamond itself and captured a glitzy close-up. The pics

7

had subsequently been uploaded to Instagram, Facebook, and Twitter with umpteen wedding-appropriate hashtags. I'd burbled on about my impending wedding and imminent name change. You see, I'd wanted the world to know. Everyone else seemed to have shiny perfect lives, and now I had one too. Hooray!

I rubbed my temples. Despite Sue's words of reassurance, I could feel a headache starting.

'Do you understand?' Sue prompted.

'Yes,' I whispered uncertainly.

'I can tell you're not convinced. Okay, let's go over the facts.' There came the sound of sizzling as rashers began to brown. 'When you were a slip of a girl, you walked down the aisle to wed Teddy who, just like a certain band's song, thought he was far too sexy for his shirt, his trousers, *and* his boxers and frequently shed the lot to cavort with other women throughout your twenty-five-year marriage. Teddy would then come back to you with his tail between his legs, promising it would never happen again. But Teddy only kept half his promise, in that it never happened again with the same woman. So, when you found out about his latest conquest in a rather public way, you knew it was time to either put up and shut up, or bail out. You chose the latter and, for a while, enjoyed not having your nerves jangling with dropped phone calls on the home landline. Then you met George in the chiller aisle of Kings Hill's biggest supermarket while shopping for a lonely meal for one, and he asked you out. Initially you weren't interested, but he persisted. Also, George was different to Teddy. He wasn't

8

loud. And, unlike Teddy, he wasn't sexy.'

'Oh, thanks.'

'You know what I mean,' said Sue hastily. 'You felt secure with George–'

'Because of his boring looks and boring ways,' I cut in.

'Look, Soph. Let's be realistic here. I have nothing against George, but everything about him is… *grey*.'

'What do you mean?' I gasped.

'He has grey hair. Grey eyes. Grey suits. Grey jeans. He even drives a grey car.'

'The car is silver,' I objected. 'Just like George's hair. You know, male magazines refer to these guys as *silver foxes*. That sounds rather glamorous to me.'

'If you say so.' I sensed the shrug in her voice. 'George eventually popped the question but, from what you've told me, the proposal was casual and lacked any romance.'

'It was sweet enough,' I protested. 'Just like him.'

'George isn't sweet,' Sue countered. 'He's *safe*. Men who are safe and look like George do not have a harem of women lusting after them.'

'Well, I lusted after him,' I squawked.

'No, you didn't.'

'W-What?' I stuttered. 'Sue, that's absolutely not true.'

'Yes, it is.' There came the sound of a spatula banging against a pan. 'From what I can gather, you've never once ripped his clothes off. In fact, from what you shared about the first time you both did it, I seem to remember you being rather put out because you'd missed the first half of Coronation Street.'

9

I opened my mouth, then shut it again.

'I'm fifty, Sue. Not fifteen. Women of our age don't go around ripping off their man's clothes.'

'Don't they?' I sensed Sue arching an eyebrow as the sound of a plate rattled down on her worktop. 'Speak for yourself. Charlie and I still go at it like a couple of teenagers.'

'You can't possibly.'

'We do, and you'd better believe it.'

I felt momentarily flummoxed. Was there something wrong with me? Time under the duvet with George wasn't adventurous. It was very perfunctory.

Very boring? enquired my inner voice.

I recoiled in horror. George was *not* boring. He was, as Sue said, safe. Safe was safe. Safe wasn't boring.

Isn't it?

'So stop fretting about a ridiculous message from Tabby Twitface –'

'Thomas Tabby Cat,' I corrected.

'Him too' – Sue exhorted – 'and know that when you marry George this Saturday, all will be well.'

'Yes,' I said slowly. 'It's going to be a lovely day.'

'Of course it is.'

I stared into space thinking about my big day. It wasn't going to be a grand event. Not at our age. After all, we'd both been married before. Sadly, neither of us had children, nor parents or siblings. Consequently, George had been adamant about not wanting a fuss. Instead, we were each inviting a couple of close friends to the local registry office – Sue and Charlie on my side, and Graham Rollinson and his wife Jackie on George's side.

Afterwards, the six of us would have a celebratory *wedding breakfast* at Little Waterlow's pub, The Angel. George had booked one of the pub's two function rooms. It would be a small affair.

And rather boring, said my inner voice.

Nonsense!

'It will be intimate and classy,' I said to Sue.

'Indeed,' she agreed. 'And I know George wanted to be conservative with his pennies and not splash out on a hideously expensive wedding, but at least he didn't hold back for the honeymoon. I'm quite jealous of you jetting off to the Amalfi Coast immediately afterwards.' Sue's voice took on a wistful tone. 'I've heard it's stunning.'

'Yes,' I said, properly smiling for the first time since reading the troll's message. 'I'm really looking forward to that bit.'

'Surely, you're looking forward to your wedding day, too?' asked Sue curiously.

'Of course,' I quickly answered.

But after we'd said good-bye to each other, I wasn't sure who I'd been trying to convince the most. Sue, or myself.

Chapter Two

I'd barely ended the conversation with Sue when my mobile rang. I glanced at the name on the screen and my heart sank. Teddy Fairfax. My ex-husband.

'Hello,' I said cautiously.

'How's my favourite ex-wife?' he said jovially.

'Your only ex-wife,' I pointed out.

'And that's why you're my favourite,' he quipped. 'How are you, darling?'

'Honestly, Teddy? None the better for hearing your voice.'

'Oooh, that's harsh. Very harsh.'

'What do you want?'

'That's my girl. Straight to the point. You were never one to beat about the bush.'

'Unlike you. That's probably because you spent a lot of time *in* the bush, having your wicked way with your latest conquest.'

'That's all in the past.'

'Ah, a sentence that tells me you're currently between girlfriends.'

'You're right. Fancy a quick one?'

'Are we talking about a drink or sex?'

'Sex, of course.'

'No.'

'Bet you don't say that to George.'

I sighed. Teddy always had the ability to exasperate me. I began to quickly dress, trying to ignore my stomach which was starting to growl with hunger.

'Teddy, you've been calling me a lot lately, and I wish you'd stop. What if George had been here?'

'Then I'd have behaved honourably and asked his permission to give you a quick one.'

'You're not funny.' I headed towards the steep staircase inside my two-up-two-down. Like most of the old cottages in the village of Little Waterlow, the ascent and descent in these properties required one's full attention and utmost caution. 'I'll ask you again. What do you want?'

'I want to persuade you not to marry George.'

'Again?' I sighed, walking into the kitchen.

Teddy had been aghast when he'd found out about my engagement. Not that it had been a secret. In a village like Little Waterlow, gossip was a pastime. At one point or another, nearly everyone fell under the spotlight of scrutiny because that's just the way my village was. A resident couldn't change their washing powder without it being discussed. I could still remember Mrs Bates, two doors down saying, "I heard you'd gone off Persil, Sophie. Is that true?" And me replying, "Yes, it seemed a bit pointless buying it after having all my dirty laundry washed in public." This was a reference to when villagers were gossiping about Teddy and me when our marriage – which had always been on a

13

slippery slope – had finally ended and in a most public way.

We'd been having a drink at our local. Teddy had barely set his lager down at our table when he'd excused himself to go to the Gents. Unbeknownst to me, he'd then attempted buying contraceptives from the machine on the wall. Unfortunately, the machine had swallowed his money without delivering the goods. He'd promptly had a private word with the landlord but, from my seat, I'd managed to catch the gist of the conversation.

Shocked, I'd waited for Teddy to return to our table before shrilly asking why he'd bought contraceptives when I'd gone through the change. Regrettably I'd been overheard by Little Waterlow's biggest gossip, Mabel Plaistow. She'd been having a quiet Guinness with her husband Fred, out of sight at the table behind me. She'd leant across to tap me on the shoulder, intent on getting my full attention. "I'll tell yer what yer man wants 'em for," she'd declared. "To put on 'is willy when 'e's playin' away."

No shit, Sherlock!

I'd subsequently picked up Teddy's pint and, in front of astonished customers, tipped it over his head. Leaving Teddy open-mouthed and dripping, I'd calmly walked out of the pub. That night I'd ignored Teddy's familiar pleas for forgiveness, and slept in the spare room.

The following day I'd made an appointment with Gabe Stewart, a local no-nonsense solicitor who specialised in divorce. And the rest, as they say, is history.

Teddy had always played around. I'd spent years forgiving, but never quite forgetting. The issue with the

14

contraceptive machine at The Angel had simply been the last straw.

My ex-husband and I now lived at opposite ends of the village. It was inevitable that our paths sometimes crossed. Teddy had wanted to remain friends and – after twenty-five years of marriage and no close family members – I'd felt the same way. Also, it was easier to love him as a mate rather than a philandering husband. However, there was a world of difference between occasionally bumping into him and now having him telephone on an almost daily basis.

'This is the fourth time this week,' I said, using my shoulder to wedge the phone against my ear while filling the kettle. 'Why don't you want me to marry George?' I plonked the kettle on its electric base, then flipped the switch.

'You know why.'

'No, I don't.'

'Yes, you do. The man is a berk.'

I reached into a cupboard and extracted a mug.

'You don't *know* George, so how can you possibly hold such an opinion?'

'I've seen him around.'

'Oh, really?' I went to the fridge. Extracting a loaf of bread, I dropped two slices into the toaster. 'And have you ever bothered to say hello to him?'

'Of course not.' Teddy sounded indignant. 'Why on earth would I want to associate with a man who wears a grey suit?'

I rolled my eyes.

'What's wrong with a grey suit?'

15

'Grey suits are for boring people.'

Oh God. First Sue. Now Teddy.

'I see. Do you think George would be more likeable if he wore a loud pinstripe, like your good self?'

Teddy was a business consultant with a fine line in patter and an eye for expensive cloth that made a statement.

'I simply take pride in the way I look,' he pointed out.

'Is that why you went to Turkey last year for a hair transplant?'

'I need to look my best to succeed in wooing you back.'

'You'll never woo me back and, anyway, Sue says men who have hair transplants are vain.'

'Says the woman who's had more filling than a sandwich shop.'

'I think you mean *filler*,' I corrected, just as the toaster violently ejected my breakfast on to the worktop. I grabbed it and reached for the margarine.

'That too.' Teddy cleared his throat, an indication that the subject was about to be changed. 'Anyway, never mind Sue. I'm talking about George. Call off the wedding. If you go through with it, darling, you'll be making a terrible mistake.'

I paused from my toast buttering.

'What did you say?'

'You heard. The guy simply isn't your type.'

'And what, exactly, is my type? Someone like you who behaves like a dog with six dicks?'

'You'll be bored to tears if you marry George Baker.'

'That's fine,' I said, reaching for the marmalade and

lathering it over the toast. 'It will be my pleasure to be bored to tears, because it means I'll never be stressed wondering what George is up to behind my back.'

'Don't count on it,' said Teddy darkly. 'Sometimes it's the quiet ones that need to be watched.'

'Oh, don't be so ridiculous, Teddy,' I snapped. 'I'm now ending this conversation. If I were you, I'd take a good long look at yourself before you start casting aspersions about other people.'

Annoyed, I abruptly ended the call and aggressively bit into the toast.

It was only when I was later walking to work, that a thought occurred to me. Might Teddy be the author of that strange Instagram message?

As I bowled along the leafy lane covering the distance from my cottage to another not so very far away, the possibility that my ex-husband was Thomas Tabby Cat seemed more and more likely.

Chapter Three

'Hi, Sophie,' trilled my boss. Ruby reversed out of a floor-to-ceiling stock cupboard, a grin on her face. 'How are you this morning?'

I shut the door to the tiny hair salon and shrugged off my jacket.

'Not so bad,' I said, forcing a smile.

Ruby paused for a moment, her arms full of tin foils, hair dye and bleach brushes. She gave me an appraising look.

'Hmm. You look like my mum when she's been walking one of her four-legged doggy clients and had a run-in with an off-lead hellraiser.'

'Oh?'

'In other words, you have a face like a slapped bum.'

'Gee, thanks, Rubes.'

Ruby was only nineteen and said things how they were. Her mother, Wendy, was a lovely woman who'd recently remarried. Ironically, Wendy's new husband had turned out to be my divorce lawyer. Wendy's life had fallen under the gossips' spotlight when her first husband had… well, let's just say there had been some eyebrow-raising tittle-tattle.

Wendy had gone on to buy a dear little house called Clover Cottage but, since marrying Gabe, she'd permanently loaned the cottage to her daughter. Ruby had recently qualified as a hairdresser and gone on to turn a small outbuilding into a tiny hair salon. Her business had taken off almost immediately thanks to Little Waterlow's high street salon – my original workplace – going into administration.

Following my redundancy, I hadn't wasted a moment, and hotfooted over to Ruby's place to see if she needed another pair of hands. Happily, she had.

Despite our age gap, we got on well. Occasionally I babysat Mo, Ruby's little girl, if she and her partner Simon wanted a night out. They were a lovely little family and it made me wistful for the children I'd always hoped to have with Teddy but which, despite our many attempts at IVF, had never come along. Perhaps – looking back at our bumpy marriage – that had been a blessing in disguise.

'So come on then,' said Ruby, scrutinising my face. 'What's up?'

I hung my jacket over the coat stand in the corner.

'It's something and nothing.'

Ruby dumped the foils and hairdressing paraphernalia on the tiny reception table, then stuck her hands on her hips.

'Forget the *nothing* and tell me the *something*. In fact, hold fire while I put the kettle on. We've got ten minutes before our respective clients arrive, so sit down for a minute and take some deep breaths. I can tell you're rattled.'

She disappeared into a small backroom that housed a loo, miniature washbasin, a washing-machine-cum-tumble-dryer, and a slither of worktop upon which sat a kettle and a microwave.

I flopped down on the chair by the washbasin and stared through the window. The view was of Ruby's home. Clover Cottage was chocolate-box pretty, especially with its arc of pink rambling roses framing the back door. The beautiful blooms gave off the sweetest fragrance throughout the summer months.

I gazed at the roses, my mind wandering to some different flowers. Namely, my bouquet. George had suggested I go for something in silk, claiming they'd make a nice keepsake. Together, we'd trawled through a website. He'd paused to consider some artificial lilies.

'These are nice,' he'd enthused. 'I *love* them in this colour.'

They'd been grey.

I'd since visited Daisy Kingston, another resident of Little Waterlow, who had her own florist shop in the heart of the village. She'd promised to give me a bouquet of mixed blooms in a riot of different colours.

It had struck me – briefly – that George could, at times, be somewhat controlling. However, I'd then dismissed the thought. So long as I agreed to whatever George wanted, there wasn't a problem. That said, I wasn't too sure what he'd say about my choice of bouquet.

Ruby interrupted my musings.

'Here we are,' she said, handing me a mug.

'Thanks, sweetheart.'

I took the drink from her, sipping gratefully as she settled down on the cutting stool. Her gaze met mine. She was an extraordinarily pretty girl with a shocking pink crop that set off bright blue eyes and elfin features. She beamed at me over the rim of her cup.

'So, go on. Spill the beans. Think of me as your personal agony aunt.'

'Hmm. Okay.' I set down my cup and pretended to type, my fingers wiggling in the air. 'Dear Aunty Ruby. I have a problem. I'm getting married this Saturday–'

'Indeed, and I'm doing your hair,' she dimpled. 'Oh, sorry. I've interrupted. Carry on.'

I continued air typing and talking.

'My best friend thinks my fiancé is boring, and my ex-husband says I shouldn't marry George–'

'What's it got to do with either of them? Oooh, sorry. I've done it again. Continue.'

'Something happened this morning. Something that *really* rattled me–'

I paused as my eyes suddenly brimmed.

'Yes?' prompted Ruby, alarmed at a possible display of waterworks.

I frantically blinked the tears back into their ducts.

'I had a message from Thomas Tabby Cat.'

Ruby frowned, cupping her hands around her mug.

'You've lost me.'

'On Instagram.'

'You follow a cat?

'He follows me.'

'I'm not following.'

'I don't follow him either.'

'Sophie, what the heck are you talking about?'

'It was an anonymous message from someone calling themselves by that name.'

'Oh, I see. A promoter, right?'

I shook my head.

'No, a troublemaker. They told me that George was a cheater.'

'*Whaaaat?*' she squawked.

'And now I feel deeply anxious. It's triggered me. You know, after all the shenanigans when married to Teddy.'

'Look, I don't know your George. I mean, I've met him a couple of times when he's popped in here to see you after work, but – first impressions and all that – he doesn't strike me as someone who would muck a woman about. After all…' she trailed off.

'Yes?'

'Well, don't take this the wrong way, Sophie, but he's quite an ordinary looking guy. I privately thought he was punching when you introduced him to me.'

'Punching?'

'Yeah, you know. Punching above his belt. After all, you're way better looking than him.'

'What are you talking about? I'm nothing special. In fact, I'm very ordinary.'

'No, you're bloomin' not,' Ruby snorted. 'Look at yourself!' She jabbed a finger at one of the two huge mirrors on the opposite wall. 'Look at that reflection. You're gorgeous.'

'Ruby, I'm fifty. My face looks like it needs ironing.'

'You have a few laughter lines, that's all. It shows you

have a sense of humour. But never mind them. Look at the rest of you. You have a cloud of long, dark hair. Flawless skin that glows with good health. Beautiful brown eyes. You remind me of Nigella Lawson, and my Simon has always fancied her. You're still very attractive. Whereas George…' she trailed off again.

I finished the sentence for her.

'Isn't.'

'No, sorry, he definitely isn't. In fact' – she took a deep breath and looked a bit sheepish – 'I privately wondered what on earth you saw in the guy. I can see he drives a big car and heard he has his own company. I put the attraction down to his bank balance.'

'Bloody hell, Rubes. I'm not that shallow,' I protested. 'I fell for George because' – I floundered for a moment – 'well, because he's a nice guy.'

'So is my dustman but I wouldn't want to marry him.'

'George is dependable. And' – I hesitated for a moment before ploughing on – 'yes, if I'm honest, he's a tiny bit boring. But that's fine by me.'

'In which case you must agree that George isn't the swaggering, cheating type.'

'Yeah,' I sighed. 'It was my first husband who was like that.'

'Teddy. Yes, I've seen him about the village. He's still a good-looking guy. Are you sure you're doing the right thing marrying George?'

'Why? Do you think Thomas Tabby Cat is telling the truth and giving me a genuine warning?'

23

'Er, no.' Ruby shook her head. 'I meant that you don't sound like you're in love with George.'

I opened my mouth in shock.

'Ruby, that's not true. I love George to bits.'

'Not the same thing,' she said, shaking her head.

'What do you mean?'

'I mean, are you *in love* with George?'

I was saved from answering the question thanks to the arrival of our first two clients of the day.

Chapter Four

'Mornin',' wheezed Mabel Plaistow.

Little Waterlow's oldest resident trundled over the threshold, closely followed by her ancient husband, Fred.

'Good morning,' said Ruby warmly.

Fred and Mabel were my boss's immediate neighbours and, consequently, regulars in the salon. Pleased with Ruby's hairdressing skills, they'd gone on to recommend her to all their golden oldie mates, which had somewhat astonished Ruby. She hadn't anticipated having so many pensioners on her books.

After qualifying, bubble hairdos hadn't been quite the look she'd been hoping to regularly create. However, business was business. Until Lady Gaga popped by wanting a diagonal bob in platinum blonde and black, Ruby had made sure senior citizens were half price.

'Come over to the basin,' Ruby said to Mabel. 'Fred, I'll leave you in Sophie's capable hands.'

'How nice,' he leered.

'Fred Plaistow' – Mabel barked as she folded the salon's protective gown around her ample midriff – 'stop yer flirtin'. Sophie ain't interested in an old timer like you.' She sat down and leant back against the basin. 'She's already spoken for. Ain't that right, love?'

'We've seen your George,' said Fred.

'Yes, I think most of the locals know of my fiancé.' I fastened a gown's tie at the back of Fred's neck and indicated he take a seat in front of the long mirror. 'The usual?' I asked, picking up my scissors.

'Yes, short back and sides, please. Meanwhile, I'll let you into a little secret.' Fred winked at me in the mirror's reflection. His expression was one of furtiveness. 'My Mabel reckons I look a bit like your George.'

My scissors hovered mid-air as I stared back at Fred. Oh, my goodness. He wasn't far wrong. Both men had similar jawlines and slightly crooked noses. I gulped. Was this how George might look in his mid-eighties? My eyes flicked to Mabel. Ruby was applying the weekly blue rinse. In time, would I look like Mabel? Would George and I sit together every evening in front of the telly, me impersonating a battle-axe as I commandeered the remote control and henpecked George into submission?

'You *will* watch Countdown with me and that's the end of it.'

Would we then retire to bed with our mugs of cocoa and gossip about the latest scandal in Little Waterlow? Who was sleeping with who? Who was trying to murder who? Oh yes, it all happened in this village. Might George and I eventually find ourselves the new King and Queen of the rumour mill? I suppressed a shudder and began snipping,

'You're getting wed soon, aren't you?' said Fred.

'Yes, that's right. This Saturday.'

'An' you'll make a right bonny bride, love,' said Mabel, hand on a towel turban as she sat down heavily on the chair beside us.

'Thank you,' I smiled, not so keen on the word *bonny*.

Like Nigella – who Ruby had earlier compared me to – I had wide hips and a generous bottom. When you reached fifty, such a figure went with the territory.

'Where are you going for your honeymoon?' asked Fred.

'The Amalfi Coast.'

'I dunno where that is, love, but it sounds nice,' said Mabel.

'Italy,' said Ruby, deftly sectioning Mabel's hair and securing a roller.

'We went to Bognor for our 'oneymoon,' said Mabel. 'It poured with rain all week. We 'ad to make our own entertainment,' she guffawed.

Fred reached out and patted Mabel's hand.

'That's right. We made love almost every night.'

'We did,' Mabel nodded. 'An' we still do. *Almost* on a Monday. *Almost* on a Tuesday. *Almost* on a Wednesday…'

Chapter Five

George texted me between clients, just as I was hastily cramming a sandwich into my mouth.

No cooking for you tonight. I'm taking you out! Xx

Oooh, lovely. We hadn't made any arrangements to see each other this evening. I loved a surprise, especially when it was spur of the moment. The impromptu message also reassured me. It wasn't the text of someone having an affair. If George was playing away, he'd surely want to utilise every spare minute for a clandestine meeting, not take his future wife out to dinner.

Nor would he be marrying you this Saturday, reminded my inner voice.

Well, quite.

I'd already made up my mind to tell George about the weird Instagram message. He had a right to know. After all, it was about him. He'd probably laugh his head off at the very idea.

I quickly texted back.

Fab! Where are we going? Xx

Seconds later my phoned dinged with a reply.

It's a surprise! Dress to impress. See you at seven'ish xx

I replied with a smiley emoji wondering which restaurant

George had in mind. Dress to impress, eh?

As I greeted my next client and made small talk, a part of my brain detached and floated off. Namely, back to Catkin Cottage. More specifically, the wardrobe in my bedroom. My mind's eye watched the door gently swing open so I could set about inspecting the garments within.

Hmm, what did we have here? A little black dress. *Little* being the word. It showed rather a lot of thigh and quite a lot of billowing cleavage. I wished George hadn't been so secretive about the venue. If it were a flashy wine bar – like one or two over at West Malling – then I could carry it off. However, I'd look a bit daft if we ended up going to the local pub. Jeans and simple tops were the general attire round here. Indeed, it was considered dressy if you teamed jeans with heels instead of wellies.

I sighed and continued to mentally push clothes hangers apart. Little red dress? No. Little blue dress? No. Oh, wait, what was this? A calf-length purple dress which would have been demure if not for the split running up the front.

The dress had a square neckline. I could wear it with my balcony bra, thus showcasing my bust in a classy way, rather than a spilling-over-one's–dinner-plate kind of way. Yes, sorted.

I'd glam it up with some costume jewellery. If the restaurant turned out to be on the rustic side, then I'd be sure not to cross my legs, thus avoiding any exposure of a bare thigh. Plus, I could always whip off the bling and slip it into my handbag. Yes, good idea, Sophie.

Halfway through the afternoon, the sun beat relentlessly

29

against the windowpanes. After a lengthy stint of Ruby and I using hairdryers at the same time, the temperature within the salon had risen enough to justify leaving the door open for some air.

There was a mini drama when two bees flew in. My client – phobic about stinging insects – shot off her chair so speedily it was as if someone had pressed an ejector button. She then attempted to do a four-minute mile in a confined space, all the while screaming at the top of her lungs. Mabel Plaistow, back home and next door, despatched Fred to see what all the commotion was about. Fred kindly used a butterfly net to gently guide the insects outside again. After that, the door remained shut.

By the end of the day, I was decidedly damp under the armpits and looking forward to a shower before going out for the evening.

With trills of toodle-oo and see you tomorrow, I hastened home on foot, grateful that Catkin Cottage was only a short walk away. Right now, in the early evening sunshine, it was a pleasure to commute using my own two feet. I wasn't too sure how enjoyable this journey would be in the winter when the bad weather arrived, and the nights drew in.

There was no street lighting or pavements along the lane. It didn't herald a pleasant walk come winter, and likely not a particularly safe one either. I did have a car, but parking was a premium at Ruby's salon. She wouldn't want her employee monopolising one of the customer's parking bays.

Haven't you forgotten something? prompted my inner voice.

What?

Come winter, you won't be walking to work from Catkin Cottage. After this weekend, your address will be Kings Hill. You'll be living in George's house.

Ah, yes. Silly me for forgetting that.

I sighed. Oh well, perhaps I could ask George to drop me off in the mornings before he went on to the office. Or maybe I could invest in a bicycle. Yes, that was a good idea. I could leave the bike in Ruby's garden while I did my hairdressing.

Preoccupied, I didn't initially spot George parked outside my house. I wondered how long he'd been waiting, and why he hadn't driven the extra mile or so to pick me up. Perhaps he'd only just arrived. His fingers were drumming the top of the steering wheel. Upon seeing me, he buzzed down the driver's window.

'Hey,' I grinned. 'You're early.'

'Not really. It's half past six. Hop in.'

My smile wavered.

'You said seven.'

'Seven'*ish*. That means give or take a portion of minutes.'

'But George, you're half an hour early and I'm simply not ready. You said dress to impress. I can't possibly go to some smart restaurant wearing these trousers and a sweaty t-shirt.'

I was very aware that my armpits were damp and that my cheap deodorant had let me down.

'Sophie, stop procrastinating and get in the car.'

Uh-oh. George was getting ratty. That was one of the negatives about my fiancé. If one could measure patience in terms of miles or even yards, George's would be somewhere around the length of a ruler. A child's ruler at that.

'Sorry, but I really do need a shower,' I protested.

Ignoring me, George leant across the handbrake and opened the passenger door.

'You look fine,' he said.

'Well, I don't feel it. Can I at least go and change into a dress? I'll be two minutes.'

'Make it one,' he said between gritted teeth.

'Oh, for–'

I legged it up the path to Catkin Cottage. Scampering up the stairs, I shed clothes as I went. Pushing against my bedroom door, I hastened to the wardrobe. Thank goodness I'd thought about what to wear earlier.

Plucking the purple dress from the rail, I slipped it over my head. Phew. I'd forgotten how warm this material was. Hell. It also had long sleeves – hardly the thing to wear on a warm June evening.

I was just about to rip the dress off when George tooted the car's horn. Yes, okay. I'm coming. Just give me a few more seconds.

My collection of shoes lay on the floor of the wardrobe. I grabbed a pair of strappy sandals, rammed my feet into them, then dashed to the bathroom for a spritz of deodorant. Damn and blast. I should have done that before putting on the dress.

Grabbing the canister, I flicked up the hem, gathering

yards of material. Pointing the aerosol in the direction of my pits, I squirted lavishly. The ensuing scent told me I'd used sticky hairspray.

'Shit,' I swore, just as George tooted again.

Catching sight of myself in the mirror, I cringed. So much for hoping to titivate with makeup. Instead, I'd have to tone down my hectic complexion with talc.

I puffed some into one palm, patted it over my cheeks, then sneezed violently. Slightly better. Lippy… lippy… where was the shade I wanted? Ah, in my bedroom, on the dressing table. George tooted again. Feeling like a Countdown contestant, I instead rummaged in the bathroom's vanity drawer. Bingo. An old cerise-coloured lipstick. It would have to do. I ran it over my lips, belatedly realising that it clashed violently with the dress. Too bad.

Risking my neck, I belted down the steep staircase, charged out the front door and practically threw myself into George's Mercedes. His foot was on the accelerator before I'd even buckled up.

'Well, this is a nice surprise,' I chirruped, trying to lighten his mood. His irritated expression told me that now wasn't the time to share chit-chat about the earlier Instagram message. 'Which restaurant are we off to?'

'We're not going to a restaurant,' he said, his features softening slightly. 'We've been invited for dinner at my friends' house.'

'O-Oh, really?' I stuttered, trying to ignore the sinking feeling in my stomach.

George had a lot of acquaintances, but they were just

33

that. Colleagues and business contacts. Actual friends were people he could count on one hand. Or, to be absolutely precise, two fingers. I didn't need to ask any further questions about where we were going or who was hosting.

We were off to Graham and Jackie Rollinson's abode, an immaculate property that also happened to be in Kings Hill. It was similarly decorated to George's place, but in shades of magnolia rather than grey. Fortunately, Kings Hill was a big place. I was grateful that the Rollinsons weren't George's immediate neighbours and, therefore, wouldn't be mine either when I moved in with my new husband.

George had known Graham since school days, hence Graham being elected as George's best man. Jackie also got on famously with George. However, much I'd tried – and I really had, I promise – I'd failed to bond with her. Some women preferred the company of men, and I'd told myself that Jackie was one of them.

I stared through the car's passenger window, a part of me wishing the evening was over before it had even begun.

Chapter Six

'George!' said Jackie, her face lighting up. She embraced my fiancé, winding her arms around his neck, squeezing tightly. Ever the touchy-feely flirt. 'Come in, come in.'

She released him and stepped aside, allowing George to cross the threshold. I followed behind. Enticing cooking smells were wafting into the large hallway area.

'Hello, Sophie.' Jackie quickly air-kissed the space either side of my cheeks, before turning her attention back to George. 'It really is *so* lovely to see you.'

'You too, sweetheart,' said George, looking at her fondly.

'Graham is in the lounge. Go on through. You know the way.'

Neither of us were wearing jackets on this warm evening, so there were no garments to hang in the coat cupboard. Jackie followed George into the lounge while I brought up the rear.

'Hello, matey,' boomed Graham, coming over. He pumped George's hand. Graham was quite a bit older than Jackie and reminded me of Brian Blessed. He had the actor's same theatrical voice. 'Come and get a Scotch in you and tell me how your takeover plans are going. A little bird told me you've made a successful bid for Percy's Pencils. Oh, hello, Sophie. Didn't see you there.'

No, well, you wouldn't with your wife blocking the doorway.

'Hello, Graham,' I smiled, after Jackie had stepped to one side.

'I'll let my good lady wife look after you, my dear.'

Super.

'I'm on gin and tonic,' said Jackie. 'Is that all right for you?'

'Lovely.'

I couldn't bear the drink but didn't want to appear awkward.

Jackie disappeared off to the kitchen to sort out the tipple and check simmering saucepans, while the men moved across the room, immersed in business talk. I dithered on whether to join them, but their body language indicated otherwise, so I remained where I was.

Feeling like a spare part, I settled for studying the cream walls with the same intensity as one might scrutinise a Van Gogh painting. I could imagine, if Sue were here, the pair of us mucking about, giggling naughtily as we took the micky out of the Rollinsons' decor:

'Amazing brushwork, eh?'

'Absolutely. Do you think Graham used a six-inch bristle head on this expanse of blandness?'

'Nah, more like a nine-inch roller sleeve. After all, he's deliberately created a subtle textured effect adding a touch of drama to an overall sense of nothingness.'

Cue much snorting behind our hands. Like me, Sue loved bright colours and a bit of clutter. Her house was full of ornaments and giant plants, and every single wall within was smothered in framed prints or treasured photographs. By comparison, this house was positively sterile.

Just like George's place, came an intrusive and unwelcome thought.

'For you,' said Jackie, returning with a jingling tumbler full of ice and lemon.

I could smell the gin from two paces and deduced it was a triple. The Rollinsons enjoyed drinking almost as much as they loved entertaining.

I had no idea how Jackie kept her figure, which was the bony side of thin. Everything about her was glacial – from the platinum-blonde hair and pale blue eyes to the cold shoulder she always gave me. This evening she was wearing a white dress which added to the icy overall effect. If I was fanciful, I'd say she'd just stepped out of the wardrobe after visiting Narnia.

As I opened my mouth to compliment her on the delicious cooking smells, she turned on her heel and joined Graham and George. A second later she'd seamlessly crowbarred her way into their conversation.

'Absolutely splendid news about Percy's Pencils,' she gushed, manoeuvring herself between the two men. She lightly touched my fiancé's forearm. 'Very well done, George. *Very* well done indeed. You'll earn a small fortune out of that venture.'

'Thanks, Jackie,' George beamed, basking in her praise.

'It won't be long before I'm exchanging the Merc for an Aston Martin.'

I swished the ice around my glass before taking a glug of the horrible gin. *Dutch courage*, I told myself. Taking my cue from Jackie, I moved across the room to join them.

'George has a wonderful business head on him,' I said, planting myself opposite Jackie. I noticed she was still touching my fiancé's forearm. I copied and touched George's other arm. For one surreal moment, he looked as if he were about to be seduced by two women.

'And it's a good thing I'm such a high earner' – he told Graham and Jackie, while gently shrugging off my hand – 'because we'd never make ends meet on the pittance Sophie earns.'

Stung, I didn't know how to respond. Instead, I gulped down some more gin. Didn't George realise how belittling his words were? Surely such a put-down had been accidental?

'Ah, yes, how is your little hairdressing job?' asked Jackie with a patronising smile.

Bitch.

I swallowed down some more gin before replying.

'There's nothing little about it,' I replied, slurring slightly. It had been a long time since lunch and drinking a hefty gin on an empty stomach was having an effect. 'It's been manic all day long. Ruby Walker – that's the owner – is only nineteen, but the salon's phone never stops ringing. The appointments diary is crammed.'

'I guess someone has to do the hair of the local yokels,' Jackie sniffed. 'I don't suppose the likes of someone so young and inexperienced could even *begin* to measure up to my guy in London. Clive has been approached by the Beeb, you know.' She looked at George, eyes wide. 'A sort of reality programme, from what I can gather. A fly-on-the-wall camera picking up all the gossip from the celebrities that frequent the place. Kate has already paid a visit. I wonder what might be overheard if *she's* there when the crew are discreetly in situ.'

'I'm not usually into reality telly, but I'd make a point of watching that one,' said George, sucking up to Jackie. 'Just imagine the royal beans that might be spilt.' He gave the three of us a keen look. 'It would certainly redress the balance after Meghan and Harry's Netflix deal. Perhaps enough material could be gleaned to make a feature film.'

'Yes, they could call it *Gone with the Windsors*,' I quipped.

'Don't be fatuous,' said George. 'I think Kate and William have had a very stressful time.'

'I didn't hay they sadn't,' I retorted.

My tipsily jumbled words hovered in the air. For a moment, there was an uncomfortable silence. Graham was the first to jump into the awkward gap.

'We're *so* looking forward to the wedding this Saturday,' he said to me. 'How are you feeling about becoming Mrs Sophie Baker?'

'Delighted,' I said truculently. 'I wouldn't be marrying George if I wasn't.'

'I'll bet,' said Jackie slyly. 'After all, you'll be the wife of a very rich man.'

Somehow, she'd made it sound as though I were a gold digger.

'What's that supposed to mean?' I said boldly.

'Sorry?' said Jackie, looking startled.

'I'll have you know' – I waggled a finger at her – 'that I'm my own person when it comes to money. I've worked all my life, and I have no intention of stopping.'

'Jolly good for you,' said Graham, sensing tension. 'Jackie is the same.'

'Really?' I snapped. As far as I was aware, Jackie hadn't worked for years.

'Oh, absolutely,' Graham nodded. 'It's a full-time job running this house, overseeing the garden, hosting business dinners, and looking after me. Consequently, Jackie is on my payroll. And she earns every penny, don't you, angel heart!'

Jackie swivelled her pale blue gaze to Graham and gave him a sweet smile. It was about as authentic as the fake fur in my wardrobe.

'I certainly do, my darling bobble-wobbles.'

Bobble-wobbles? I boggled into my gin.

'In fact' – she continued, fluttering her eyelashes – 'I think I should have a pay rise.'

'I'll sort it out, my little cupcake.'

'Mwah-wah-wah,' she replied, blowing noisy kisses from the palm of her hand.

'Graham is blessed to have a woman like you in his life,' said George gallantly. 'Oiling the wheels, so to speak.' He paused briefly, before plucking another well-used idiom from the ether. 'You're a woman who keeps all those cogs running smoothly.'

Someone give me a paper bag.

'Just like *me*!' I asserted, deciding to point out my own qualities in the absence of George mentioning them. I prodded him playfully in the chest. 'Who's a lucky, *lucky* boy!' I turned to Jackie, eyes wide with innocence. 'Forget the wheels and cogs. I'm the one who keeps his balls rolling.'

Chapter Seven

'I've never been so embarrassed in all my life,' ranted George. He started the car, doing lots of unnecessary engine revving. 'Your behaviour was appalling.'

The car shot backwards, wheels squealing slightly as we accelerated off the Rollinsons' driveway.

Jackie and Graham suddenly appeared, standing in their open doorway. They raised their hands by way of farewell.

'Wave back,' instructed George.

'Will two fingers do?' I enquired mildly.

'What on earth's got into you?' George growled as we sped off into the night.

That was obvious. Too much gin. In fact, the car's motion was making me feel nauseous.

'Shorry,' I said contritely.

'Not good enough. Tomorrow, I want you to phone Jackie with an apology.'

'For what?' I said, feeling a frisson of alarm.

'For telling her that her décor was rubbish.'

'I didn't say it was rubbish,' I protested. 'I simply said her colour scheme was a little bland for my liking.'

'It amounts to the same thing.'

'No, it doesn't.'

'*And* you criticised her cooking.'

'*Her* cooking?' I scoffed. 'You know as well as I do, she employs someone to do all the prep work. Then all she has to do is stick the meat in the oven and keep an eye on a couple of simmering saucepans. And I didn't criticise anything.'

'You didn't need to. Your face said it all.'

'Oh, for goodness' sake, George. The lamb was bleeding all over my plate and practically baaing. When meat is *that* rare, it puts me off.'

'You could have shut your eyes.'

'What, and looked like I was meditating my way through the meal?'

'Why not? You might have received some enlightenment on how to behave. How would you feel if I treated Whatshersame and Thingybob like that?'

I swivelled my head and glared at George.

'Are you, by chance, referring to my best friend, Sue, and her husband, Charlie?'

'That's right.'

'To answer your question, yes, I'd feel irked,' I confessed. 'But not as annoyed as right now when you can't even remember the names of two people whom I love and hold dear, especially when you've now met them several times.'

'More's the pity,' George muttered under his breath.

'I heard that,' I snapped. 'They'll be attending our wedding, George. What are you going to do when we all sit down together and make conversation? Turn to them and say, "Sorry, remind me again who you are?"

'Possibly,' George admitted. 'After all, neither of them made any lasting impression upon me.'

My mouth dropped open.

'I can't believe you just said that.'

'I can't believe you're even friends with such people.'

'What's that supposed to mean?'

'Sue is a complete airhead and Charlie carries on like he's an overgrown schoolboy. He's the sort of guy who probably thinks it's funny to try and set fire to his farts.'

'Well at least they are genuinely nice people.'

'Are you saying Graham and Jackie aren't?'

'Graham is okay, but Jackie is…'

'Yes? Go on, don't stop now,' George goaded.

'Okay,' I said, taking a deep breath. 'She's a self-satisfied, self-absorbed, smug–'

'Oooh, what a lot of words beginning with S. Can't you think of words beginning with a different letter?'

'Two-faced, bitchy, anally retentive c–'

'Don't,' George warned.

'COW!' I roared.

'You're bang out of order.'

'No, I'm not. It's true. She's one of those narcissistic females who takes absolute delight in undermining another woman. "*Oh, Sophie*" – I mimicked in a silly voice – '*my hairdresser rubs shoulder pads with the Queen Consort. Tell me, who's the most famous person you've ever welcomed at your itsy-bitsy salon?*"

'She was talking about Kate, not Camilla, and was there really any need to tell her that Ken Barlow visits Ruby

Walker's salon?'

'Why not? He has surely been the King of Coronation Street *and* likely a national treasure.'

'But you know full well that William Roache has never frequented your workplace.'

'No, but Fred Plaistow does, and he could easily pass for Ken.' Well, only if you screwed up your eyes and looked at him side-on. 'My point is, Jackie repeatedly belittled me, and she always has done. It would have been nice if you'd stuck up for me. The fact that I must share my wedding day with her looking down her nose at me is not something I'm relishing. If she says anything out of place, I swear I'll end up ramming my bouquet down her throat.'

For a moment my words seemed to reverberate around the car's cabin. I gulped. Oh Lord. I'd gone too far. I'd never criticised George's best friends before, nor had he ever let me know how he truly felt about Sue and Charlie. Possibly I'd provoked him. Yes, of *course* I had.

I rubbed a hand across my forehead, as if to wipe away the silly argument. My mind felt sober, but my brain needed to catch up. Right now, I had a thumping headache and felt horribly sick.

George cleared his throat, then reached across the divide between our seats. His hand took mine and enfolded it within his.

'Let's not argue,' he said gruffly.

'Okay,' I quickly agreed.

I'd said what I'd wanted to say. It may have been the drink talking, but nonetheless I'd made my point. I didn't care for Jackie. Never had. Never would.

George squeezed my hand.

'Let's draw a line under this conversation. Put it down to pre-match nerves, eh?'

'Okay,' I said again. My mind wandered back to the Instagram message. I cleared my throat. 'George?'

'Yes?'

'Are you…'

'Am I what?'

'Would you…'

'Would I what?'

'Do you…'

'For heaven's sake, Sophie. What are you trying to say?'

'Okay, er, well, um, do you like tabby cats?'

George frowned.

'Why? Do you want one after we're married?'

'Not particularly.'

'So… what sort of question is that?'

I turned my head away. Gazed out the window.

'I don't know,' I sighed. *Don't let some online troll upset you.* 'Ignore me.'

George's voice was tender when he next spoke.

'I think you need to sober up, darling.'

'Yes, you're probably right.'

I looked down at his fingers curled around mine. Everything was fine. *We* were fine. I'd simply let an annoying female and half a bucket of gin upset my equilibrium.

The drive back to Catkin Cottage passed in an amicable

silence, each with our own thoughts. When George eventually pulled up outside, he didn't suggest coming in.

'Tomorrow is Friday,' he said. 'Are you still happy with our original plan not to see each other the day before the wedding?'

I nodded.

'Yes, and anyway I still have a few things to do.'

That said, the page in my diary wasn't particularly busy. George, ultra-organised, had already packed his suitcase for the impending honeymoon. He'd left it at my place, along with the airline tickets and his passport. I, on the other hand, more last-minute-dotcom, had pre-booked the day off work to leisurely pack my own suitcase and oversee any last-minute requirements while relishing the last day of being Sophie Fairfax.

Relishing? piped up my inner voice.

Okay, that was the wrong word. I just wanted to, well, savour my last day of being a singleton and all that went with it. To be alone with my thoughts, as it were. And anyway, I wasn't clinging on to my surname. No, not at all. After all, Fairfax was my old married name from the years I was with Teddy.

'In which case' – George scattered my thoughts as he leant over to deliver a perfunctory kiss – 'I'll see you in your finest at the registry office on Saturday afternoon.'

'You will,' I said, pecking him back.

'Let me be old-fashioned and walk you to the door,' said George impulsively. He opened the driver's door, trotted around to the passenger side, then offered me his elbow. 'Ms

Fairfax, would you allow me to escort you home?'

'Why, I'd be delighted, Mr Baker,' I giggled, unfolding my legs, and taking his arm.

How delightful. How romantic. So much for the likes of Sue and Teddy telling me that George was boring. How dare they!

I put the key in the door and let it swing open, then closed my eyes, waiting for George to take me in his arms, tip me sideways like a *Strictly* dancer, then glue his lips to mine.

'Oh dear,' he said instead.

My eyes pinged open. George was peering into the hallway, looking faintly horrified. I followed his gaze to see a trail of female garments littering the staircase – the clothes I'd shed in haste earlier when George had been impatiently tooting his horn.

He cleared his throat.

'Sophie, I've noticed that you have a predilection to being somewhat messy. I do hope you will put your clothes away once we are married.'

Chapter Eight

Thanks to the gin overload, I slept all the way through the night without even getting up to spend a penny. I was eventually awoken by the alarm going off a little before nine.

I made a cartoon long-arm from under the covers and blindly patted several buttons around the clockface. When the wretched thing continued to shriek, I emerged from under the duvet ready to hurl the object across the room. That was when I realised the noise was coming from elsewhere. Someone was leaning on the doorbell.

'God's sake,' I growled, swinging my legs over the side of the bed.

Standing up, the room momentarily spun. I grabbed the edge of the bedside cabinet and steadied myself, just as my head began to throb. Deep joy. A hangover.

'Coming,' I yelled over the din, wincing from the effort of shouting. The throbbing turned into a relentless pounding.

Gingerly, I made my way down the stairs, clutching the banister rail with one hand and my head with the other. Flinging wide the front door, I was dismayed to see Teddy standing on the doorstep.

'At last,' he grinned, taking his finger of the doorbell.

My ears still seemed to be ringing. Heaven's above. Was

I suffering from tinnitus? It reminded me of what Sue had said when she'd experienced the problem following a head cold. "I'm not particularly musical, but I suspect I'm hearing EEEEEEEE sharp."

'Behold!' Teddy continued, beaming away. 'A vision with bed hair and mismatched pyjamas.'

'You woke me up.'

'In the nick of time, by the looks of things. Didn't anybody ever tell you not to stick your fingers in electrical sockets?'

'What do you want?' I squinted, wishing I had a handy pair of sunglasses. The early morning sunshine was threatening to burn my retinas.

'Can I come in?'

'No.'

'Why not? After all, George isn't here.'

'How do you know?'

'Because his car isn't outside.'

'Teddy, why aren't you at work?'

'Took the day off,' he said carelessly.

'Whatever for?'

'To see you. Now, are you going to step aside, or do I have to get all masterful?' He grinned impishly. 'I could lift you into my muscular arms, stride across the lounge, then deposit you on the chaise longue leaving you to swoon prettily while I put the kettle on.'

My headache was threatening to go to the next level. I needed caffeine. Now. And as Teddy had disturbed me, he could flipping well oversee the drinks.

'You know where the kitchen is,' I scowled, moving to one side.

'Coffee or tea?' he said amiably, stepping into the hallway. 'Oooh, dear.' He stopped and peered into my eyes. 'Look at those peepers. Red-rimmed roadmaps. A double strength coffee for you.' He sailed off to the kitchen, for all the world as if Catkin Cottage was his abode. 'We'll forego the instant. Only the real stuff will do when you look like you've spent the night tossing and turning.'

I trailed after him, then collapsed down on a chair.

'Try not to make so much noise,' I said, as Teddy clattered about.

Mugs clunked alarmingly as he removed china from the cupboard. Filling the kettle, it sounded like Niagara Falls flowing from the tap. The contents of the fridge door jingled as he located the milk. I winced as Teddy chucked coffee beans into the electric grinder, then flicked the switch.

'Heavy night?' he asked solicitously, after the racket had subsided.

'Yes, although it wasn't meant to be.'

'Ah, the words of a woman who was drinking to drown her sorrows.'

'Hardly. I was drinking to numb the monotonous drip-drip of *another* woman I don't care much for.'

Teddy pushed the plunger on the cafetière.

'Oooh, tell me more' – he affected a camp voice – 'because I love a good gossip.'

'Not much to tell,' I said miserably. 'George took me to his best mate's house.'

'Life in the fast lane again, Soph?' he teased.

'They're nice enough people really,' I said defensively, knowing that Teddy was revving up to shred George's friends.

'But *nice* also translates as *boring*,' he pointed out.

'Well, sometimes,' I conceded. 'Also, Jackie – that's the wife of George's pal – is one of those women who is so flipping pleased with herself. What must it be like to be so self-satisfied?'

'Loving yourself is important' – Teddy adopted a wise expression – 'as long as you wash your hands afterwards.'

'Oh, for goodness' sake,' I tutted. 'Do you always have to bring everything back to sex?'

'Now you're talking,' said Teddy gleefully. 'Would you like some? I hear it's fantastic for seeing off hangovers.'

'Thanks for the offer, but I'll stop you right there.'

'You sound like my computer.'

'Eh?'

'I put in a new password yesterday. *MyPen*s*. The screen flashed up a message that said: *Error, not long enough*. Ah, you're smiling. Go on, Soph. Go mad and allow yourself to dissolve into giggles.'

I shook my head but flashed him a grin. It was impossible to be cross for long with Teddy. He busied himself pouring the coffee, then set a mug down before me. I took some rapid sips, alternatively blowing on and slurping the scalding liquid, relishing the caffeine rush.

'So, why are you really here?' I eventually asked, cupping my hands around the mug.

'Well, being that I was unsuccessful in talking you out of marrying George—'

'Yes?'

'I thought, instead, we could spend the day together. A sort of hen night. Well, not a hen *night* because it's daytime. Instead, a hen *day*. What do you think?'

'I think you're talking crazy language. Sorry to state the obvious, but a hen only goes on a jolly with females.'

'Then let *me* pretend to be the hen. After all, you constantly ruffled my feathers when we were together.'

'Ha, funny! Nothing to do with you ruffling mine due to all the women you bedded throughout our marriage.'

'It wasn't that many.'

'Really? How many do you think it was, Teddy?'

'No more than four.'

'Hmm, I get a different answer every time I ask you that question. I'll bet there were so many you can't even remember.'

'I remember they weren't a patch on you,' said Teddy gallantly.

He reached across the table, took my hand, and gave me one of his best puppy-dog looks. Once it would have had me melting faster than a snowball in a microwave. I tutted and shook my head. Teddy always behaved like this if the past came up in conversation.

'It's true,' he said smoothly. 'That's why, ultimately, I always came back to you.'

'But I must have been doing something wrong if you felt the need to wander.'

'It was never your fault,' he said softly, playing with my fingers. 'I give you my word that, when we were together, I was the happiest married man on the planet. Unfortunately, I share my life with Dick and, as we both know, Dick is a total pleb. He was the one who led me astray.'

'Perhaps I should have chopped Dick off,' I mused.

Teddy winced.

'Honestly, darling, those women never meant anything. It was just sex. I was an idiot who took a long time to grow up.'

'And are you now grown up?'

'Yes, totally,' said Teddy earnestly. 'In fact, I'll prove it. Dump George and marry me instead. No need to cancel the registry office. I mean it.'

I stared at Teddy in disbelief.

'I can't believe you just said that.'

'Cross my heart. I've never been more serious.'

The Instagram message floated through my brain. I cleared my throat.

'I need to ask you something.'

'Ask away.'

'Are you Thomas Tabby Cat?'

'Darling, I'll be anyone you want me to be.' He batted his eyelids disarmingly, clearly oblivious to what I was talking about. 'So, what do you say, Soph? Marry me tomorrow. Please? *Pretty* please?'

'I say no,' I said, nonetheless smiling.

Gently, I extracted my fingers from his hand. Teddy was one of those men who could charm the birds from the trees, but I much preferred him as a friend than a husband. He gave me a sad smile then shifted in his seat. A regrouping gesture.

'So, back to our hen day.' He rubbed his hands together, his face full of glee. 'Don't dismiss it. In my humble opinion, you should have had a knees-up with Sue and all your girly friends. Why didn't it happen?'

I took another sip of coffee and considered.

'It was George's decision, really. He thought we should forego a hen and stag night because–'

'He's too boring?'

'No, because I'm fifty and he's–'

'Past it?'

'Of course not. We just felt that, at our time of life, it was–'

'Too exhausting?'

Whilst Teddy could be amusing, he could equally be very annoying. I gave him a stern look over the rim of my cup.

'George is in his fifties, and I celebrated the Big Five-Oh earlier this year.' I shrugged dismissively. 'Somehow, whooping it up with our respective friends didn't seem appropriate.'

'So, what you're saying is, from now on it's all downhill. A gentle slide into a premature old age. Exchanging your silk robe for a sensible fleecy down-to-the-ankles affair with matching *His 'n' Hers* slippers.'

'Sounds all right to me,' I said sulkily.

'Well, it doesn't to me.' An edge had crept into his tone. 'What's got into you, Soph?'

'Nothing,' I tutted.

'I thought as much. Isn't George delivering? You could always buy a nine-inch joy toy.'

I rolled my eyes.

'Sex again? Don't you ever get bored talking about it?'

'Nope. Do you?'

'I don't – and by that, I mean I don't *talk* about it.'

'Not sure I believe you. Are you honestly telling me that you and Sue don't discuss your men over a cuppa and choccy biccy?'

We did, but I wasn't telling Teddy that.

'Anyway,' he continued. 'You might be fifty, but you still look terrific.' He glanced at my pyjama bottoms. 'And you have a great pair of legs under those hideous granny-style tartan stripes.'

'Teddy, you don't need to flatter me because we're still not having sex.'

He adopted a wounded look.

'Can't I pay my wife a compliment?'

'Ex-wife, and no.'

He drained his cup.

'Come on, drink up.'

'Whatever for?'

'Because' – he sighed theatrically – 'if you're absolutely adamant about us not having sex, we need to crack on with our hen party for two. Get dressed and I'll take you out for brunch.'

My stomach chose that moment to rumble loudly.

'Okay,' I said, dramatically caving in. An image of a Full

English floated through my brain. Crispy bacon. A couple of eggs with big fat golden yolks fried to perfection. Hash browns. Baked beans. Mm. Maybe a couple of pieces of toast smothered in real butter. 'You've talked me into it.'

Teddy beamed at me across the table.

'Good girl.'

'I'll pack my honeymoon suitcase when we get back. After all, I'll have the rest of the day to do it.'

'Of course you will,' he said, not quite meeting my eye.

Chapter Nine

'Where the heck are we going?' I said, as Teddy's open-top sportscar hit the motorway.

'For brunch,' he shouted, over the roar of the engine.

'Have you forgotten that Chloe's Café is on Little Waterlow's High Street?'

'We're not going there,' said Teddy dismissively. 'My wife deserves better.'

'Ex-wife,' I once again reminded, pushing windswept hair from my eyes.

'Wife… ex-wife.' He took one hand off the steering wheel and made a see-saw motion. 'We married in church and vowed to be together until death do us part, so I say *pah* to any decree absolute.'

'We also vowed to be faithful and true,' I pointed out. 'A promise you didn't keep.'

'I've already told you' – Teddy briefly took his eyes off the road to flash a winning smile – 'it was Dick's fault.'

'I'm starting to think I should have named Dick Fairfax as Co-Respondent in our Divorce Petition.'

Our paperwork had been drawn up before recent changes in law that now granted couples *No Fault* divorces.

'Let's leave the past in the past,' said Teddy.

'Okay. There's nothing to be gained from rehashing the moment I found another woman's knickers in our bed.'

'Absolutely,' said Teddy stoutly. 'After all, I've forgiven you for all those mega naughty words you screamed at me, so we're quits. Meanwhile, sit back, and relax.'

My stomach briefly shot into my oesophagus as Teddy floored the accelerator. The car powered past a motorist hogging the middle lane.

'When are you going to tell me where we're going?' I asked after Teddy had shunted the car back to an empty inside lane.

'I'm not,' he said. 'It's a surprise, so stop asking.'

I shook my head imperceptibly and instead settled back in the bucket seat. The warm wind had thankfully blown away the last of my hangover. Bliss. I closed my eyes against the overhead sun, enjoying its warm rays kissing my skin as my hair whipped about my face. In this moment, I felt inexplicably young and carefree. Well, certainly more so than lately. Recently George had made me feel every one of my years. I instantly felt disloyal to my fiancé.

Teddy had been a nightmare to be married too, but he'd also been a lot of fun. I realised that now, as we zoomed past a lorry. Unfortunately, the fun bits were still mostly buried under all the tearful bits − of which there had been many − but, maybe now, as friends, I could view the fun moments again and this time with joy. I remembered we'd once spent an entire day reading the Sunday papers in bed and eating chocolate buttons for sustenance. There another time when, on a whim, we'd bought a kite. We'd taken a trip to

London's Greenwich Park to fly it, laughing as the gaily coloured diamond had taken off, trailing its colourful ribbons, and almost immediately tangled in a tree. Then there had been the time Teddy had whisked me off to Venice for a surprise weekend. He'd even serenaded me as we'd glided along a canal in a gondola. Later, he'd waltzed me around St Mark's Square while a pavement orchestra played, tourists looking on in bemusement.

Don't put on your rose-tinted glasses, warned my inner voice. *Not on the eve of your second marriage.*

I sighed, remembering the moment I'd removed some black fishnet knickers caught up in our duvet. His other women had always been keen to leave a sign. On another occasion it had been a six-inch curly blonde hair stuck to Teddy's black shirt. Then there was the earring in the passenger footwell of Teddy's car. Also, a lipstick in a shade I'd never worn, left on the sink in our bathroom. I'd loved Teddy with all my heart, but after that experience in The Angel with the faulty contraceptive machine, I'd ended up hating him too.

Hatred doesn't benefit anyone. It's like a poison. You can't see it. You can't touch it. But your body feels it and responds accordingly.

I could remember suddenly being taken ill. It had come from nowhere. I'd thrown up and up, and up some more, until in the end I'd been dry heaving. As soon as I'd made the appointment with Gabe Stewart's law firm, the nausea had stopped. My body had recovered, and I'd never been poorly since.

'Hey, wake up,' said Teddy, patting me on the arm.

'I'm not asleep,' I said, opening my eyes.

'You've been snoring for the last forty-five minutes,' he laughed.

I blinked and stared around. The car was crawling along in city traffic but, to our right, a navy-blue sea glittered under a big fat sun.

'What on earth–?' I blinked again.

'Welcome to Brighton,' said Teddy.

Chapter Ten

'Hold my hand,' Teddy instructed as – having finally found a parking space – we waited kerbside to cross the busy road.

'I'm not a child,' I retorted.

'Just do it,' he said, grabbing hold of me and breaking into a run. 'You take your life in your hands trying to cross a stretch of tarmac like this one.'

'We could have used the pedestrian crossing,' I puffed, scampering along beside him. I jumped as an irate motorist braked sharply and blared his horn.

'I'm not waiting half an hour for the red man to change to a green one,' Teddy countered, pulling me along. Patience had never been my ex-husband's virtue. 'Keep up, Soph. Pretend we're Batman and Robin on a mission.'

'Except any moment now we might become Flatman and Ribbon,' I gasped, as a bus bore down upon us.

I had a fleeting vision of us both being mown down together. The last thing I wanted was to expire before my wedding day. Apart from anything else, what the hell would George say? "Why was my fiancée in Brighton with her ex-husband?"

The village would have a field day nattering about it, no doubt putting two and two together and coming up with six-hundred and eighty. I could imagine Mabel Plaistow, joining in the gossip. "I always wondered if that Sophie Fairfax still harboured a soft spot for her ex. I remember Teddy. He once visited Ruby's salon and Sophie got all in a dither. She knocked over the trolley, scattered hair rollers everywhere, tripped over a fallen can of hairspray and then forgot to breathe." The reality was that Teddy had accidentally elbowed the trolley over in his haste to take a call from a girlfriend.

'We made it!' Teddy shouted, punching the air with his free hand.

We sprang onto the pavement, only narrowly avoiding a female cyclist. She took to her bicycle bell like an irate customer summoning Basil Fawlty to reception.

'After that experience, I think I need a lie-down,' I said faintly.

'Now you're talking,' said Teddy happily. 'I can find us a sumptuous B&B with bedsprings designed to accommodate the most robust of lie-downs.'

'Oh, *please*,' I sighed, rolling my eyes.

'No need to beg,' he winked. 'The Grand Hotel is just along the waterfront. I'll use my good looks and smooth patter to book us in for some afternoon delight.'

I shook off his hand.

'I meant *please* as in *give over.*'

'What's that?' Teddy feigned sudden deafness. 'Did you say *leg over?*'

I let out an exasperated sigh.

'I'm starting to think that coming out with you was a

bad idea. Quit the fooling around and take me to whatever greasy spoon you had in mind, because I'm starting to feel *hangry*.'

'Ah, I seem to remember not liking my wife when she gets both hungry and angry.'

'Ex-wife,' I growled.

Teddy backed away in mock alarm.

'Uh-oh. It's happening. Quick, follow me. There's not a moment to lose.'

He took off at a sprint, catching me unawares. Feeling increasingly annoyed, I darted after him, dodging strolling tourists, office workers buying sneaky take-out cappuccinos, and chattering young mums blocking the pavement with baby buggies.

Dodging the latter, I skidded to a halt, then glanced wildly about. Where had my ex-husband gone? Movement caught my eye. Ah, there he was. Teddy had taken a left turn into Ship Street, part of the historic Lanes.

I dashed after him just in time to see a flash of shirt disappear within a beautiful Grade II listed building. The old post office, no less, but now named *The Ivy*. I shot through the door and nearly cannoned into the back of him as he conferred with the maître'd.

'This way, Soph,' he beamed, before following the young man. I hastened after them both, nearly bashing into Teddy again when the maître'd abruptly stopped at a table for two. A chair was pulled out for me.

'Madam.'

'Thanks,' I muttered, sitting down heavily. I felt hot,

bothered and out of sorts.

'What would you like to drink?' asked Teddy.

'A bucket of water comes to mind,' I gasped.

Foolishly I'd left home without a bottle of Evian. Post hangover, the earlier black coffee and warmth of the day had left me feeling horribly dehydrated.

'A pot of tea and a bottle of champagne,' said Teddy smoothly.

'Oh, Teddy, I don't think–'

'And we'll both have your Full English, please, and as soon as possible as my good lady here is ready to pass out from hunger.'

'Of course, sir,' said the maître'd, looking bemused.

As the waiter melted away, Teddy gestured with one hand.

'So, what do you think?'

I glanced about, taking in the opulent bar, high ceilings, and exotic palm leaf wallpaper. The latter was smothered in nature prints and an overload of mirrors.

'It certainly has the wow factor,' I said.

'They say their décor is inspired by the nearby Royal Pavilion.'

'I can believe that,' I nodded. 'Listen, this is very nice of you to bring me here, but it really wasn't necessary.'

'I wanted you to have a lovely last day of freedom.'

'Don't say it like that,' I tutted. 'You make it sound as if I'm about to go down for ten years.'

'You know what I mean,' Teddy smiled. 'Listen, Soph.' He took my hand across the table. 'It's okay,' he assured, catching the look on my face. 'I'm not about to chat you up or bombard you with further suggestions of a sexy romp. I'm being serious.'

'Okay,' I said cautiously. 'What is it you want to say?'

He took a deep breath.

'Once upon a time we were husband and wife, and despite me being a lousy partner, I still care deeply about you, okay? So, I simply want to say that if George ever treats you badly, then you tell me, right?'

'What would you do? Bop him on the nose?'

'Maybe,' he shrugged. 'Just remember that I'm always here for you.'

I regarded Teddy across the expanse of white linen. He was still a good-looking man. Thanks to his trip to Turkey, he had a full head of hair. It was flecked with grey, but it made him look distinguished. I gave his hand a grateful squeeze, acknowledging his caring words.

'That's a very sweet thing to say, Teddy. And thank you. However, George is very reliable, and I don't anticipate ever needing to lean on anyone other than him.'

'You're probably right,' Teddy sighed. 'I'm jealous that he is the one marrying you tomorrow. However, nothing will change my opinion of him. I still think George is a boring old fart.'

'Right,' I said, giving my ex-husband a benign smile.

'I guess a fart is like success. It only bothers you when it's not your own.'

'Ah, a Teddy Fairfax pearl of wisdom.'

'Oh, I have plenty of those,' he said, suddenly morose.

66

'One day you'll find Mrs Right,' I said warmly.

'I had Mrs Right, but stupidly, I let her go.'

My eyes momentarily brimmed. Occasionally, my ex-husband said something that tugged at my heartstrings. This was such a moment. Sometimes Teddy could be such a sweetheart.

'Aye–aye, things are looking up,' he beamed, breaking the moment.

He straightened in his seat. I was well acquainted with such body language having witnessed it many times. It usually happened when he'd spotted an attractive member of the opposite sex. He'd follow up with a smouldering look. Sure enough, a pretty waitress was heading our way, bearing tea and champagne.

I smiled to myself. At other times, Teddy could be such a knob.

Chapter Eleven

'That was superb,' I said, as we later strolled along Brighton Pier.

'A late breakfast at The Ivy,' said Teddy with satisfaction. 'Far more civilised than Chloe's Café, don't you agree?'

'Careful,' I warned. 'You're in danger of sounding like a roaring snob.'

Chloe was a lovely girl – well, if you could refer to someone in their forties as a girl. Little Waterlow's diner was a cross between a trucker's greasy spoon and a cake shop. Chloe did all her own cooking, from sausage, bacon, and egg, to featherlight sponges and mouth-watering cheesecakes.

'I'm not dissing Chloe or her café,' Teddy protested. 'I just wanted to, er, well, you know, give the place a bit of distance for now and–'

I stopped walking and stared at Teddy in amazement.

'Oh, for heaven's sake. I get it. You recently made a play for Chloe.'

'Um, maybe.'

'And she turned you down.'

'Er, sort of. Oh, okay. Yes, she did. But in the nicest possible way,' he added defensively. He paused by a pop-up refreshment stall selling lurid pink and blue drinks that were little more than coloured ice. 'Want one?'

I shook my head.

'No thanks.'

'I'll grab one. Hang on a mo.' He fished in his pocket for change, then his wallet for a note. Upon finding neither, he presented the vendor with his bank card.

As I waited for him to pay, I thought about Teddy asking Chloe out. It didn't surprise me. She was totally his type, meaning everything was enhanced – chest, eyelashes, nails, lips. Even her teeth looked like they belonged to a reality star. Rumour had it that she'd run away from her bully of a husband and changed her identity.

Fred Plaistow had once dared to ask Chloe if her name was a pseudonym. The old man had been rewarded with a cool look and the question had gone unanswered. Mabel Plaistow had gone one step further telling anyone who'd listen that Chloe had likely murdered her husband, thus stoking the flames of speculation.

'Do you think I'm losing my touch?' said Teddy, looking worried. 'I miss not having a pouting girlfriend telling me I'm her Teddy Bear. In fact, I haven't had a girlfriend for ages.'

'Define *ages.*'

Teddy took a slurp of his slushy ice drink as he considered.

'At least a week or so.'

'Is that all?' I hooted with laughter. 'You're being silly. Do you know, after we went our separate ways, it was months before I even *thought* about going on a date with a guy.'

'That's the difference between you and me,' said Teddy sagely. 'You're very fussy.'

'No, it means you're a tart and I'm not. Oh, look.' Ahead, and set to one side of the pier, was an old-fashioned gypsy caravan. 'A fortune teller!'

The caravan was charm itself in summery shades of pastel pink and sky blue. Large red roses were painted around the entrance.

'Come on.' I said excitedly, tugging on Teddy's forearm. 'Let's find out what the future holds.'

'I can tell you straight away that it involves a loss of money.'

'Don't be so negative,' I chided, moving towards the half dozen steps to the entrance.

'It's true,' Teddy protested. 'I'll bet this so-called psychic's fees are at least thirty quid.'

'So? We can both afford it. And anyway, I thought today was meant to be my hen day. A bride-to-be gets to choose what she wants to do.'

'Oh, go on then,' Teddy grumbled.

I peered at a sandwich-board sign resting at the foot of the steps.

Madam Rosa

If it's truth you seek, you're in the right place,

But if you're unsure, then do an about-face.

Teddy, reading over my shoulder, groaned aloud.

'What a load of bull–'

'Teddy!' I reprimanded, just as a female appeared at the top of the steps.

She looked as ordinary as the next person, so I took her to be a departing customer.

'Is Madam Rosa any good?' I enquired.

'Spot on,' she replied. 'She's the woman who knows everything.'

Teddy gave her his best I-want-to-have-sex-with-you smile.

'Did she tell you that you look like an angel seconds away from meeting her soulmate?'

The woman looked Teddy up and down.

'*I'm* Madam Rosa,' she said brusquely. 'And today isn't your lucky day, Mr Fairfax. Or should I say *Teddy Bear*? I gather that's what you like the ladies to call you.'

Teddy's jaw dropped.

'How on earth–'

'I just told you' – she gave Teddy a disdainful look – 'I'm the woman who knows everything. Now, are you having a reading, or not?'

'You're the psychic, you tell me,' Teddy quipped nervously.

'I-I'd like one, please,' I stammered, interrupting the tension zigzagging between this no-nonsense woman and my gobsmacked ex-husband.

Madam Rosa's eyes swivelled from Teddy to me. For a few uncomfortable moments, she didn't speak. Was she scanning my aura, or something?

'Very well,' she eventually said. 'You certainly look like a woman who needs some straight-talking advice.'

'Really?' I quavered, as my stomach inexplicably

contracted.

'Meanwhile, Mr Fairfax' – she turned her attention back to Teddy – 'why don't you take your drink and sit in a deckchair while waiting for your ex-wife.' She gave him the ghost of a smile. 'You can keep an eye out for an angel whose seconds away from meeting her soulmate.' Teddy had the grace to blush. Madam Rosa's eyes flicked back to me. 'Come in,' she invited. 'Let me tell you more.'

'Okay,' I whispered, suddenly feeling ridiculously nervous.

Tentatively, I climbed the wooden steps.

Chapter Twelve

'Oh God,' I wailed to Teddy. 'What if everything she said comes true?'

'Don't be ridiculous,' he scoffed.

We were back in his sportscar, heading home to Little Waterlow. The wind tugged at my hair. The day was still warm, but a chill seemed to have settled around my heart.

'But she *knew* things,' I pointed out.

'Coincidence,' he said dismissively.

'She called you by your name. Mr Fairfax.'

'Yes, I was pondering over that and I've sussed how she pulled that off. If you remember, I'd just paid for my drink at that nearby pop-up stall.'

'And?'

'I was still holding my debit card. Madam Rosa must have somehow read my name from the plastic.'

'Oh, right, no doubt using her superhuman razor-sharp vision,' I said scornfully.

'Perhaps she was wearing really strong contact lenses.'

'What, like a pair of magnifying glasses taped to her eyeballs? She'd have needed something like that to have read from that distance.' I pulled a face. 'That aside, how do you explain her knowing that past girlfriends have called you

Teddy Bear?'

'Because' – Teddy's voice took on a tone of exaggerated patience – 'if you cast your mind back, I mentioned it. I said I missed not currently having a girlfriend calling me *her Teddy Bear*. Remember?'

I did. Right... right, okay. I was silent for a moment. Things still didn't stack up.

'So, how did she know I was your ex-wife?'

'I don't remember Madam Rosa saying that.'

'You surely must. It was when she suggested you find a deckchair to sit in while waiting for me. That was when she referred to me as your ex-wife. I mean, why not just say *wife*?'

Teddy shrugged as we roared along a slip road and joined the motorway.

'Madam Rosa made a lucky guess,' he said, accelerating over to the outside lane.

I shook my head, my mind going back to Teddy and me on the pier and the moment we'd stopped by Madam Rosa's caravan. I began to replay the conversation we'd been having at the time. We'd been talking about the proprietor of Little Waterlow's café – Chloe – and how Teddy had asked her out but been rebuffed.

I mentally rewound my memory, pressing the pause button on Teddy saying... what? I screwed up my face in concentration. *What* had he been about to reveal? I pressed the play button again, this time slowing the memory down, until it was frame by frame and... there!

I forensically scrutinised the mental scene. There was

Teddy slurping on a pink and blue drink. Hm. Coincidental. It matched the gypsy caravan's paintwork. He'd also been lamenting about it being ages since he'd had a girlfriend. *A week or so*, had been his precise words. And I'd poo-pooed the comment. I'd stated that, after we'd separated, it had been months before I'd dated a guy. In fact, my exact words had been *after we went our separate ways*. Bingo! I'd found the moment where an outsider listening in would have known I was Teddy's ex-wife.

'Cracked it,' I trilled gleefully. 'It *did* come up in our conversation. You know, about me being your ex.'

'Are you sure?'

'Definitely,' I said, exhaling with relief. 'Also, I've just twigged something.'

'Oh?'

'That pop-up stall, where you bought your drink–'

'What about it?'

'Well, I reckon the vendor was in cahoots with Madama Rosa.'

'How do you work that one out?'

'Because' – this time it was my turn to adopt a tone of exaggerated patience – 'the first clue is that both your drink and Madam Rosa's caravan were pink and blue.'

'Don't open your detective agency just yet, Soph,' said Teddy, dissolving into giggles.

'Second' – I persisted, ignoring his mirth – 'both the drinks stall and the caravan were quite close to each other. Therefore, Madam Rosa might possibly have overheard our conversation.' I nodded to myself, warming to my task.

'Third–'

'Oh, there's a third clue?' Teddy asked, eyes wide as he feigned astonishment.

'Third' – I repeated – 'the vendor and the fortune teller likely know each other, meaning that the vendor probably texts Madam Rosa pertinent details on customers' bank cards so that Madam Rosa looks super-intuitive coming out with a person's name when she's never before met them!'

Teddy briefly took his hands off the steering wheel and gave me a quick round of applause.

'My goodness, Soph. You have to get up early in the morning to get one past you, eh!'

I smirked, then looked out the side window. We were whizzing past fields of sheep, the animals unperturbed by traffic noise. I watched them grazing, looking so peaceful. How delightful. Now another field, this time full of cows. Lovely. And, oh look, yet another meadow, this time with horses, and two of them had darling little foals hugging their flanks. I felt a wave of contentment wash over me. All was well in the world.

Or was it? I let out a strangled squeak.

'What's the matter now?' asked Teddy, glancing at me in alarm.

'That still doesn't explain how she knew about Thomas Tabby Cat, or–'

'Whoa, hang on a minute.' Teddy made a back-peddling gesture with one hand. 'Earlier on this morning, at your place, you asked me if I was Thomas Tabby Cat. Who the heck is this guy?'

I took a deep breath.

'Thomas Tabby Cat is an anonymous person with a fake Instagram account who sent me a horrible message informing me that George was a cheater.'

'WHAAAAAT?' Teddy roared, nearly driving up the backside of a van. 'Don't tell me you fell for that nonsense?'

'I can't deny that the message upset me.'

'Is that why you wanted to see a fortune teller? Because you wanted Madam Rosa to tell you that George is a faithful nerd who wears grey suits to match his grey hair and his even greyer personality?'

'I guess so,' I snapped.

'Well more fool you for wasting your dosh, because I could've told you that for free. George isn't shagging around. What woman in her right mind would even give him a second glance?' Teddy caught me looking daggers. 'Sorry, sorry,' he added quickly. 'I didn't mean to offend you, but I've privately wondered how he managed to pull a bird like you. The guy is punching.'

'What do you mean?' I scowled, shifting uncomfortably in my seat. Ruby had recently used that same word. *Punching*.

'You're beautiful.'

'Teddy, I'm fifty years old. I'm not beautiful.'

He sighed, and it seemed as if the weight of the world was suddenly on his shoulders.

'What the eff has age got to do with beauty?' he said in annoyance. 'So what if you're fifty. *So bloody what?* You're gorgeous. Abso-bloody-lutely *gorgeous.*' He made a tutting sound. 'This is all my fault.' He shook his head sadly. 'All those years of me playing away knocked your self-confidence. In other words, you haven't got any.' He slapped his forehead. 'It's so obvious to me now. That's why you've settled for a man like George. Mr Ordinary. Mr Play-It-Safe. My lovely Sophie accepted Mr Boring Fart's marriage proposal because she knew her heart would never get smashed to smithereens again. And I'll bet Madam Rosa didn't have to dig too deep to unearth that little gem.'

I didn't answer.

'I knew it,' Teddy growled. 'What else did this fraudster say?'

'Plenty,' I muttered.

'Did she advise you not to marry George?'

'Sort of,' I said, my voice flat.

'Did she tell you to wait because your soulmate was on the horizon?'

'Sort of,' I repeated.

'Isn't it obvious?'

Teddy had inadvertently slowed the sportscar right down and we both jumped as another motorist undertook us, horn blaring. Teddy floored the accelerator again, and I clutched the sides of the bucket seat as my head momentarily whipped back.

'Isn't what obvious?' I prompted.

Teddy reached across the divide and grabbed my hand.

'We should never have split up. *I'm* your soulmate, and *I'm* the one you're meant to marry tomorrow morning.'

Chapter Thirteen

I lifted my suitcase onto the bed and unzipped it. As the lid flopped back on the duvet, I reached for my prepared list of what to pack.

Moving around the bedroom, I began to methodically open drawers, removing things from within. There was a small pile of beautiful lingerie, not yet worn, bought specifically for my honeymoon. There were also new dresses for the evening, old t-shirts and shorts for sightseeing and – I fingered some shiny blue fabric between my thumb and forefinger – my very first all-in-one swimsuit.

Previously, I'd always worn bikinis when holidaying, but a little while ago George had made a negative comment that had rattled me. He'd said that middle-aged women shouldn't wear bikinis, and that men found flabby midriffs a massive turnoff.

I'd filed the comment away. Taken note. I'd never had children, so didn't have visible *recti divarication* – abdominal separation – but there was no denying the creping belly skin. When leaning forward, my stomach pleated like the cheeks of an old lady.

I folded the sensible navy-blue costume complete with Hattie Jacques built-in cups and popped it within the suitcase.

Okay, it made me look like someone's maiden aunt, but at least my midriff wouldn't put off any man getting to grips with his cornetto.

Teddy had left half an hour ago, hugging me affectionately and wishing me all the best for tomorrow. I'd thanked him for the lovely impromptu hen day, and he'd told me not to worry about Madam Rosa's reading.

'She really put the wind up me,' I'd said, prior to waving him off.

'Thus confirming' – Teddy had quipped – 'that George truly is a boring fart.'

As such, Madam Rosa hadn't talked about George. Instead, she'd mentioned a man who lived where the sun was hot, who had a passion for fine wine and good food. This man had dark hair and eyes that often twinkled with mischief, danced with merriment, and smouldered with love.

'This man is your future. You will live and work side by side and be incredibly happy,' she'd declared with unwavering certainty.

'Sorry,' I'd said, trying not to bristle. 'You're wrong. Tomorrow I'm marrying a man called George Baker.'

Ha! Madam Rosa had come across as a clever clog smoothly coming up with my ex-husband's name, but she hadn't been able to do that with my fiancé, had she! Nor had she been able to tell me the name of this so-called future love interest.

'Sometimes I must be careful with what I say because of the laws of karma,' she'd said mysteriously. 'Even so, Fate tends to look after itself. You can't interfere with it. Nor can you change it. It makes not a jot of difference if you get married to George Baker tomorrow because I see you, eventually, with someone else. All will be revealed when the moment is right. Oh dear, I can see my words have upset you, and I apologise. But karma or not' – Madam Rosa had made a dismissive gesture with one hand – 'I cannot have it on my conscience not to be truthful. The universe has already given you a warning.' She'd given me a strict look. It had also been a telling look. 'Thomas Tabby Cat.'

I'd violently flinched.

'How can you possibly know about that?' I'd whispered.

'How many times must I reiterate that I'm the woman who knows everything?'

'What's this week's lottery numbers?' I'd feebly joked, while trying to calm my racing heart.

'I'm not allowed to reveal such information, or it would jeopardise my gift. Now, back to Thomas Tabby Cat. You know this person. What's more, their message was one of truth.'

I'd jumped up so quickly I'd banged my head on the gypsy caravan's low ceiling.

'Thank you, Madam Rosa, but I'd now like to end this session. Your reading isn't quite what I was expecting.'

'You were anticipating froth and frivolity,' she'd nodded. 'Everyone does. However, I'm not a seaside charlatan, and that's why I have a printed warning by the caravan's steps. My readings are not for the faint-hearted.'

'Thank you for your time,' I'd said stiffly.

'I'd like to leave you with some wise words. Someone

once said to me, *what if the worst thing that ever happened to you turned out to be for the best.'*

I looked at her, dumbstruck. What sort of ridiculous comment was that? If, for example, a doctor gave you a week to live, how could that possibly be a blessing? Madam Rosa's gaze was unwavering.

'Remember those words as you go through the days and weeks ahead.'

Oh, the woman was barking. Absolutely doolally. Not to mention emotionally cruel. Her printed warning should be rewritten, and more appropriately so:

If you want your day to go without a hitch,
Do not visit this psychic because she is a bitch!

Well stuff you, Madam Rosa.

Irked, I picked up a bottle of Factor 20 suncream and popped it into the suitcase alongside the matronly swimsuit. Tomorrow I *would* marry George Baker and, what's more, I was going to have a fabulous day and a totally brilliant honeymoon. So there.

Chapter Fourteen

'Here she is!' cried Ruby, as I walked into the salon on Saturday morning.

Today, young Meg was in situ. Ruby and Meg had met at hairdressing college. Meg was a Saturday morning fixture, providing a nail gelling service.

'Hi, Sophie,' Meg dimpled.

'Hiya, girls,' I chirped, doing my best to sound like an excited bride-to-be.

'It's just the three of us for the next couple of hours,' Ruby beamed. 'Let's start with a mini celebration.' Like a magician, she produced a flute of champagne. 'Here, get this down you.'

'Oh, Rubes, you shouldn't have–'

'Don't protest,' she admonished, wagging a forefinger. 'This is a special day. A *life*changing day.'

I stretched my smile even wider, hiding the frisson of alarm at Ruby's last sentence. It was indeed going to be a lifechanging day. After today, I would always sleep next to George Baker, the man who wore grey silk pyjamas to bed, always mindful of colour-coordinating his nightwear to his bedroom's soft furnishings.

'Cheers,' I said, mustering enthusiasm.

What was the matter with me? Outside, the sun had dipped behind a cloud. In an instant the sky became the same colour as George's hair.

'All the best for later,' said Ruby, clinking her glass against mine and Meg's. She took a few greedy glugs. 'Mm, that's good. I wish every day could start so decadently.' She put the flute down and produced a protective gown, waving it through the air like a matador getting a bull's attention. 'There,' she beamed, as the cape whirled around my torso. She did up the tie at the base of my neck. 'Come and park your botty by the basin and let your Aunty Ruby get to work with the shampoo.'

And so the wedding preparations got underway.

I left the salon with my cloud of dark hair transformed into a sleek curtain trailing down my back. My nails looked so elegant I had to keep checking my hands, not quite able to believe they were really mine.

Once back at Catkin Cottage, I carefully put on a spa headband and set about applying bridal makeup.

My wedding outfit awaited. Currently it was hanging from the bedroom door, in a protective wrapper. The pretty cream dress artfully hugged my bust and generous curves. It gave the illusion of voluptuousness rather than too much time spent in the company of Mr Kipling's cakes. A bolero jacket, satin heels and matching clutch completed the elegant ensemble.

The doorbell rang halfway through an application of mascara. I gave my lashes a last upward swipe, before hastening down the staircase to see who it was.

'Becky!'

I smiled a greeting at our local florist's assistant.

'Special delivery,' she beamed. 'One very beautiful bride's bouquet.' She held a long slim box aloft.

'Can you take it through to the kitchen and pop it on the worktop?'

'Of course,' she said, stepping into the hallway. 'Through here, right?'

I nodded and followed behind her, holding my breath in anticipation as Becky reverently set the box down and then opened the lid.

'Oooh, that's stunning,' I gasped, marvelling at the exquisite cerise roses, perfect lemon dahlias, elegant cream orchids, feathery purple carnations, and finger-like fronds of lilac all set off by bright emerald foliage and a froth of Baby's Breath. 'The colours are straight out of Aladdin's Cave. I love it.'

'Good to hear,' Becky smiled. 'I'll leave the lid open. Flowers don't like being in the dark.' She made her way back to the hallway. 'Have a fabulous day!'

'Thank you.'

I shut the door and was just about to return upstairs when the doorbell rang for a second time. It was Sue and Charlie.

'Please tell me you're early,' I shrieked, clutching my heart.

'Yes, yes, we're early,' Sue assured.

She stepped over the threshold, her avuncular husband bringing up the rear. Suddenly the hallway seemed to shrink in size. Three people in this space was one too many.

'Go through to the lounge,' I said, flapping a hand. 'Make yourself a drink or something. I haven't finished my makeup and need to get a wiggle on.'

'Panic ye not,' said Charlie. 'I'd love a small G & T, Sophie. Your chauffeur is allowed one small tipple without exceeding his alcohol limit while on driving duties.'

'For heaven's sake, Charlie,' said Sue, planting her hands on her hips. 'Make your own gin and tonic. Sophie needs to finish herself off.'

'If you don't mind,' I said, making for the staircase again.

'Hang on.' Charlie summoned me back. 'You haven't seen the motor,' he gently admonished, all the while looking mighty pleased with himself.

I moved to the window, peered out, then gasped aloud. Charlie's car was polished to within an inch of its life and now sported a beautiful white ribbon on the bonnet.

'Oh, my word, it looks amazing. Thank you,' I said, giving him a hug. Sue joined us, smiling fondly. I released Charlie and embraced her too. 'I'm so grateful to have my dearest friends with me today. Charlie, thank you for being my chauffeur. And Sue, thank you for being my Matron of Honour and best friend. You've been a rock, especially when I was going through some dark days. You kept me sane, pointing out that feeling down wasn't due to a blocked chakra.'

Sue laughed.

'Your divorce and redundancy played a part too.'

'I'm better at unblocking drains than chakras,' Charlie

pointed out, but he was visibly palpitating with pleasure. 'Does that mean you'll now make me a gin and tonic?'

'No!' said Sue, giving him a little shove. 'Go and make it yourself and, while you're at it, do one for us too.'

'I'm fine,' I protested. 'I'm not a fan of gin and had some champagne earlier. I don't want to be tipsy when I arrive at the registry office.'

'Nonsense. Make one for Soph anyway,' Sue instructed Charlie. 'I'll drink it if she doesn't. Meanwhile, I'm going to look at the dress and titivate. Also' – she took me by the arm and steered me down the hallway – 'I want a little chat.'

'Oooh, that sounds ominous,' I joked.

'It's meant to,' she grimaced, as we went upstairs. 'I want a heart to heart.'

'About what?' I asked, feeling a flutter of panic.

'I have a question for you, Soph. Are you sure you're doing the right thing marrying George?'

Chapter Fifteen

'Sue!' I protested, as my bestie frogmarched me into the bedroom. 'Of *course* I'm doing the right thing in marrying George. Fancy even asking such a question on my wedding day.'

'I just want to be sure that *you're* sure,' said Sue. 'The other day your nerves were like stretched knicker elastic.'

'No, they weren't,' I protested.

Sue arched an eyebrow.

'Thomas Tabby Cat,' she pointed out. 'Does that ring any bells?'

'Oh that,' I said dismissively. 'I thought we'd agreed it was a nasty little troll.'

No way was I telling her about my jaunt to Brighton and Madam Rosa's prediction.

'Yes, more than likely,' Sue nodded, walking over to my dress. She let out a low whistle. 'Very nice, Soph. I can't wait to see you in this. Let me help you with the zip.'

'Hang on,' I said, grabbing my lipstick and carefully slicking the gloss around my mouth. 'Okay, ready.'

'Oh, wow,' said Charlie as, ten minutes later, I entered the lounge. 'You look beautiful, sweetheart.' He came over and gave my arm a squeeze. 'If I didn't have the lovely Sue in my life, I'd marry you myself.'

'Thanks, Charlie,' I beamed.

'You look an absolute doll,' said Sue approvingly. 'Let's finish our G & T's, then head off.'

'Oooh,' I gasped, as a netful of butterflies took off in my stomach. 'I suddenly feel a bit nervous.'

'It's not nerves.' Sue shook her head before necking the rest of her drink. 'Rather, excitement.'

'Yes, of course,' I said, not entirely convinced as I drained my own glass.

'Don't forget your bouquet,' said Charlie, pressing the flowers into my hands.

I tried not to clutch them to my chest like a lifebuoy.

'Hold it there,' said Sue, whipping out her mobile. 'Let me take a quick pic. Smile, Sophie. After all, you're getting married, not going to a funeral.'

I bared my teeth at the camera, willing them not to chatter. Why was I suddenly so nervous? I hadn't felt like this when I'd married Teddy.

Charlie led the way out of the cottage, then gallantly opened the car's passenger door.

'Bride in the front,' he said, as Sue moved to the rear door. Seconds later, the three of us were buckled up. 'And we're off,' Charlie beamed.

The car purred down the lane before taking a right turn, heading off in the direction of the registry office.

Fifteen minutes later, Charlie pulled over kerbside to let me and Sue out. George was already there, waiting on the pavement with Graham and Jackie. The three of them were chatting animatedly. George looked smart in a brand-new charcoal grey suit. Graham was similarly attired while Jackie looked svelte in a tailored beige ensemble.

'You're here,' George grinned as I got out of the car.

I smoothed down my dress with one hand.

'Were you worried I'd stand you up?' I bantered, planting a kiss on his cheek.

George's smile faltered.

'Have you been drinking?' he asked, leaning in and sniffing.

Jackie and Graham looked embarrassed and moved away, pretending not to have overheard.

'Well, I–'

Sue put a hand on my arm, indicating I say no more, then flashed George an *up yours* look.

'We all had a glass of Dutch Courage before leaving Catkin Cottage,' she explained. 'I expect you've had a little tipple too, eh?'

'No.' George shook his head and frowned. 'I hope you don't fluff your lines, Sophie.'

'I won't,' I soothed. 'You look very handsome, darling.'

'Thank you,' said George, not returning the compliment. Instead, his gaze fell upon my bouquet. 'Good God,' he muttered, eyeballing it in horror.

'W–What?' I said in alarm.

'Those… those *flowers*,' he spluttered. 'They're hideous.'

'I have to agree,' said Jackie, coming over. 'What on earth possessed you, Sophie? The colours are so gaudy.'

90

'What are you talking about?' said Sue, outraged. 'They're absolutely beautiful, just like Sophie.'

'They're tacky,' countered Jackie, giving them a disdainful look.

'Nobody asked for your opinion,' said Sue sharply.

'They look like something you'd buy from a garage,' said George, ignoring Sue. 'Why didn't you ask the florist for neutral tones?'

'Because I like them,' I said in a small voice.

'Too late to do anything about it now,' snapped George. 'Just make sure they don't appear in the photographs.'

'Ladies and gentlemen,' interrupted Graham, ignoring the fraught atmosphere. 'I think we should be making our way inside.'

'Where's my husband?' said Sue, immediately distracted.

'He's parking the car,' said Graham smoothly. 'In his absence, I'm happy to escort you inside the building.' He valiantly proffered his elbow. 'I'm sure my good lady wife won't mind in the least.'

'In which case' – said Jackie testily – 'George will have to do the honour of escorting your *good lady wife*.'

And with that Jackie linked arms with my fiancé, letting him lead her up the steps to the old town hall while I trailed awkwardly behind.

Chapter Sixteen

'Good afternoon,' trilled a female voice.

I shuffled past Sue, who was still holding Graham's arm, just in time to see the female registrar greeting George and Jackie.

'Hello, Sophie and George,' said the registrar. 'I'm Glenda Wales, your marriage officiant. Are you both excited?'

'Thrilled to bits,' drawled Jackie. 'But I'm not the bride.'

'Oh,' said Glenda, looking taken aback. 'Um, are you Sophie? she asked Sue.

'Try again,' I said, waving my bouquet for attention.

'I do apologise,' said Glenda. She gave Jackie a fleeting look of bewilderment, before switching her attention back to me. 'Sophie, can I ask you to stand alongside George. That's it,' she nodded, as Jackie finally relinquished my fiancé's arm. 'Is everyone here?' she asked George.

'They are now,' called Charlie, hastening over. 'Sorry to be late, folks. The car park was rammed.'

'Right,' said Glenda. 'Everyone, please follow me.'

A few minutes later, Glenda was stationed beside an ornamental desk in a pleasant ceremony room. The space was filled with lots of silk flowers and several rows of chairs for guests. Sue and Charlie were seated in the right aisle, with Graham and Jackie sitting to the left.

Vivaldi's *Four Seasons* suddenly filled the room. George whisked me down the short aisle so quickly, the introductory music seemed to continue playing for an eternity.

As the violins joyfully depicted a musical explosion of flowers blooming, butterflies dancing and birds endlessly trilling and warbling, Glenda stared at a point on the ceiling. I glanced nervously at Sue and Charlie. Both seemed to be enthralled with their shoes. A sneak peek at Graham and Jackie revealed Graham transfixed by a giant orchid while Jackie studied her nails.

I stood next to George inwardly cringing at the awkwardness of the moment. He gave my arm a subtle squeeze. Thinking he was being affectionate, I returned it with one of my own.

I glanced up at him, relieved all was well again. However, George was regarding me with a grim expression. He jerked his head at my bouquet. Inwardly sighing, I passed the flowers to Sue just as the interminable music finally faded to silence.

'Good afternoon, everyone,' began Glenda. 'We are gathered here today to witness the marriage of George and Sophie.'

And we were off.

In no time at all Glenda had whizzed us through the traditional vows, with us solemnly declaring there was no lawful impediment why we shouldn't be joined in matrimony. I experienced a split second of hysteria, imagining my bouquet being able to speak, and quivering with indignation at George's rejection. "My advice is to leaf him."

There was a pause while Jackie read a poem called *My True Love* by Sir Philip Sydney. As she delivered each line in a mournful voice, her gaze was firmly on George. I discreetly looked at Graham, wondering if he thought this somewhat odd, but he was busy with his own fixation. Namely, Glenda's sizeable chest.

Jackie sat down, and Glenda cleared her throat.

'And now it is time for the personal marriage promises. Face each other, please.' She smiled at George. 'George, do you promise to respect Sophie as an individual, support her through difficult times, rejoice with her through happy times, be loyal to her always and, above all, love her as your wife and friend?'

'I do,' George intoned, his gaze on someone in the aisle behind me. Graham? Or Jackie? What was going on here? Why wasn't he looking at me?'

'Sophie, do you promise to care for George above all others, to give him your love and friendship, support and comfort, and to respect and cherish him throughout your lives together?'

'I do,' I said, looking up at George, whose focus remained elsewhere.

'Lovely,' said Glenda. 'George, please repeat after me. I give you this ring, Sophie, as a token of my love and friendship...'

And suddenly the pair of us were wearing shiny gold

bands and it was time to do the signing of the legal schedule.

Glenda picked up my bouquet and artfully set it down on the ornamental desk, thus including it in the photographs. George immediately gathered it up again. He passed it to Jackie, who tossed it onto a nearby seat. Sue promptly scooped up the bouquet and returned it to the desk. George gave Sue a baleful look. Sue glared back. Charlie's eyes flicked backwards and forwards between the two of them, clearly baffled why everyone was suddenly playing a floral version of *pass the parcel*. Graham, familiar with both his wife and best mate's preference for neutral colours, nervously backed away, while Glenda looked on, mystified at the sudden sub-zero temperature. George was about to reach for the bouquet again, but I beat him to it.

'Thank you,' I said, snatching up the flowers and giving George a challenging look. 'As my bouquet cost a small fortune, I'll keep hold of it.'

George's mouth pursed, but he didn't reply. We dutifully posed for the pictures that followed, although I was aware that the pair of us were smiling through gritted teeth.

We departed from the ceremony room to the sound of Barbra Streisand singing *Evergreen.* As I listened to her warbling away about love being like a rose, I looked at my brightly coloured bouquet and experienced a feeling of unease.

Outside, on the steps of the town hall, Sue removed a packet of confetti from her clutch bag and flung it at George and me.

'Smile,' she shouted, snapping away as the pink paper

petals whirled through the air.

For a moment we forgot about the silent dispute over the wretched bouquet and grinned away. It was our wedding day, and we'd just got married. Hurray!

'Stop that.' Jackie's voice was like a pistol shot as she rounded on Sue. 'Can't you read? There's a large sign over there that says *No confetti throwing.*'

Chapter Seventeen

'Sorry, George' – Sue didn't sound remotely apologetic – 'but your best man's wife is the most miserable woman I've ever had the misfortune to meet.'

George and I were now sitting in the back of Charlie's car. Sue's head had swivelled one hundred and eighty degrees to see how my husband was taking this little homily. Not well, judging from the way his mouth had disappeared into a thin line.

'Lovely wedding,' said Charlie, diplomatically steering the conversation down a different path. He signalled and pulled out, sharply accelerating after the Rollinsons' car, so that we were now travelling in tandem to The Angel for the wedding breakfast. 'You've been lucky with the weather too,' Charlie prattled. 'The sun hasn't stopped shining.' His gaze met mine in the rear-view mirror. *Let's keep this conversation going*, his eyes implored.

'The weather has been perfect,' I agreed, determined to forget about Jackie appropriating George prior to the ceremony and then snatching Sue's box of confetti immediately afterwards. 'Although it's meant to be changing tomorrow. It's going to get a little unsettled.' A bit like the hostility between Jackie and Sue.

There had been something of a standoff between the two women as we'd all stood on the steps of the town hall. After Jackie had appropriated the confetti box from Sue, my bestie had promptly snatched it back. She'd then sweetly enquired if the drama Jackie was trying to create would have an interval, whereupon Jackie had told Sue not to be so rude. Sue had then put her hands on her hips and said, "Whatever. I've been called much worse by far better." Whereupon Jackie had retorted, "Keep rolling your eyes. You might find your brain back there."

Charlie, aghast at the altercation, had promptly tried to laugh the whole thing off. He'd then grabbed Sue's arm, propelling her down the steps, his smile fixed as he'd said, "Come with me, darling. I need some help reversing the car after parking it in a tight spot."

The moment they were out of earshot, George had rounded on me.

'And you say she's your best friend, Sophie? After today, I think that's one friendship that should be knocked on the head.'

'What do you mean?' I'd gasped.

'Exactly that,' George had declared. 'That woman has no class, and I would prefer you not to associate with her.'

Jackie had smirked and moved away to talk to Graham.

My eyes had flashed with indignation.

'Please don't tell me who I can and can't be friends with,' I'd hissed. 'I wouldn't dream of telling you not to further associate with Jackie, even though I can't stand her.'

It had then been George's turn to look thoroughly

gobsmacked. There had been no further cross words about the respective women we didn't care for. However, there had been a loaded silence. It now prevailed as Charlie chauffeured us back to Little Waterlow.

Fifteen minutes later, the six of us alighted from our respective cars and walked through The Angel's bar area. The landlady was the first to greet us.

'Congratulations,' trilled Cathy.

She was possibly the second biggest gossip after Mabel Plaistow, likely because her pub was the rural equivalent of *EastEnders'* Queen Vic. Many a village drama had unfolded within its whitewashed walls. The Angel's popularity meant there was always an audience to soak up any public theatre, and plenty of tongues to fuel new gossip.

Cathy guided us through the bar area to Function Room 2, the smaller of the occasion suites reserved for special events.

'Here we are,' she said, opening the door. 'I hope you like the decorations me and my Frank have done for you, Sophie.' She beamed at me expectantly.

'It looks wonderful,' I said truthfully. Coloured balloons and banners were dotted about the place. In the centre of the room was a large table. It had been laid with crisp white linen and polished silver, with a large floral centrepiece. It matched my bouquet perfectly.

'I know you said your colour scheme was eau-de-nil but, honestly, it looked so bland that me and Frank decided to add a bit of oomph.'

'I'm glad you did,' I said warmly, all the while ignoring

George.

In my peripheral vision I could see the look on his face. I caught him doing an eye-meet with Jackie. She returned it with an expression of sympathy. Blasted stuck up woman. Mind you, what did that say about my husband? Evidently, he was a roaring snob too.

Meanwhile Graham had buttonholed Charlie. He was complimenting Charlie on his motor, telling him that it had made a splendid wedding car. Charlie, relieved that Graham hadn't taken umbrage at their respective wives' fall out, visibly swelled with pride. Charlie then began to earnestly tell Graham about the best liquid car polish on the market.

Jackie stalked out of the room, presumably to use the Ladies. George dithered whether to join Graham and Charlie, but then turned on his heel, ostensibly to visit the Gents.

'I'll let you freshen up, Sophie,' said Cathy. 'Frank is just popping the cork on some champagne. He'll be with you in a couple of minutes.'

'Lovely,' I said.

'Come on,' said Sue, taking me by the arm. 'I could do with a wee and I need you with me for protection. Her Royal Highness went off to the loo and I don't want to clash with her again. Bloody cow.'

'Let's just put it behind us,' I said, as we made our way along the corridor, passing Function Room 1 enroute to the Ladies. I paused for a moment. 'When you see her, just smile, and don't say anything. Know that you're the bigger person.'

'I *am* the bigger person,' said Sue mockingly. 'Have you not noted her figure? I've seen lollipop sticks with more fat

100

on them.'

'Shh,' I hissed, as I pushed against the powder room's swing door.

However, the six cubicles within were uninhabited. Nor was anyone standing at the row of sinks opposite.

I exhaled with relief. I didn't want any further locking of horns between Jackie and Sue. I made a mental note to make sure both women were seated as far apart as possible when we returned to Function Room 2.

However, as we stood at the basins washing our hands, Sue couldn't resist bitching.

'I've seen ice cubes with more warmth than that woman.'

I regarded Sue in the overhead mirror's reflection.

'Are you talking about Jackie?'

I rummaged inside my clutch and withdrew a lipstick.

'Of *course* I'm talking about Jackie.' She moved away from the hand dryer and opened her own bag. Removing a tiny glass atomiser, she gave herself a couple of squirts behind each ear. 'If I were to say she had a face like a slapped arse, it would be an insult to backsides all over the country.'

I examined my lipstick application, then pressed my lips together.

'Yes, she is a little chilly,' I acknowledged, chucking the lippy back in my clutch.

'Chilly?' Sue's eyes widened. 'What an understatement. I'll bet she leaves Graham with frostbite after oral sex.'

'Shh,' I hissed, terrified that Sue's voice might carry beyond the restroom. 'Jackie could come in here at any moment.'

'No, I won't shush,' said Sue defiantly. She chucked the mini atomiser back in her bag and regarded me in the mirror. 'Why on earth is George friends with those two? I mean, what's the attraction? She's a cow, and Graham is a buffoon.'

'George went to school with Graham, so they've known each other for years. As for Jackie, I think she's just the type who gets on better with men. Some women are like that.'

Sue pulled a face.

'I can't stand females like that.'

'Look, I don't care much for her either, but try not to make it too obvious, eh?' I said, moving away from the mirror. 'Come on. The champagne is waiting.'

We exited the Ladies, but as we stepped into the corridor, we could hear raised voices. They were coming from Function Room 1.

'Blimey,' muttered Sue. 'Is that Cathy tearing her Frank off a strip?'

'He is a bit of a henpecked husband,' I giggled. 'Shall we be naughty and listen?'

'Yeah,' Sue grinned mischievously.

As we pressed our ears against the door, I had a moment of wondering if this was what Mabel Plaistow did when she was on the scent of a good story. As Sue and I earwigged, it became apparent that Cathy was warming to her task.

'You are pathetic,' she exhorted. 'A total knobhead.'

'What are we like?' I sighed, trying not to titter. Sue and I were almost nose to nose as we stood there, heads bowed together. 'I wonder what Frank has done wrong?'

'Shh. Hopefully we'll know in another minute or so,' whispered Sue.

We held our breath as one, and continued eavesdropping, but the next juicy delivery had my brow furrowing.

'Why did you marry her?' Cathy demanded.

Sue froze, and my heart lurched as realisation dawned. That voice didn't belong to Cathy. It wasn't The Angel's landlady on the other side of this door – which surely meant it wasn't her henpecked husband being berated.

Sue eyeballed me in horror.

'It's Jackie,' she said gruffly, stating the obvious. 'Who the hell is she talking to?'

Please, God. Don't let this be what I think it is.

But God wasn't listening.

'I'M TALKING TO YOU,' Jackie bellowed. 'So, answer my question. Why did you marry her?'

'Because YOU wouldn't!' George retorted.

Chapter Eighteen

Sue looked at me anxiously.

'What the f–?' she muttered.

I put a trembling finger to my lips, unable to speak and desperate not to miss a word of what was being said on the other side of the door.

'The reason I didn't marry you' – Jackie screeched – 'is because I'm *already* married. Being a bigamist isn't quite the career move I was looking to make.'

'You could have left Graham and filed for divorce,' George shouted. 'God knows I asked you enough times.'

'Why should I have dumped Graham when you showed no intention of giving up Sophie?'

'Sophie and I would have gone our separate ways the moment you'd left Graham. I wanted you to prove yourself to me. That you weren't *all talk and no do* which, let's face it, has been your track record to date. So why are you now giving me a hard time?'

'I WAS going to leave Graham,' Jackie asserted. 'I was simply waiting for the right moment.'

'And when would that have been? I waited long enough. Over two years. What was I meant to do? Put my life on hold until Graham had made his next million and you had more rich pickings to relay to your divorce lawyer? I was honest and up front with you from the moment Sophie came into my life. You know she doesn't make my heart sing the way you do, but I was never going to stay by myself. I was lonely, Jackie.'

'And how do you think that makes me feel, knowing that the man I love is sleeping with another woman?'

'Probably the same as how I feel,' George retorted. 'After all, you still share Graham's bed.'

'What are you two doing?' said an unexpected male voice.

Startled, Sue and I physically jumped and banged our heads together.

'For God's sake, Charlie,' Sue whispered. 'Go away.'

'But–'

'Now is not the moment,' she hissed.

'But Graham is wondering where everyone is. I said I'd go and have a look around and–'

He broke off as Graham appeared at the other end of the corridor. Oh no. The last thing we wanted was him booming away in that Brian Blessed voice asking what the three of us were up to outside Function Room 1.

'Shh!' I waved a hand, signalling urgently. Graham gave me a thumbs up, indicating he understood. Comedy-style, he tiptoed with exaggeration along the corridor.

'This reminds me of a joke,' he snickered foolishly.

'There's nothing funny about what we're listening to,' Sue muttered, rubbing her forehead.

'Then let me cheer you up,' said Graham sotto voce,

oblivious to the expression on my face. 'Why are corn farmers good at eavesdropping?' He looked expectantly from Charlie, to Sue, to me. 'Because they have ears everywhere!'

Graham opened his mouth to roar with laughter, but Sue was too quick for him. Springing upright, she clamped a hand over his mouth and pushed him away from the door.

'Do not laugh,' she warned, as his eyes bulged. 'You keep this' – she jerked her head meaningfully at Graham's mouth – 'tightly shut. Comprendez?'

Graham gave a series of rapid nods, his eyes wide with fear. Sue was a terrifying force when she wanted to be.

'Will one of you tell me what the hell is going on?' Charlie whispered urgently.

'If you shut up and listen, you'll find out,' said Sue hoarsely.

Suddenly there were four of us hunched together with our heads pressed to the door.

'You've wrecked my life,' Jackie bleated shrilly.

'Not intentionally,' snapped George in exasperation.

Graham's back stiffened, but he made no comment.

'Look, darling.' George's voice dropped an octave, and everyone leant in closer to catch what he was about to say next. 'This is getting us nowhere. Today of all days is not the time to announce that you regret not leaving Graham for me. *You're* married, and now *I'm* married. We'll just have to make the best of the situation and carry on seeing each other as and when we can.'

'I'm not up for that,' Jackie cried, before dissolving into noisy sobs.

106

I leant on the door handle, causing the four of us to fall into the room.

'Me neither,' I declared.

Chapter Nineteen

There was a moment of shocked silence where everyone regarded each other.

Sue's nostrils were flaring, as if a bad smell was under her nose. Graham was blinking rapidly, as if such action might clear the image of his wife clinging to his best mate. Charlie was slack jawed, and I... well, I was aware of a terrific heat taking over my body. Presumably red-hot molten anger.

'You BASTARD!' I rasped. My voice was harsh, and the accusation seemed to hang in the air with an underlying menace. 'And as for YOU' – my eyes bored into Jackie like twin laser beams – 'the identity of Thomas Tabby Cat is revealed. Oh, yes. You're the author of that anonymous message via Instagram. A cowardly notification informing me that George was a cheater. You thought you'd put the cat amongst the pigeons, didn't you? But your dirty little trick didn't work in time. What a shame. To think I could have been doing something so much better today – like my laundry – instead of getting hitched to a two-faced prat or sharing air space with a narcissistic twat.'

There was a collective inhale as I delivered that last word. Wow. I'd never said that before, but it had felt so good.

'Twat,' I repeated, warming to my subject. 'And did you know you have a face like one too?'

'That's enough, Sophie,' said George.

'Oh, he speaks!' I hooted. 'Well, you can fuck right off.' Omigod. I couldn't remember the last time I'd said two bad words in as many seconds. 'Not only have you wrecked our new marriage, but you've also sabotaged your oldest friend's relationship. What a breathtakingly shitty way to treat your best mate. You and Jackie are welcome to each other. Here' – I tugged at the shiny new wedding ring on my left hand and threw it at George – 'give this to twat-face.'

As the ring bounced across the carpet, it seemed to shock Graham out of his stupor. Suddenly he was striding over to George with a balled-up fist. The punch connected to George's jaw, propelling him backwards. He crashed into the table, knocking over a chair in the process, then sprawled across the floor, momentarily motionless. Jackie screamed, while Charlie's hands flew to his face in horror.

'Don't just stand there, man,' boomed Graham to Charlie. 'I've hurt my hand. Throw another punch for me.'

'Oooh, *Sue*,' wailed Charlie, sounding just like Frank Spencer, and looking not dissimilar as he crossed his legs and wrung his hands. 'Help! *SOMEONE HELP!*'

'On it,' shouted Sue, spinning on her heel. There was a stunned very brief pause, only broken by Sue reappearing with my bouquet in her hands.

'Good girl,' I cooed, grabbing the flowers from her. I strode over to Jackie. 'You didn't like my bouquet, did you? Well, this is for looking down your nose at me and my flowers. Take this.'

And with that I began thrashing her over the head with the blooms, putting all my anger, hurt, humiliation and embarrassment into the job with every ounce of my being. As she tried to deflect the blows with her hands, the air filled with flying petals. Flowerheads began to litter the carpet, and I wondered if it was possible to kill someone in such a way. I could imagine the local press getting whiff of the scandal and hotfooting over to the pub before the police arrived. What would a journalist write?

WEDDING DAY WAR!

Little Waterlow resident Sophie Fairfax's marriage to George Baker lasted less than an hour when she discovered the best man's wife was also George's mistress. Jackie Rollinson, for nefarious reasons also known as Thomas Tabby Cat, met both her match and her Creator when George's jilted wife used her bouquet as a weapon of mass destruction and sent Jackie off for reincarnation via a hundred carnations. Sophie is now taking stalk of her life from a police cell while George is in hiding from his ex-best friend who wants to take a leaf out of Sophie's book and kick George in the bud. When we tracked down Graham Rollinson, he declined to comment saying it was a thorny subject. Meanwhile, George has claimed that his so-called cheating only extended to using his tulips for kissing and that he only ever wanted somebudy to love.

Suddenly a shadow fell across the room. Like an avenging angel, landlady Cathy was standing in the doorway. Her face bore a thunderous expression as she took in the chaos.

'WHAT THE BLOODY HELL IS GOING ON IN MY PUB?' she roared.

Chapter Twenty

Cathy's voice was like a pistol shot.

I instantly stopped thrashing Jackie with my flowers but didn't hang around to answer the landlady's question. George and Jackie could have the pleasure of explaining why Function Room 1's carpet looked as if someone had duelled with the contents of a florist's shop. They duplicitous pair could also explain why one of the dining chairs was upturned, how the groom had ended up flat on his back with the best man massaging his fist, and why the best man's wife literally looked like she'd been dragged through a hedge backwards.

Instead, I tossed aside my annihilated bouquet, spun round, and charged past a startled Cathy. This galvanised Sue into legging it after me with the hapless Charlie bringing up the rear.

'Sorry,' I heard him call to Cathy as he belted after me and Sue. 'George will explain.'

'*Somebody* better had,' Cathy screeched. 'And someone had better put their hand in their pocket and pay for that chair. It's broken.'

'Stop her,' I heard George yell, evidently recovered enough to speak. 'SOPHIE!' His words followed me along the corridor. 'COME BACK. IT WAS A MOMENT OF LUNACY. WE CAN WORK THIS OUT.'

Ignoring him, I burst into the bar area, startling some locals who were having a quiet pint. Hastening past curious faces, I catapulted through the main door, and exited into the car park with Sue and Charlie hot on my heels.

Graham's booming voice floated after the three of us, informing anyone within hearing distance that he would be filing for divorce first thing on Monday morning. Shrill female sobbing swiftly followed.

I risked a quick glance over my shoulder to see that Graham had nearly caught us up. He sent the exit door crashing back on his hinges as he strode into the parking area. Jackie was clinging on to her enraged husband's coattails, shrieking her head off.

'*Please,* Bobble Wobbles. I *beg* you. Don't leave me.'

'Hurry, Charlie,' I gasped, as I caught sight of George, back on his feet and limping after everyone. 'Get your zapper out.'

'Steady,' Sue snorted. 'That's my line.'

'This isn't the time to joke,' I panted, as Charlie popped the central locking. We practically threw ourselves into the vehicle. 'Quick, lock us in!' I bawled.

Charlie pressed the button just as George made a superhuman effort to reach the car and wrench open the rear door. He rattled the handle impotently.

'Open up,' he yelled, his free hand slapping the window. 'Sophie, darling. Come back. I love you.'

'Hit the accelerator,' ordered Sue.

Her tone dared Charlie to disobey. The car screeched backwards causing George to jump out the way. Charlie hunched over the wheel, intent on emulating Jeremy Clarkson on a crazy day out with Richard Hammond and James May.

For one horrible moment, I wondered if George might prostrate himself across the bonnet. He lunged forward, but Charlie leant on the horn. Everyone jumped, including George.

Suddenly we were roaring away from The Angel in a cloud of exhaust. I swivelled round in my seat, peering through the rear window, aghast to see that everyone in the bar had now come out to watch the street theatre taking place between Graham, Jackie, and George.

Oh dear. Graham had delivered another blow to the treacherous groom. Once again, George was flat on his back. Jackie momentarily stooped over him, apparently dithering what to do. Meanwhile, Graham was abandoning the pair of them to make his own getaway. As Charlie's car rattled around a bend, the three of them disappeared from sight. I exhaled gustily, and suddenly realised I was shaking.

'You okay, Soph?' said Sue, peering at me anxiously.

'Not sure,' I quavered. 'Are you?'

She blew out her cheeks.

'Dunno. I mean… bloody hell, Soph.'

'I know,' I said unsteadily. 'Bloody hell.'

We stared at each other, white faced and wide eyed.

'We'll never be able to go to The Angel again,' said Sue.

'That's fine, because I never *want* to go to The Angel

again,' I said with feeling.

'Is anybody going to ask me how I'm feeling?' said Charlie, gripping the steering wheel so hard his knuckles had turned white.

Sue looked at her husband and frowned.

'Why?'

'Because I feel most peculiar. It's not every day you attend a wedding reception and watch it go pear-shaped in a matter of minutes. I don't think I will ever erase the sight of Sophie going berserk with her bouquet. She looked terrifying.'

Sue leant across the space between her and Charlie and patted his leg.

'Now, now,' she soothed. 'Just console yourself with the fact that it was a bouquet and not a machine gun. Just think of the damage our Sophie could have done with *that*,' she grinned.

'Don't.' Charlie momentarily squeezed his eyes shut. 'I hope I don't have nightmares tonight. By the way, where are we going? I haven't a clue.'

'Surprise us,' said Sue.

I stared out the window, trying to still my trembling body.

'I don't think I can take any more surprises today,' I muttered.

'Sophie is right,' said Sue. 'Let's recalibrate. Pull over at the next lay-by, Charlie. Let's get our bearings and then we'll find a pub and have a stiff drink. I think we all need one after that bit of hoo-ha.'

'I can't drink and drive,' Charlie bleated. He was no longer looking like Jeremy Clarkson, more like Mr Bean after a disaster. Which I suppose was only fitting.

'Oh dear,' said Sue. 'Let me program the satnav and we'll go back to ours instead. We have some brandy in the cupboard. Sophie, you stay the night with us. You've had one hell of a day and need looking after.'

I was feeling decidedly odd. It was probably shock catching up with me. That and using a bucket of adrenalin while walloping Jackie.

'A brandy might be nice,' I murmured, leaning back in my seat.

I closed my eyes and momentarily drifted, until my mobile burst into life. My eyes pinged open again. The caller display announced it was George. Switching the phone to silent, I once again closed my eyes.

How would I ever again hold my head up high in Little Waterlow?

Chapter Twenty-One

The three of us wearily filed up the path to Sue and Charlie's house. Once inside, we drooped into the kitchen. Charlie made a beeline for the corner cupboard.

'Cooking brandy,' he announced, making a face. 'However, this is an emergency.'

'Oh, Charlie, that's filthy stuff,' Sue protested.

'The filthier the better,' I said, collapsing down on a chair at the kitchen table.

'I agree with Sophie,' said Charlie, pouring three glasses.

Sue sat down opposite me and sighed heavily.

'I wonder what's happening at The Angel?'

Charlie set the glasses down on the table, then pulled out a chair.

'I would imagine that Cathy has summoned her hubby to drag George back inside and cough up the dosh to pay for the damage. I wouldn't want to get on the wrong side of Frank. He's a big chap.'

'Forget Frank.' I gave a mirthless laugh. 'It's Cathy who wears the trousers in that marriage, make no mistake. *She's* the one to be terrified of.' I took a swig of the brandy, taking comfort in the burning trail down my throat. 'Oh God,' I gasped. 'I hope Cathy doesn't come after *me*. I mean, I'm the one that made a mess of the place with my bouquet.'

'Don't fret,' Sue reassured. 'A vacuum cleaner will take care of that. What were you supposed to do? Say, "Terribly sorry, Cathy. Go and fetch your Dyson while I finish giving this Jezebel a makeover."'

'Maybe,' I sighed, before taking another fortifying sip. My shoulder muscles were starting to unkink. 'Do you really think that chair was broken?'

'Don't know,' said Charlie. 'But it was hardly a priceless antique. I'm sure it won't cost George more than a hundred quid to replace. I feel bad that I didn't try and break up the fight between the two men. After all, I've done Tai chi. It's meant to diffuse stressful situations.'

'Right,' said Sue with a wry smile. 'I'm not sure how things could have changed by stepping between two men in slow motion.'

'It's just as well that you kept out of it, Charlie,' I said. 'You could have inadvertently been injured.'

Sue's stomach chose that moment to rumble.

'Your lovely wedding breakfast,' she lamented. 'I wonder what will happen to all that uneaten food.'

I shrugged.

'Perhaps Cathy will sell it as posh bar food.'

'Remind me again what we would have been having.'

I twirled my brandy glass between my fingers as I thought back to the conversation I'd had with George about the menu. In the end he'd chosen everything because – as he'd succinctly pointed out – he was the one paying for it.

'Dorset crab with asparagus, lemon and baby leaves,' I

intoned. 'Followed by chargrilled leg of lamb with saffron couscous, Mediterranean vegetables and a honey jus, finishing off with salted caramel brownie and a warm chocolate sauce.'

Charlie licked his lips.

'Stop. You're making me hungry.'

'I can rustle up some cheese on toast,' Sue suggested, getting to her feet.

'Sounds good,' he said.

I wasn't sure I could eat anything just yet. My stomach was still churning.

Reaching into my clutch, I checked my mobile. It was still switched to silent. Oh Lord. Twenty-two missed calls. All of them from George. Fifteen voicemails. George again. I caught Charlie watching me.

'Are you going to respond?'

'I'll have to at some point.' I pulled a face. 'After all, we need to discuss divorce.'

'Perhaps you can get the marriage annulled,' Charlie suggested.

'Maybe,' I nodded. 'I'll investigate.'

I pressed the voicemail icon and clamped the phone to the side of my head. George's recorded message instantly hit my eardrum.

pleading *Sophie, darling. Please phone me...*

begging *Call me. Please...*

imploring *We can work this out. We can. We really, really can...*

solemn *Jackie means nothing to me. Promise...*

desperate *Sophie, I'm going out of my mind...*

119

perplexed I'm at Catkin Cottage. Where are you?

Ah, yes. Where am I? Well, George. I'm with my good friends. Friends that you dissed. Friends whose names you couldn't even commit to memory, never mind their address – despite being invited to their home and enjoying their hospitality.

tearful Sophie, please, this is ridiculous. It's our wedding day!

sobbing I'm a broken man. I'm going home. Please respond…

more sobbing

sniffing This is mental cruelty…

Did he really just say that?

annoyed If nothing else, can you have the decency to return my calls?

Decency? DECENCY?

My lip curled as I continued to listen.

exasperated We are husband and wife. Let's put this behind us…

authoritative You are Mrs Baker. Come home. Now!

assertive Sophie, have some heart, eh?

pissed off For fuck's sake. You've made your point. CALL ME!

No, George. I will not call you. Right now, you can flaming well stew.

Sue returned to the table with melted cheese on thickly buttered slices of toast. Despite initially thinking I wouldn't be able to eat, suddenly I was ravenous. The three of us tucked in.

'Such a shame about the honeymoon not going ahead,' said Sue, between mouthfuls. 'What a waste of money.'

I stopped chewing and stared at her. Omigod. The honeymoon. What with all the fracas, it had completely slipped my mind. I glanced at my watch. The flight to Naples was leaving in precisely two hours and forty-five minutes. Our respective suitcases, plane tickets and passports were stowed away in my bedroom at Catkin Cottage.

'What?' prompted Sue, looking at me. 'I can tell the cogs of your brain are whirring.'

'I'm thinking… maybe… no, definitely… well, I'm not sure… yes I am… or maybe not… oooh, but I really want to–'

'For goodness' sake, woman,' said Sue in exasperation. 'Spit it out!'

I looked at Sue fearfully.

'I'm thinking of going ahead with the honeymoon. By myself, obviously.'

Well, why not? It had cost George a pretty penny and, as Sue had pointed out, it was a shame to waste it. Also, George wouldn't be able to follow me. Not without his passport. And he couldn't retrieve his passport because he didn't have a key to my house. At the time of him not wishing to give me a spare key to his place, I'd been miffed, so had followed his example. Now I thanked George from the bottom of my heart for his funny little ways. It meant I could take off to Italy safe in the knowledge that he wouldn't be able to follow me.

'Are you serious?' asked Charlie.

121

I wavered for a second, then made my decision.

'Never more so,' I asserted, cramming the last bit of toast in my mouth.

'Attagirl,' said Sue, rearing up from her chair. 'Come on, Charlie. Don't take another sip of that brandy. We need to get Sophie back to Catkin Cottage to collect her case. There's not a moment to lose. If George is there, I'll deflect him.'

'How?' I asked, suddenly alive to the fact that George could still be hanging around, despite his voicemail saying he was heading home.

Sue gave me a determined look.

'I'll kick him in the goolies, thus rendering him incapacitated.'

'I've a better idea,' I said, reaching again for my phone.

Quickly I tapped out a text.

Hello, George. Happy to talk, but it will have to be tomorrow. I'm mentally exhausted and want a clear head when discussing any possibility of a future together.

I pressed send. I had no intention of sharing my future with a cheater, but right now it was important to let George believe otherwise. He replied almost immediately.

Thank you, thank you, thank you. Come to mine in the morning. I love you xxxxxxx

I didn't bother with any further reply. The man didn't know the meaning of love. Indeed, he was a two-faced prolific liar. I glanced up at Sue and Charlie.

'Sorted. He won't be bothering us. Meanwhile, I just want to say that you two are amazing. I don't know what I'd have done without you both by my side today.'

'That's what friends are for,' said Sue stoutly.

'Come on,' said Charlie, squaring his shoulders. 'Let's do this.'

Chapter Twenty-Two

Charlie rose magnificently to the occasion, roaring over to Catkin Cottage without flattening anyone or anything.

Once indoors, I belted up the staircase, transferred my ticket and passport from George's man-bag to my clutch, and grabbed my suitcase. Clattering back downstairs, I ensured the front door was double-locked, then hastened back to a waiting Sue and Charlie.

Slinging the case in the boot, I'd barely shut the car's passenger door before the motor's tyres left rubber on tarmac. I fumbled with the seat belt as we screeched off. This time our destination was Gatwick Airport.

'Flipping heck,' I breathed. 'I'm really doing this.'

Sue swivelled round in her seat.

'This is so exciting,' she beamed. 'I feel like we've just helped you bust out of jail or something.'

'I know what you mean,' I agreed. 'You know, even if today's hoo-ha hadn't happened, I have a horrible feeling that, in time, I'd have felt suffocated living at Kings Hill with George.'

'I did ask you earlier if you were doing the right thing,' Sue reminded. 'Words to that effect, anyway.'

I groaned.

'Nobody likes to admit they were wrong. Even if Jackie hadn't been in the equation, I think sooner or later I'd have realised that I'd made a mistake.' I sighed. 'However, out of today's shambles, there is one thing I *am* pleased about.'

'What's that?'

'Knowing that I won't ever have to wake up in a house where everything is grey.'

Sue nodded her agreement.

'You can't say that about Catkin Cottage. It's a riot of colour, and gorgeous with it.'

'Thanks,' I said gratefully.

'So what are you going to do while you're in Italy?'

'Oh, you know. Stay in my room. Curl up in a ball. Mope.'

Sue looked aghast.

'Are you winding me up?'

'Of course,' I grinned. 'I can tell you exactly what I'm going to do. Alternate between sunning myself and exploring. George had made an extensive itinerary—'

'You're kidding.'

'Never been more serious. He'd printed it out, too. All six pages.'

'What a dick.'

'Yeah,' I agreed. 'It was an organised schedule itemising where we'd be visiting. What days. Times. You get the picture. I didn't bother bringing it with me. I shall let each moment unfold without overthinking it and travel around as the mood grabs me.'

'Perfect,' said Sue, nodding with approval.

The car bucketed along. In no time at all we were on the M25 heading south. The traffic was light.

I breathed a sigh of relief that George had insisted we leave for the honeymoon directly after the wedding breakfast. If we'd waited until a weekday morning, then right now Charlie's getaway-style driving would've been hampered by rush hour traffic.

We were now cruising along in the fast lane, overtaking a series of vehicles. Every now and again, another motorist would do a doubletake at Charlie's car. The white ribbon was still secured to the bonnet, rippling in the wind. Necks craned as drivers hoped to glimpse a blushing bride within. Upon seeing a weary fifty-year-old in a crumpled suit, they instantly lost interest and looked away.

My eyes momentarily brimmed, and I quickly blinked away the tears. There was a time and a place to cry, but it wasn't now. I knew that when the tears were permitted to flow, they would probably be of epic proportions. Niagara Falls eat your heart out.

Meanwhile, all that mattered was Charlie safely delivering me to the airport, pulling up the handbrake outside *Departures* and me hitching up my hemline and legging it to baggage drop off. Once free of my suitcase, I'd need to get through security as swiftly as possible before the relevant gate closed. There would be no time to check out Duty Free, or sit down and enjoy a coffee, or browse in WH Smith's book section. There wasn't even a spare moment to pay a visit to the Ladies.

My bladder chose that moment to let me know the latter

was becoming quite pressing. I shifted in my seat and crossed my legs. This was one wee-wee that would have to wait.

Chapter Twenty-Three

At the airport, I said goodbye to Charlie and Sue with swift, fierce hugs.

'Text me,' Sue urged, while Charlie retrieved my suitcase from the boot. 'Let me know you've arrived safely.'

'Will do,' I promised.

'I think it would be more prudent to let us know you caught your flight,' said Charlie. He released the suitcase's handle and pushed it into my hand. 'Now go,' he urged. 'There's not a moment to lose.'

Heeding his words, I scampered off towards the pedestrian crossing.

Stepping off the kerb, a bus angrily sounded its horn.

'And try not to get run over,' Charlie yelled after me.

Oh Lord. I hadn't even seen that bus. Probably because I hadn't looked. What was that saying? Oh yes. More haste, less speed. How true. I wouldn't be going anywhere if I got flattened by a vehicle.

Cringing, I raised a hand in apology to the bus driver, then dashed over to the other side. Blending in with a group of people, I briskly headed towards an escalator.

At the top of the moving staircase, more people fell in alongside me. We were all heading towards some vast automatic doors. Once inside the airport, I became part of a huge crowd that seemed to constantly come together before splitting apart.

For a moment I stood in the middle of this shifting formation, disorientated and out of sorts, as people rushed in all directions. Seeing an overhead information board, I moved towards it, screwing up my eyes myopically to read the details. Oh, help! The gate was already open for boarding.

The next forty minutes was a blur of pushing and shoving, lifting and dumping, running and dodging, before setting off the alarm through security. This was followed by a pat-down search before finally... *finally* charging down the jet bridge towards the waiting aircraft, my feet all the while painfully protesting. Stilettoes were never designed for high-speed sprints through airports.

I catapulted through the plane's doorway, cannoning into an air stewardess. Apologising profusely, I hobbled along the aisle behind some squabbling children and their bickering parents.

Looking left and right, I kept an eye out for my designated seat, at the same time noting the faces of other passengers. He was excited. She was tense. He was bored. She couldn't care less. He looked thrilled to bits. She looked terrified. Such were the readable expressions of those who awaited our pilot's skills at steering this metal bird down a runway and into the sky.

Finding my seat, I flopped down into it, noting the empty one alongside me.

Ha, George! The silver fox was outfoxed.

'Seat belt on,' said an air stewardess, lightly touching my shoulder as she carried out her final check.

'Have I got time to use the loo?' I asked, just as the PA system crackled into life.

'Cabin crew, arm doors and cross check,' said a brisk male voice.

'Sorry' – the stewardess paused for a moment – 'you'll have to wait until we're up in the air and the seat belt sign has been switched off.'

I buckled up and, once again, firmly crossed my legs just as my phoned dinged with a text. Ah. That would be Sue wanting to see if I'd made the flight. I'd better reassure her before switching the phone to Airplane Mode. But as I glanced at the screen, my burgeoning bladder contracted with apprehension. Clenching my pelvic floor muscles, I clicked on the message from George.

I took a chance on trying to talk to you sooner rather than later, and drove over to Catkin Cottage. However, the place looked deserted. Your curtain-twitching neighbour informed me you'd left earlier and been in a tremendous hurry. Apparently, you had a huge suitcase in tow. Can I presume you're on your way to Italy without me?

I took a deep breath and tapped out my reply.

You presume correctly.

George's reply was immediate.

I will personally make sure you regret this.

I momentarily closed my eyes before giving my response.

Don't threaten me, George.

I pressed the send button and then went offline.

Chapter Twenty-Four

After the wedding shambles, I'd fled to Gatwick Airport fired up and full of gung-ho. However, after receiving George's text prior to take off, the sense of scoring a small point over my cheating new husband, was starting to dissipate. He'd said I would regret such action.

Now, at Napoli Airport, his earlier words had left me with a sense of foreboding.

What can he do? my inner voice reasoned. *He's over a thousand miles away and his passport is locked inside Catkin Cottage.*

Exactly. George's threat was an empty one. Nothing more than bluster. Too bad I'd done a runner and evaded him. After all, he had no one else to blame for this situation but himself. Well, him and *her.*

As I stood by the allotted baggage reclaim area, waiting for the carousel to deliver my suitcase, I used my passport as a makeshift fan. Naples was an hour ahead of London but, even though the Italian time was nearly ten o'clock in the evening, to say it was hot was an understatement. Didn't this airport have any air conditioning? Apparently not.

I wondered what was happening back at Little Waterlow. I'd assumed that Jackie and George would immediately run off together. It seemed I'd got that bit wrong. Instead, George had headed over to Catkin Cottage to reason with me, so he'd evidently gone there alone. Did that mean that Jackie was still frantically back peddling with *Bobble Wobbles*? Was she somehow holding out on supergluing her marriage back together?

I wondered how Graham was. My heart squeezed for him. He'd looked so shocked. So utterly devastated. It was bad enough knowing your wife had betrayed you, but to discover it was with your oldest friend was a painful double whammy.

The conveyor lurched into life, and a throng of people swarmed around it, reminding me of angry wasps fighting over the pickings of a rotten apple. For a moment I felt overwhelmed by the general chaos and stuffy air. Telling myself I'd feel better when outside in the fresh air, I focussed on the conveyor. My spirits lifted when I spotted the first suitcase coming through the plastic strips. It was mine. Last case on, first off. Either that or a stroke of good luck.

Grabbing it, I pulled up the handle, took a deep breath, then pushed through the milling crowd. George had pre-booked a taxi to avoid any hassle. As I approached the Arrivals areas, I was relieved to see a man – a dead spit for Danny deVito – holding up a sign.

MR AND MRS BAKER

I gulped down a sudden lump of emotion. *Mrs Baker.* Except I wasn't Mrs Baker. Well, maybe officially, but not for much longer.

Don't think about it, Sophie. Not here. Not in this

132

chaotic airport in thirty degrees of heat. The last thing you want is a public emotional meltdown.

I trundled over to my driver.

'Hello,' I said, pasting on a bright smile.

'*Signora* Baker?' enquired Danny.

'Yes.' For now. 'That's me.'

'*E Signore?* What you do with him?' Danny enquired with a heavy accent. 'You keel him, eh?' he wheezed, before cracking up with laughter.

'Ha, ha!' I chortled along with him. 'That's right.'

Danny's smile broadened.

'You joke. I know he alive.' He pointed to the toilet sign. '*Nel bagno.* We wait.'

'No, no, he's not in there. He, er…'

Danny's expression switched to mortification.

'Oh no. He really die?' he asked, looking horrified.

'No!' I protested. 'He, um, simply missed the flight.'

'*Veramente?*' Danny looked incredulous that two people, travelling together, should suddenly find themselves in a situation where only one of them had managed to board the plane. 'How that happen?'

'M-My husband has a false leg,' I stuttered. 'And, er, it fell off.'

Danny's eyebrows shot up to his bald head.

'*Mio Dio.* And Meester Baker, he no put it back on again himself?'

'Oh, no.' I shook my head emphatically. 'It's a very complicated procedure. It needs a doctor. There's lots of, um, screws and pins and fiddly bits, you see. One of the

133

airport staff had to use the emergency phone to summon Special Assistance – they're the people who drive those funny little golf carts–'

'Golf? Meester Baker play golf at airport?'

'No, I was referring to the mode of transport. You know, electric go-cart thingies which make funny noises' – I raised my voice a couple of octaves to demonstrate – 'BLEEEEP BLEEEP. And everybody rushes to get out of the way in case they get run over.'

'The bleeeep–bleeeep squash people?'

'Um, well, hopefully not. But the bleeeep–bleeeep rushed to George and picked up his leg. However, nobody could find all the screws and pins. A passing doctor advised that George had to go to hospital.'

'Ah, for operation,' said Danny.

'That's it!' I said, nodding emphatically. 'An operation.'

Why hadn't I just said that in the first place? That George was suddenly taken ill. A rotten appendix or something.

Or even a rotten heart? my little voice wryly enquired.

'Too bad,' said Danny, taking my suitcase from me. 'Okay, we go. Follow please.'

I trotted after Danny who, despite having extremely short legs and a large rotund belly, could shift.

Sticking close to his side, I let him guide me through the throng and through the main doors. Outside, cooler air rushed to greet me. Despite the hour, it was still warm.

As a welcome breeze lifted my hair, I inhaled greedily. Seconds later I choked on the diesel fumes of a coach passing the airport's taxi rank.

We entered the main car park, and Danny stopped by a shiny black Mercedes. Popping the locks, he opened the rear door for me.

'Thank you,' I said, gratefully sinking down on the leather seat.

'*Prego,*' he replied, before shutting the door after me.

Leaving Danny to transfer my suitcase to the boot, I leant back and momentarily closed my eyes. I felt bone weary and severely out of sorts.

My eyes pinged open again as Danny opened the driver's door and eased himself behind the steering wheel. As the Mercedes set off, a tiny part of me – we're talking microscopic – perked up. No matter how awful the circumstances, I'd made it. I was here. In Italy. And come hell or high water, I was going to make the most of it.

Chapter Twenty-Five

'How long will the journey to Maiori take?' I asked Danny.

He made a see-saw motion with one hand.

'One hour. Maiori not far. About feefty kilometres. But Lattari Mountains make journey slow.'

'Oh,' I said in a small voice.

Mountains? I gulped nervously. Such roads were famously winding and narrow, with hairpin turns. They were extremely challenging to drive. Right now, Danny was pumping the accelerator and seemed determined to overtake everything in sight. This wasn't currently an issue because we were travelling on some sort of Italian freeway. But later?

Don't fret, my inner voice assured. *Danny wants to welcome tomorrow just as much as you do. I'm sure he will slow down when we get to the latter part of the journey.*

As the Mercedes ate up the miles, I sat back and tried to relax. I must have drifted off for a while, exhausted from the day's events. I came to with a sudden queasy feeling yoyoing between my stomach and throat.

'You awake,' said Danny. 'We now travel the *Costiera Amalfitana.*'

Ah, Danny was talking about the Amalfi Coast.

'Splendid,' I said, peering through the window, but there

was little to see in the darkness.

'You come again, eeen daylight. Thees Italy's most scenic stretch of coastline.'

I could believe him. From what I could see in the car's headlights, we were currently passing through a pastel-hued village terraced into the hillside and travelling along a steep, ribbon-thin road.

As the Mercedes swung through a bend that doubled back on itself, I experienced a horrible sensation in the pit of my stomach. I stared grimly ahead, glad of the inky night hiding what I knew to be on the left – a sheer drop.

I dared to peek at the road's edge. Where was the safety barrier? The headlights momentarily revealed a low sweep of metal which, from my perspective, looked no more than twelve inches high. What idiotic workmen had erected this? A bunch of midgets? Surely a twelve-foot-high solid metal wall would have been more appropriate?

We were now rushing towards another hair-raisingly sharp bend. As the Mercedes whooshed sideways, nausea once again swept over me.

'The night hides the mountains,' said Danny. 'They sooo beautiful. All covered in green.'

Right now, the only green thing around here was my face.

An overhead light momentarily filled the car. It was another vehicle's headlights. I craned my neck to see. Uh-oh. A Fiat was approaching from the opposite direction. Judging from its speed, the car was being handled by a daring driver determined to show off his behind-the-wheel bravado. Even worse, our paths were going to cross at the next hairpin bend. And was it my imagination, or was Danny speeding up?

As the Mercedes – in the righthand lane – swung out to the farthest point of tarmac, I closed my eyes, swallowed hard, and waited for the moment where the tyres must surely leave the road.

I had a horrible premonition of the vehicle freefalling, engine screaming, wheels spinning, as we plunged down... down... down, with Danny conversationally saying, "And now we fly past Vesuvius, active volcano which geeves some of continent's largest eruptions and presents beeg danger..."

'Arghhhhhh,' I screamed, as the Fiat and Mercedes shot past each other with barely a millimetre to spare.

'You worry,' said Danny laughing. 'No need.'

'Can we possibly slow down?' I croaked.

'No point,' Danny shrugged. 'We nearly there. Look.'

'Where?' I gasped, craning my neck again.

'Over there,' he pointed.

Having spent so much time climbing up the mountain, it appeared that we were now rapidly going down the other side. To the right, twinkling lights were coming into view. I took a breath. Maiori.

George had referred to the pretty southern Italian town as the perfect picturesque address. Its sand-and-shingle beach, nearly a kilometre long, was known by locals as *Lungomare Amendola*. George had spouted about sea-view cafés, shops, and restaurants, and easy access to postcard-worthy towns – Minori, Cetera, Positano, Ravello, Amalfi and Maiori itself.

As the road levelled out and the Mercedes travelled along a promenade, I looked to both left and right, drinking in the sight of locals, despite the late hour, eating al fresco.

Ornate chairs were set on pavements. Lovers held hands across candlelit tables. On the other side of the street, couples strolled arm in arm. On the marina's edge, boats bobbed. Sea the colour of night reflected the orange glow of streetlights.

My stomach lurched again as the Mercedes went up a sharp incline. Oh no. Not another mountain road? Ahead, I could make out a huge building. It appeared to be clinging to a rocky peninsula overhanging an expanse of black water full of furiously crashing waves.

Danny swung the car left and it came to an abrupt stop.

'We arrive, *Signora* Baker. *Il Castello.* Your hotel.'

Chapter Twenty-Six

With one hand, I tried to smooth out my heavily creased wedding outfit. The garment now looked how I felt. Tired and dishevelled. Danny retrieved my suitcase from the boot.

'*Signora*,' he said gravely, passing me the case. 'I hopa your husband is reunited with meesing leg soona.'

'Oh, er, thank you.'

'*Buona sera*,' he said, walking back round to the driver's side.

'Bonner Sarah,' I replied, trying out some Italian.

I tottered through some glass double doors and found myself in a scruffy foyer. The tiles on the floor were careworn and chipped. Overhead, a large chandelier attempted to twinkle through layers of cobwebs and dust. To the left was an old chaise longue with motheaten upholstery. To the right was a reception area which contained a battered desk with a built-in counter.

I glanced around in surprise. The foyer looked like a worn–out version of the internet picture George had previously shown me. *That* image had clearly been photoshopped to convey old-fashioned charm from a bygone era. How disappointing. It didn't bode well for the rest of the hotel. From what I could see of the place so far, it wasn't so much tired as exhausted.

I wheeled my suitcase over to the counter. A man was seated behind the desk. Head down, he was engrossed in a computer printout of figures. A badge was pinned to his black waistcoat. *Luca Lamagna.*

As I waited for Mr Lamagna to look up, I found myself surreptitiously studying him. Strong hands were resting lightly on the desk. No sign of a wedding ring. From this angle he reminded me of Andrea Bocelli in his heyday. Thick dark hair flecked with grey curled over his shirt collar. Long dark lashes cast spiky shadows over tanned skin. As the seconds went by, I wondered what colour his eyes were. After a full minute, I started to wonder if Luca Lamagna was even aware of my presence. I cleared my throat and gave a little cough.

'Bonner Sarah,' I said crisply.

My words echoed around the hallway, but the man didn't look up. Instead, he picked up a pen and circled one of the figures on the sheet of paper. And then it dawned on me. Andrea Bocelli had been unfortunate to suffer blindness. Clearly this man had an affliction too. A hearing problem.

I cleared my throat and tried again.

'BONNER SARAH,' I shouted.

The man put down his pen and looked up. Ah, thought so. Poor chap was a bit *mutton Jeff.* He had the most amazing eyes. Light hazel with green and gold flecks. In fact, he was a bit of a babe. I wondered if the deafness interfered with his personal relationships. After all, it couldn't be much fun wining and dining a woman and having to shout all the time.

'DARLING, YOUR PRETTY EYES ARE BLUER
THAN THE SKY. CAN YOU PASS ME THE SALT?'

Not very romantic. No pun intended, but hadn't he
heard of hearing aids?

'BONNER. SARAH,' I enunciated, to assist his lip
reading.

The man grimaced.

'Are you trying to tell me that you have a reservation in
the name of Sarah Bonner?'

I stared at him in surprise. His English was impeccable
with no trace of an Italian accent.

'I thought you were deaf.'

'No, I was simply immersed in some complicated mental
maths and didn't want to lose my train of thought. However,
your shouting put paid to that.'

I bristled. Okay, the man wasn't deaf. He was simply
rude.

'You could've used a calculator,' I pointed out.

'Yes,' he drawled. 'I could have. Unfortunately, it's
broken. Like everything else around here. I gather you're
familiar with such problems.'

'Sorry?' I frowned.

'I overheard your taxi driver. Something about your
husband mislaying his leg. Is that why you're travelling
alone?'

My cheeks reddened. I wasn't answering that question. It
was none of this guy's business where George was.

'I'd like to check in, please.'

'Certainly. Your name?'

'Sophie Baker.'

The man's expression changed in a flash. Suddenly he was no longer bored and disinterested. Instead, he looked hacked off and angry.

'Mrs Baker,' he growled. 'No, you may not check in.'

'I beg your pardon?'

'Are *you* a little deaf? Would you perhaps like me to shout?'

'No,' I retorted. What was the matter with this guy? I'd heard of people with chips on their shoulders, but clearly this man had a few boulders strapped to his. 'I'd simply like to go to my room.'

'Well, you can't.'

'Now you listen to me,' I snapped, as my temper began to unravel. 'I've had one hell of a day, Mr Lasagne–'

'La*magna*,' he corrected.

'Whatever' – I waved a dismissive hand – 'and what I *don't* need right now is an arrogant upstart like you telling me what I can and can't do. Understand? Now let me check in or I'll report you to the manager.'

'I *am* the manager–'

'Then I'll report you to the owner.'

'I *am* the owner.'

'I don't believe you,' I countered.

'Whatever' – now it was his turn to wave a dismissive hand – 'but there's a very good reason why you can't check in.'

I planted my feet wide and placed my hands on my hips.

'And what, precisely, is that?' I demanded.

'Because your husband telephoned earlier.'

My face instantly drained of colour. Luca Lamagna watched with interest as the dawn slowly came up.

'Ah, Mrs Baker. I can see that you've worked it out. That's right. Mr Baker cancelled the reservation.'

Chapter Twenty-Seven

George had cancelled the reservation? I was silent as my brain processed this bombshell. Had I travelled all the way to Italy for nothing?

I stared at Luca Lamagna who was looking both smug and delighted at the series of emotions playing out across my face. Incredulity. Horror. Disbelief. From the look on his face, I could almost read his mind:

Take that, you uppity female, coming into my hotel, shouting at me in rubbish Italian and insinuating I was named after a popular pasta dish.

The inside of my head was starting to feel like a washing machine that had done one too many spin cycles and was about to go on the blink. And that was exactly what I was about to do in this hotel foyer. Break down. Or, more precisely, have a full-on meltdown.

I took a deep breath to say something but couldn't formulate the words.

'Huhhh,' I gasped, as my entire body began to quiver.

'Pardon?'

'Oooh.'

Luca peered at me.

'Are you okay?' he reluctantly enquired.

'Noooo,' I wailed, as all the pent-up emotion of the day condensed into a whirling ball of energy.

It started at the bottom of my feet, then moved up my legs, through my torso, then ripped into my oesophagus with a never-experienced-before force, finally hitting my tonsils like a mallet striking a gong.

'GAHHHHH,' I shrieked.

My eyes were suddenly doing an excellent impression of Gazza in that old Walkers' crisps ad. Tears were literally spurting across the reception counter as well as running down my face and dripping over my wedding suit.

'OH OH, HUH HUH HUH, EEEEEE, AH AH AH.'

Oh God. Now my nose was joining in with my eyeballs. That was all I needed – an embarrassing waterfall of snot dripping everywhere.

Fortunately, Luca was alive to the situation. He grabbed a box of tissues sitting alongside a pot of pens.

'Here,' he said gruffly, thrusting the box at me.

'HUH HUH HUH,' I replied, snatching up a handful and pressing the whole lot to my face. 'IT'S TOO MUCH,' I bellowed.

'Then use one at a time,' he said gravely, pulling out a single sheet from the box.

'IT'S NOT THAT,' I bawled. 'IT'S GEORGE.'

'Look, do you want to sit down for a minute and compose yourself?'

'N-N-N-N-' I stuttered.

'No?'

'I DON'T KNOW,' I shrieked, before trumpeting into

146

the tissue.

I seemed to be drowning in water. It was everywhere. Pouring down my nostrils. Gushing from my tear ducts. Even the inside of my ears felt wet from such an emotional overload.

I removed the sodden wad from my face, aware that little pieces had come away and were now stuck to my cheeks. I was momentarily reminded of my father. He'd always cut himself when shaving. My mother had tenderly stuck bits of toilet paper to his face to mop up the blood. How I wished my parents were still around.

'Can you tell me why you're so upset,' said Luca irritably.

'I MISS MY PARENTS,' I fog-horned.

Luca looked perplexed.

'Have they recently died?'

I shook my head.

'No, it's everything else… HUH HUH HUH… my life is a mess… OH OH OH… today I married George but George loves Jackie and Jackie wants Graham and Graham punched George and Charlie panicked and Sue grabbed my bouquet and I walloped Jackie and then' – my voice rose an octave – 'WE ALL RAN AWAY.'

Luca stared at me for a moment, then leant across the counter and patted my hand.

The effect of his touch was both unexpected and violent, like a doctor touching a dying patient with shock paddles. My entire body visibly jerked and whatever words I'd been about to say next shrivelled and died on my lips. Even my tears and snot seemed to pause mid-flow. I snorted attractively.

'I think you need a stiff drink,' he said, getting to his feet. 'Stay right there.'

Behind the desk was a door marked *Privato*. Disappearing into the back office, Luca left me standing alone, stunned and immobilised. I was incapable of going anywhere. Indeed, I seemed to be rooted, like a tree, to the floor. I was also starting to feel most peculiar.

My face, from such a loud outburst of emotion, was doing some very weird things. An entire network of nerves was now fizzing and popping all over my cheeks. It felt like a bad dose of pins and needles. My left eyelid was flickering uncontrollably and – oh no – now my right eye was doing the same thing. I seemed to be impersonating Chief Inspector Dreyfus after Inspector Clouseau had sent him bonkers. Omigod, what was happening to me?

'Here,' said Luca, returning with a glass of golden liquid.

I took it on autopilot, but hesitated to raise the rim to my lips. Something was wrong with my mouth. My lips and tongue felt most peculiar. Sort of… numb. Was I losing the ability to speak? I needed to test them out.

'Tething, tething,' I mumbled.

'What?'

Was I having a stroke? H-e-l-p.

Try again, Sophie. Nice and calm. Deep breath.

'TESTING, TESTING,' I bawled.

Luca regarded me as one might a deranged person.

'Oh, thank God,' I exhaled. 'I can still speak and make

148

sense.'

'That's debatable,' he muttered.

'What did you say?' I demanded.

'Look, could you just get that brandy inside you, then try talking to me again – preferably including the details of what happened before your friends fled to the four corners of the earth.'

Chapter Twenty-Eight

Having finally managed to get some movement back into my body, I was now perched at one end of the knackered chaise longue with Luca sitting at the other.

'Right' – he took the empty brandy glass from me – 'now that you've calmed down, how about you tell me your story again. After all, it's not every day I get a runaway bride in my hotel.'

And so the whole sorry story of the marriage-that-never-really-was tumbled out. As Luca listened, he looked more and more incredulous.

'I'm sorry you had such an awful experience, Mrs Baker-'

'Please, don't call me that. Sophie will do.'

'Sophie,' Luca nodded. 'Your husband… ex-husband…' – he waved a hand helplessly – 'rang the hotel earlier to advise that he'd been taken seriously ill. I don't accept short notice cancellations unless there are mitigating circumstances that require a level of compassion. Mr Baker indicated that he was in hospital after receiving a shock diagnosis.'

'He might have gone to hospital' – my voice was indignant – 'to get checked out after Graham punched him, but any diagnosis would have been along the lines of having a split lip stitched, not any life-threatening condition.'

I shook my head, appalled at George's audacity. How despicable to pretend to be so ill.

'He was very believable,' said Luca. 'He sounded genuinely distressed.'

'Only because both his new wife and lover had respectively abandoned him.'

Luca was silent for a moment, thinking back to his conversation with George.

'I told your husband that I was sympathetic to his situation and, as a result of his circumstances, confirmed the booking would be cancelled with all monies returned to his account first thing tomorrow morning.'

I was suddenly very still.

'So...' – I looked at Luca hopefully – 'at this moment in time, you haven't actually refunded him?'

Luca shook his head.

'No, and now I know your side of the story, there won't be any refund. That means there is no cancellation. You can go ahead and check into the room. I will personally make sure that George Baker doesn't get a penny from *Il Castello*.'

'Thank you,' I said, slumping with relief.

'Meanwhile, do you have the resources to support yourself while in Italy?'

'How do you mean?'

'You know, hard cash. Or a credit card. Something to pay for your sustenance. After all, your booking only includes breakfast.'

'Oh, I see. Yes, George opened a joint account

specifically for our holiday expenses. You know, spending money. I have a bank card for that very purpose.'

Luca raised his eyebrows.

'Are you sure about that?'

I stared at him in puzzlement. Then my mind zoomed back to sitting on the plane, awaiting take-off. George's final text.

I will personally make sure you regret this.

Wow, he'd already tried one devious trick. I'd severely underestimated my new husband's swiftness to both react and act. What might he do next?

My expression of bemusement changed to horror as realisation dawned. George would cancel the bank card in my purse, that's what.

I needed to think, and carefully. We'd opened a joint bank account purely for our honeymoon expenses. My hairdressing earnings were meagre compared to George's whopping salary. Through scrimping and scraping, I'd managed to cobble together a few hundred pounds, but George had added a great deal more to the holiday account.

'We don't want to be fretting about money, Sophie,' he'd stated. 'Not on our honeymoon.'

I'd been so relieved. The question now was, had he yet closed that account?

With trembling fingers, I reached for my mobile. After a long day, the battery was now down to three percent. Uh-oh.

Please, I silently willed the device, *don't die on me.*

My fingers tapped on the icon for the online banking

app. I waited impatiently for some tumbling cubes to move around the screen. Digital authorisation. Come on, come on. Now facial recognition. Oh, for heaven's sake! But a moment later, I was in.

My eyes scanned the screen. Phew. George hadn't closed the account. Yet. The funds were untouched. An oversight on his part, but it wouldn't be long before he acted.

My phone chose that moment to inform the battery was now at two percent. I dithered. Should I transfer the money to my personal account? Or was that stealing?

You and George are married, Sophie. Man and wife reminded my inner voice. *What's yours is his, and what's his is yours. Or something like that anyway.*

Wavering, I contemplated. If I moved the funds, would George report me to the police? I had a sudden vision of him making an international call to the local *polizia.*

'*Ufficiale*, my wife has stolen money from our joint account. Arrest her now!'

Over the years, I'd read in the newspapers many a torrid tale of warring couples emptying joint accounts without the other person's consent, sometimes even running up debt.

However, I also seemed to remember from such reports that, legally, both parties had an equal right to the monies in the account. Whilst some people might have believed this meant they only could have half of what was in the joint account, I remembered reading otherwise. It extended to the entirety of the funds. Therefore, either of the parties could empty the account, regardless of who deposited what. Moreover, they were legally entitled to do so.

That said, George could argue in court – when it came to dissolving our marriage – that he wanted the money back. However, there was no guarantee I'd be ordered to repay him. After all, his intention had been to leave me high and dry in a foreign country with not even a roof over my head – hardly reasonable behaviour.

I also seemed to recall that, in law, the word *reasonable* was very key. While staying in Italy, I would need to be able to support myself. Therefore, I had an arguably good case to justifiably use the money.

The phone's battery was now at one percent.

Hurry, Sophie, urged my inner voice. *It's now or never.'*

My fingers moved swiftly. Seconds later the app informed that only one pound remained in the joint account. The rest was sitting in my personal account.

I exhaled shakily just as the mobile's screen went black and the battery died.

Chapter Twenty-Nine

I looked at Luca in relief.

'I can now feed myself while staying in Maiori.'

'Good. There are some fabulous restaurants around here and, frankly, after the way you've been treated, I think you should take advantage. Let George pay for some slap-up meals. And why limit yourself to Maiori? You can take boat taxis to the neighbouring villages and towns and explore what the Amalfi Coast has to offer. Eat a *filetto* or enjoy some fresh catches from the sea. Then visit Positano, and watch the sun go down as you work your way through a bottle of Rioja.'

'A bottle?' I said, raising my eyebrows. 'If I drank that by myself, I'd be totally plastered.'

'Perhaps you will share it with someone,' he suggested.

He gave me a meaningful look. My eyes widened. Was he suggesting that my wine buddy might be him? In which case, good heavens, was he flirting with me?

Don't be daft, Sophie. You're fifty and, right now, looking every one of your years. When God created this man, he was in a supremely good mood.

Are you saying Luca's out of my league? I retorted.

I won't bother to answer that question since you already

know the answer.

'Sharing a bottle of wine would be nice,' I ventured cautiously. 'But I don't know anybody here to keep me company.'

Apart from you.

'I'm sure you'll make friends,' he said.

Okay, he wasn't flirting. Not that I'd been interested. After all, I was married. Well, I had been. Briefly. Suddenly, a blanket of despair threatened to engulf me.

'You make it sound very easy,' I said gloomily.

'Because it is.'

'Actually, I think I might spend tomorrow just sticking to base. I need to mentally recuperate.'

'If you stay in your room, you'll be bored within five minutes.'

'No, I won't,' I said quickly. 'I'll go up to the roof terrace. Take my kindle. Lie back on a lounger.' I could imagine the scene now. Hot sun. Drinking something tall and cool. Getting lost within the electronic pages of a feelgood romance novel. 'Then, when it gets too warm, I'll take a dip in the pool.'

In your oh-so-sexy one-piece swimsuit, said my inner voice.

Okay, maybe I'd do a bit of local shopping first. Try on some bikinis. The rooftop terrace was for hotel guests only, so hopefully my flabby fifty-year-old midriff wouldn't frighten too many people.

'Ah,' said Luca, interrupting my thoughts.

The way he'd said that one word was very telling.

'Problem?' I ventured.

'The pool…'

'Yes?'

He sighed.

'It's out of order.'

'Oh, what a shame. When will it be working again?'

'Ah.'

Uh-oh, same word, uttered with the same loaded meaning.

'Don't tell me,' I groaned. 'It isn't.'

'Not any time soon,' he said apologetically. 'Look, Sophie, there's one or two things you should know about where you're staying but, after the day you've had, I'm not sure this is the right time to tell you.'

'Nothing could make today any worse, so just spit it out.'

'Basically, this place is falling apart.' He spread his hands helplessly. 'I'm honouring existing bookings but, the truth is, those bookings should never have been taken.'

'So why were they?'

He paused for a moment, as if considering whether to share a confidence.

'Look, do you want another drink? It's a bit of a story.'

I was all ears, but my mouth had other ideas and chose that moment to give a huge yawn.

'I'm so sorry,' I said, clamping a hand over my lower face.

'You're tired. The tale will keep.'

'I'd really like to know,' I protested, just as a second

yawn ambushed me.

'Not tonight. I'll tell you another time. Come on.' He stood up. 'Let me take your suitcase up to your room.'

'It's fine,' I said, also standing up. 'I can manage.'

'Your room is on the fourth floor and there are many steps. I once counted them. Two hundred and three, to be precise.'

'Not a problem,' I assured. 'I'll take the lift.'

'Ah.'

Oh no. What now?

'Don't tell me,' I said. 'The lift isn't working either.'

'You catch on quick,' Luca grinned.

I opened my mouth to reply but found myself unexpectedly speechless. It wasn't because of the broken elevator. More because of Luca's smile. I stared at him gormlessly. He looked totally transformed. He was a good-looking guy but seeing him with his mouth now quirking upwards and how this change was impacting upon the rest of his face – and in such a good way – was making me feel quite–

Gooey? enquired my inner voice.

I ignored the question and instead noted how Luca's smile had put a light in his eyes, lifting them and accentuating the fan of fine lines at his temples. His tanned skin contrasted sharply with his teeth, which were very white and straight. What a looker. What a mouth. And I could just about see the tip of his tongue. It looked very pink. And tantalising. Inexplicably, I suddenly found myself wondering what he'd be like to kiss and–

Have you finished? interrupted my inner voice. *And is there any chance of you closing your own mouth? You currently look like a cross between a goldfish and a rabbit caught in car headlights.*

'I know what you're thinking,' he said.

'I'll bet you don't,' I muttered.

'You think this place is a bit like Fawlty Towers, and you'd not be far wrong. I can only apologise in advance.'

'Where's Manuel?' I joked feebly.

'Funny. He's actually called Luigi and due back from his break at any moment. He does the night shifts on reception.'

As if on cue, a man in his early thirties walked through the main door carrying a pizza in a take-out box. He had coal-black eyes which contrasted sharply against the palest skin I'd ever seen. Luigi could easily have passed as a relative of Dracula. It was evident that this was a man who'd turned his nights into day and rarely, if ever, spent time in the sunshine.

'*Ciao*, Luca,' said Luigi, before looking at me. 'Good evening, *signora*. Shall I take your suitcase?'

Luigi's accent was strong, but his English was perfect.

'I'll see to our guest,' Luca quickly answered. 'You enjoy your pizza, Luigi.' He picked up my case and, with his free hand, indicated the staircase. 'After you, Sophie.'

Chapter Thirty

Luca was clearly a lot fitter than me.

'Okay?' he asked, as we crossed the second landing.

He hadn't so much as paused to catch his breath, and I had a feeling he wasn't going to.

'Yes,' I wheezed, trying to ignore my burning thigh muscles.

The staircases between each floor contained many steps. Their sweeping handrails were old-fashioned and sported elegant ironwork. The steps spiralled upwards from the foyer in an ever-widening circle, reminding me of the pattern on a snail's shell.

The grace of a bygone era was evident, but its beauty was marred by battered plasterwork and peeling paint. A lack of carpet on the treads meant the sound of our footsteps bounced hollowly off the walls, echoing creepily around each landing.

'Are you sure you're all right?' Luca asked, as we finished the third flight and prepared to tackle the fourth.

I stopped and clung to the handrail, my chest visibly heaving. Speaking wasn't an option on account of sucking in air at high-speed. Now I knew why women went to aerobic classes. All that stepping up and down on plastic boxes.

Backwards and forwards. Side to side. Bouncing in time to some zippy, fast-paced pop tune. It was so they were prepared for moments like this – climbing huge flights of stairs without so much as breaking sweat.

A picture of Jackie Rollinson sprang to mind. There she was. Fitness personified. Imitating Olivia Newton-John in her heyday. Dressed in a white leotard with a loose workout-shirt knotted about her toned midriff.

My lip involuntarily curled as the lyrics to *Let's Get Physical* began to play in my head. Is that how Jackie and George had made out? Going to an intimate restaurant, then watching a suggestive movie?

Perhaps they even watched porn together, my inner voice slyly suggested.

I paled at the thought, just as an unwanted vision of Jackie – playing the part of an aerobics teacher having a private one-to-one with her pupil – began to download directly into my brain.

Noooo, stop it!

I can't. You wanted to see it, so here it is in all its technicolour glory.

I groaned aloud as Jackie – demonstrating appalling acting and vocals – showed off her stripping skills and physical assets while prancing around a half-dressed George.

'Let's get touchy-feely, touchy-feely,' she sang. 'Wanna get kissy-kissy, with my lippy. Let me see your willy work, oh willy work! I wanna bounce around your body, in the nuddy–'

'No more!' I shrieked aloud.

'Do you need an asthma pump?' asked Luca in alarm.

'S–Sorry,' I stuttered, puce in the face from both exertion and an out-of-control mind movie. I slumped over the balustrade. 'Just not… used to…' – I panted – 'being so… physical.'

GAH! Don't say that word.

'Hey, we can rest for a moment,' said Luca.

'You're very fit,' I wheezed, then instantly cringed with embarrassment. 'I mean, in good shape,' I quickly added, just in case Luca thought I was insinuating he was the other sort of fit – i.e. a sexy stud with rippling muscles.

WHY DID YOU GO THERE? screamed my inner voice. *NOW I HAVE TO PLAY YOU ANOTHER PORNO REEL.*

Oh God, noooo, I mentally moaned, as a new soundtrack started up. *You're the One That I Want.* But this time the starring roles had been given to me and Luca.

I gripped the banister tightly as my brain proceeded to show me wiggling about in the hideous all-in-one swimsuit. Luca, meanwhile, was lying flat on his back with only the tiniest hand towel covering his privates.

'I've got hills,' I warbled, indicating my cozzie's built-in cups. 'They're multiplying.' Now I was running my hand over my undulating stomach. 'And I'm com-*plete*-ly out of control–"

'Sophie, you don't look well,' said Luca.

'I think…' – I boggled at the balustrade – 'that today's events have mentally overtaken me. I feel–'

'Poorly?'

'Like I'm hallucinating or something.' I rubbed my forehead. It felt hot and sweaty. Was I coming down with something?

'Lean on me,' instructed Luca.

'No, I'll be fine in a mo–'

'This isn't a time to argue,' he said firmly. Abandoning the suitcase, he grabbed hold of my arm. 'Let go of the balustrade. Come on. One more flight to go.'

The suitcase was temporarily abandoned as Luca propelled me forward. His touch nearly had me ascending the staircase in one giant leap. What the hell was going on here? What was the matter with my body? Why was it behaving like it had been tasered?

You're tired. Overwrought. All emotions are currently heightened.

Really?

I dunno. I'm just trying to reassure you.

'Thanks,' I gasped as Luca guided me down a corridor and then propped me up against the wall.

He stuck an oversized brass key into a door's old-fashioned lock.

'Your room,' said Luca, flicking two switches.

A bare lightbulb lit the area within, casting shadows across the high ceiling. A moth, languishing on closed drapes, immediately gravitated towards it just as an air-conditioning unit rumbled into life.

I glanced around. Wow. It wasn't sumptuous by any stretch of the imagination. In some respects, it was a blessing George wasn't here. He would have created stink at this so-

163

called *honeymoon suite.*

The furniture looked like it had come straight out of Grandma's attic. A small double bed with side cabinets languished against the main wall. Opposite was a dressing table and telephone. In the corner of the room was a tallboy wardrobe. I felt like I'd stepped into a 1930's time warp.

A door to the right led to a small windowless kitchenette which was little more than a large cupboard. A strip of Formica held a kettle alongside some complimentary sachets of tea, coffee, long life milk and mini packets of biscuits. There was a tiny microwave, a couple of plates and cups, and some cutlery. There was no refrigerator or sink.

'Where do I wash up?' I asked.

'In the bathroom,' said Luca apologetically.

He pushed open a neighbouring door to reveal a similar cupboard-sized room except this one housed an ancient loo, cracked handbasin and exceptionally small shower cubicle.

'It's, er, charming,' I ventured.

'No, it isn't,' said Luca grimly. 'However, it will look marginally better in the morning when the curtains are drawn, sunlight streams in and the view is revealed. That is this room's only redeeming feature. And before you ask, yes, the telephone does work. For now, anyway.'

'You sound, um, cross.'

'As I said earlier, there's a story to tell, but now isn't the time. Let me retrieve your suitcase. I don't want a guest tripping over it and suing me on top of everything else.'

He turned on his heel, leaving me pondering about what was going on in his life to make him so irritated.

I moved further into the room and ran my hand over the dressing table's surface, then examined my fingertips. The furniture might be shabby, but it was spotlessly clean, as was the bed linen. I flopped down on the counterpane. The mattress felt hard under my bottom, but I didn't care. As soon as I could, I would peel off this suit, clean my teeth, wash my face, then curl up in a ball and sob into my pillow.

There was a thump as my suitcase bashed against the door frame. I looked up to see Luca depositing the luggage in the narrow entrance.

'Are you going to be okay, Sophie?' he asked gruffly.

'Yes,' I whispered.

'In which case, breakfast is between seven and ten. See you in the morning.'

'Thank you,' I said meekly. 'And, er, sorry about going to pieces earlier.'

'It's fine. We've all been there.'

Really? Somehow, I couldn't imagine this man striding into a building's foyer and then emotionally disintegrating.

'Goodnight,' I said.

He gave a brisk nod before quietly shutting the door behind him.

Sighing, I got up and hauled my suitcase onto the bed. Locating my washbag, I went into the bathroom. Catching sight of myself in the black-speckled mirror over the basin, I was appalled at the sight of my reflection. Eyes that resembled jam doughnuts stared back at me. They held no light, only despair. Indeed, they bore the look of someone who'd been in a battle and lost. In this light, my pallor was grey. My cheeks looked more creased than my wrinkled wedding outfit. Bits of tissue were still clinging to my skin. A large piece had adhered to my right nostril, impersonating a giant bogey.

I cringed. Whatever must Luca have thought? But then again, what did it matter what he thought? What did it matter what *anyone* thought?

I eventually crawled between the sheets, completely naked. All my nightwear was brand new and either lacy, frothy, or transparent. After all, it had been bought for seduction. Not much call for that now. If ever again.

The man I'd married had turned out to be a two-timing, duplicitous stranger. How had I got it so wrong? I'd believed George to be sincere. Genuine. I'd thought him kind. Caring. And while my love hadn't been a scorching one – like when I'd been married to Teddy – I'd nonetheless believed it had still been love. Just… a different *grade*, if that was the right word. A love that was gentle and steady, rather than fiery and passionate. A love that was suitable for an older person. Like me.

Geez, you're prattling on like a newly wedded ninety-year-old. Love is love, Sophie. It should burn brightly no matter how old you are.

Oh, sod off, I silently snarled. Just leave me alone. I've been waiting for this moment all day long. To be alone and let the floodgates finally open.

Viciously, I plumped the pillows then buried my face in the starched cotton, all ready to unleash another tsunami of tears. Instead, much to my surprise, I fell fast asleep.

166

Chapter Thirty-One

I was awoken by the landline ringing.

Groggily, I swung my legs over the side of the bed and tottered, in the dark, over to the dressing table. Pat-patting with my hands, I located the telephone and picked up the handset. Who the heck was calling me in the middle of the night?

'Hello?' I murmured.

'Good afternoon, Sophie,' said Luca.

My eyes widened in the darkness.

'Afternoon?' I repeated stupidly.

I located my mobile which I'd left charging alongside the landline phone. Good heavens. The screen's clock revealed it was a little after midday. I'd slept solidly for over twelve hours. I might have remained in the Land of Nod even longer if Luca hadn't awoken me. My stomach rumbled and I realised, with dismay, that I'd missed breakfast.

'I'm currently on reception,' said Luca. 'I have a caller waiting to be put through to you. Usually, incoming calls are transferred straight to a guest's room. However, I thought you might like to compose yourself before I put this particular gentleman through.'

'Really?' I yawned, still befuddled. 'Sorry, I'm not yet

properly awake.' I moved towards the heavy drapes. I was about to pull them back when the phone clattered to the floor. It made a loud *dinggg* of protest.

'Are you still there?' asked Luca.

'Yes,' I said, picking up the phone, then nearly garrotting myself as plastic-coated wire wrapped itself around my neck. 'Hell, I forgot this phone wasn't cordless.'

Feeling my way, I disentangled myself from the cord and stared around the darkened room. At least I knew the black-out curtains were efficient. Peering into the gloom, I located a light switch over the dressing table.

'Why do I need to compose myself?' I asked, squinting as my irises adjusted to the sudden brightness.

There was a pregnant pause.

'Because the caller is your husband.'

I gulped. Hell's bells. George was on the line, no doubt wanting to rant after discovering Yours Truly had emptied the joint account. I blinked rapidly, hoping it might help to clear my head which currently felt like it had been stuffed with cottonwool.

'Put him through,' I croaked.

There was a click and a man's voice bawled down the line.

'SOPHIE?'

I momentarily held the receiver away from my head.

'ARE YOU THERE?' asked the voice.

Hang on. That wasn't George.

'Teddy?'

'CAN YOU HEAR ME?'

'Yes, and for heaven's sake stop shouting.'

'At last,' he said, exhaling gustily. 'I've been trying to get hold of you for ages but couldn't raise you. I've been so worried.'

'Oh?' I asked nervously, reaching for my mobile. I pressed the *Focus* icon, switching off *Do Not Disturb*. Almost immediately it began pinging noisily with incoming texts.

'Little Waterlow is abuzz with the news of your wedding disaster,' said Teddy breathlessly. 'I couldn't believe what I was hearing.'

'And, er, what have you heard?' I quavered.

'Well, according to Mabel Plaistow—'

'This is going to be interesting,' I said, rolling my eyes.

'You bet. She said—'

'Teddy, can I just stop you for a moment? There's something I really need to do.'

'What?'

'Draw the curtains and make myself a cup of coffee. Can you give me a sec?'

'I suppose so,' he grumbled. 'Never mind my phone bill.'

'I also really, really, *really* need a wee and this phone isn't cordless. In other words, I can't take you with me to the bathroom to continue this conversation.'

'Go on, then,' he sighed. 'Do what you need to do. I'll hold.'

'Thanks,' I smiled, putting down the handset.

I hastened off to the kitchen first. Filling the kettle from the bathroom tap, I then plugged it into one of the kitchen's sockets before tipping coffee powder into a mug. While the kettle was coming to the boil, I relieved my bladder. Coming out of the bathroom, I discovered the kettle was still slowly whining to the boil, so hurried over to the heavy drapes and finally pulled them back.

Bright golden sunlight immediately flooded the room and... omigod... *what* a balcony and just *look* at that view!

Flinging open the door, I was amazed to see that, despite being on the fourth floor, the balcony issued on to private gardens divided up by tall privacy fences on either side. Paved slabs edged a turfed lawn, at the end of which was a wrought iron guardrail allowing an unscreened view of the sea.

Enchanted, I walked barefoot across the grass and peered over the rail. Wow. The gardens had been cleverly etched into a flat area of rock that jutted up and over the winding road far below. Beyond the road were more rocks against which waves endlessly ebbed and flowed, breaking into patterns of perpetually lacy foam. To the far right, where the hill flattened and joined the promenade, was the beach. It stretched ahead in a long curve until, in the far distance, I could glimpse the marina that housed the boats of both fishermen and millionaires.

I put my hand up to shade my eyes and watched, in delight, the progress of a large double-decker boat crammed with people. It was chugging purposefully towards the marina's jetty. That must be one of the water taxis. What a glorious way to travel.

Behind me came the faint pop of the kettle's switch. Oh

170

heavens, Teddy! For a moment there, I'd completely forgotten about him patiently waiting to speak to me. Hurrying back into the room, I grabbed the handset.

'Won't be a mo,' I said, before once again chucking the handset down. I heard a faint squawk as I belted off to the kitchen. Sorry, Teddy, but needs must.

I made the coffee, grabbed a packet of complimentary biscuits, then hurried back to the phone.

'Sorry about that,' I said breathlessly, perching on the edge of the bed. Ripping open the biscuits, I crammed one in my mouth.

'At last,' said Teddy. 'Having finally tracked you down, I reckon I've racked up a bill of fifty quid without even saying anything.'

'You now have my undivided attention,' I said, spraying crumbs everywhere.

'Right, where was I?'

'Mabel Plaistow.'

'Ah, yes. According to Mabel Plaistow, you arrived at The Angel with your wedding party and proceeded to go berserk.'

'Define berserk,' I said, washing the biscuit down with a slurp of coffee.

'Apparently, George has been having an affair with ten different women, one of whom just happened to be in the pub. You found out via an anonymous letter signed by Leo the Lion which was sent by courier to The Angel just as you were about to cut the wedding cake. You located the other woman and approached her with menace. Then your

171

bridesmaid picked up one of Cathy's potted plants and shrieked, "Kill the bitch with this." You then tried to bash the other woman's brains out. Mabel said you had to be pulled off by the other woman's husband who, in turn, snatched the plant off you and tried to brain George with it. Concussed, George staggered backwards and broke every stick of furniture in the pub, and Frank – Cathy's husband – now wants twenty grand in compensation. He's supposedly going to sue the entire wedding party.'

Thank God I was in Italy.

'Well obviously' – I took another hasty sip of coffee – 'that is a very exaggerated version, but if you strip away several layers of embroidery there is an essence of truth.'

'Oh, Soph,' Teddy lamented. 'I'm so sorry to hear everything went wrong, darling. I *knew* that man was a prat. I *told* you Madam Rosa meant that you should marry me. Do you want me to fly out to Italy to be with you?'

'Whatever for?'

'To support you, of course,' said Teddy staunchly.

'Hm, until you have your head turned by the smiling *signora* at Passport Control and want to take a crash course in Italian so you can ask her out to dinner.'

'I'm not *that* bad,' Teddy sniffed.

'You're not that good either,' I said, smiling into my coffee. I took another sip. 'I know you mean well, Teddy, but you really don't have to worry.'

'I still love you, Soph.'

'I know, and I love you too. But we both know it's the wrong sort of love.'

'Really?' said Teddy sadly.

'It's the love of good friends,' I said firmly. 'And that's wonderful. I'm very grateful to know you care about my welfare.'

'I mean it, Soph,' he said earnestly. 'You've obviously been to hell and back.'

'Yes, but I'm bearing up. Honest.'

And I meant it.

Somehow, despite the horrors of yesterday, the event had receded to a distant place in my mind. I knew it would have to be revisited at some point. Certainly, I couldn't stay in Italy forever. But, right now, the whole wedding disaster had faded to a blur. It was probably a coping mechanism. Even so, I felt disconnected from it. It was as if my heartbreak had been swaddled within an invisible comfort blanket.

Currently hundreds and hundreds of miles – plus an ocean – separated George, Jackie, and me. I felt safe. For now, anyway. For the next seven days, the only love triangle I wanted to be involved in, was one that looked like a pizza.

I was just about to chomp into another biscuit when a movement caught my eye. Out in the garden, a kitten had appeared from nowhere.

'Oh,' I cooed.

'What?' said Teddy.

'I have a visitor.'

'Don't tell me George has turned up.'

'No,' I chuckled. 'There's no chance of that.'

'Good to hear.'

173

'Hello, little one,' I said to the kitten, as it boldly strolled through the open door and into the room.

'So, if it's not George, who are you talking to?' asked Teddy.

'A cat. Well, she's a baby.'

'How do you know it's a girl?'

'Because of her colouring. She's ginger, white and black. A calico. They're always female.'

'Don't touch her,' Teddy warned. 'She might look cute but she's probably full of fleas. Or ringworm. Or both,' he added.

'I don't care if she is,' I said.

I held out one hand, inviting the kitten to headbutt my fingers. She was too nervous to come any closer.

'Look, never mind the cat for a minute,' said Teddy. 'Listen to me, darling. I'm here if you need me. Do you understand?'

'Yes,' I nodded. 'And I'm very grateful, Teddy. But you don't need to be concerned. I'm okay and I'll be home in a week.'

'Call me if you need me. I mean it.'

'All right,' I assured.

'Promise?'

'Promise.'

'Just give me the word and I'll–'

There was a loud squawk in the background followed by a woman speaking. Despite the distance, I could hear her clearly demanding to know who Teddy was talking to.

'My wife,' he replied, to which there was another loud

shriek and the sound of someone throwing something. A slipper?

'Ouch,' said Teddy. 'We're divorced... yes, you did hear me say I still love her... look, I only met you the other day... oh, for...sorry, Soph. I'll call you back. Meanwhile, enjoy the company of your new charge.'

'*Ciao*,' I said, hanging up. Some things never changed, and Teddy would always be one of them. I turned my attention back to my new four-legged friend. 'Well, this is a lovely surprise.'

'Meow,' she squeaked.

'I suppose that means *feed me.*'

'Meow,' the kitten agreed.

'Luckily for you, I have some milk.'

I went into the kitchenette and opened the long life, poured some into a dish, then returned to the bedroom area.

'Here you are,' I soothed, setting the bowl down and backing slowly away. 'You are so pretty. What shall I call you? Oh, wait. I know the Italian word for *pretty*. It's *bella*,' I grinned. 'How very apt. I shall call you Bella.'

Cautiously, Bella crept towards the saucer. Keeping her eyes firmly upon me, she began to lap. In no time at all the milk was gone.

'I shall buy you some more,' I promised. 'I guess I'd better add cat food to the shopping list. In fact, you've given me the perfect excuse to get my act together and venture into Maiori.'

The telephone rang again just as Bella jumped onto the unmade bed, loudly purring.

'My goodness, I'm popular today,' I said aloud, picking up the handset for a second time. 'Hello?'

'Sophie,' said Luca. 'It's your husband again.'

I shook my head. There was no doubt about it. Teddy was a trier. Presumably his lady friend had stormed off leaving him free to talk without any jealous interruptions. Bella was now paddling the rumpled sheets with her tiny paws, preparing to settle down for a snooze. Oh, but she was adorable. I found myself giving her a smile straight from the heart before turning my attention back to Luca.

'Put him through,' I said.

A second later, the soppy grin was wiped from my face.

'You bloody cow,' hissed George.

Chapter Thirty-Two

For a moment I said nothing. What was there to say?

Everything, said my inner voice.

And nothing, I countered.

Tell him he's a prat. A bastard. A dick. A shit. A fu–

Thanks, I cut in, but I think I can speak for myself.

'Well,' I ventured. 'I'd like to say this is a pleasant surprise, George.' I gripped the handset. 'But unfortunately, it isn't.'

'Where's the money, Sophie?' he demanded.

Ah. There was no longer any pretence of loving me or wanting to make a go of our marriage.

'In my account,' I said calmly.

'Transfer it back. Now.'

'No.' I shook my head. 'You tried to cancel the hotel reservation, George. What type of person does that? If you'd been successful, I'd have been out on the street in a foreign country. You know I don't have that sort of credit on my card, or funds in my bank, to see me through staying here.'

'That's not my problem,' George snarled. 'You should never have flown off to Italy in the first place.'

'And maybe you' – my voice was starting to rise – 'shouldn't *in the first place* have had a longstanding affair with your best friend's wife while ASKING ANOTHER WOMAN TO MARRY YOU!' I shouted.

Startled, Bella leapt off the bed and raced through the open door. A second later, she'd scrambled through a hole in the fence and vanished. Oh God. I shouldn't have shouted. I instantly felt consumed with guilt. I'd make it up to her. Somehow.

'Never mind what I should or shouldn't have done,' said George coldly. 'At least I'm not a common thief. I'm warning you now, Sophie–'

'Don't threaten me, George.'

'I'll do what the fuck I like.'

'I think you've already done enough fucking,' I said crisply. 'But of course, there's always room for a bit more, so do please take some of your own advice and FUCK OFF!'

I slammed the phone down so hard the plastic handset split in half, spilling a spaghetti of thin wires across the dressing table.

Now look what you've done, said my inner voice. *That's one more thing that doesn't work in this crumbling hotel. You'll probably have to pay hundreds of Euros to replace it.*

It was too much.

'ARGHHH,' I bellowed at the wall. 'SODDING SHIT, TWATTING HELL, STINKY BUMHOLES, HAIRY BOLLOCKS, BUGGER AND BALLS AND FUCKITY-FUCKITY-FUCK–'

I abruptly stopped ranting upon hearing a knock on the door. Oh, cosmic. No doubt it was the housemaid, come to

178

make the bed, and now she'd heard every word of the raging *senorita* on the other side of the door. She was probably nervously backing away, ready to charge down four flights of stairs to seek out Luca so she could breathlessly report that it hadn't been possible to clean Room 410 on account of the occupant being a loony. Chest heaving, I paused to see if another knock might be forthcoming.

Silence.

I collapsed down on the bed again. Had she gone away? If not, perhaps I could pretend I'd had the telly on. I glanced around the room looking for a handy remote control, then realised there wasn't one because there was no television. Fab. *Il Castello* was a hotel that just kept on giving. Not.

Maybe I could instead make out that I'd been watching a video on my mobile and that a foreign satellite orbiting this particular part of Planet Earth had caused a freak issue with the volume button so that everything had amplified tenfold and–

There was another knock on the door. This time much firmer. I gulped. I'd just have to style it out. At least the housemaid was Italian. The possibility of her speaking amazing English was slim. I brightened at the thought. Yes, it was most unlikely she'd have understood all those terrible swearwords.

'Coming,' I warbled. 'Just switching off my, er, programme.'

Taking a deep breath, I marched over to the door. But instead of greeting a housemaid who only spoke pidgin English, instead I came red face to face with Luca.

179

Chapter Thirty-Three

'Having put through your husband's calls twice' – Luca explained – 'I thought I'd pop up just to make sure you're okay.'

'Oh, er, yes. I'm fine. Thank you,' I whispered, face flaming.

'Sure?'

My chin wobbled violently.

Stiff upper lip, Sophie. Come on, do it. You're British and that's what Brits do.

Maybe I'd like to be Italian, I silently responded. After all, they're quite famous for expressing their emotions. Nobody bats an eyelid if they make a drama out of a crisis, wailing and weeping noisily before nosediving with grief into a bowl of spaghetti.

'Sophie?' Luca prompted. 'You look upset. And, er, confession time, I heard you, um, *emoting.*'

I gulped a bit more.

'Sorry about that. You'll probably have the switchboard lighting up with complaints from neighbouring guests.'

'It's fine,' he assured. 'I think everyone on this floor is at the beach, soaking up the sunshine, so you don't need to worry about your rant being overheard. If it's any consolation, I thought it was quite inspiring.'

He gave a mischievous grin, as if we were sharing a secret, and despite still being upset, I found myself mustering a sheepish smile in return.

'I have a confession too,' I said. 'Your telephone handset is now in two pieces.'

'That's fixable,' he assured. 'May I?'

'Of course,' I said, stepping aside to let him in. 'I'm not usually foulmouthed, honest.'

'You don't have to justify yourself,' he said, picking up the broken handset and aligning wires and bits of plastic. There was a clicking sound as everything snapped back together. 'There,' he said, putting the receiver back on its cradle.

'Thank you. And, um, I'd just like to explain that the first call was from my ex-husband – who tends to forget we're divorced. He was ringing to see if I was okay. But the second call...'

My voice snagged on my tonsils, and I had to pause for a moment. Recalibrate. Luca leapt into the gap.

'The second call was from the current husband.'

I nodded.

'George discovered that I'd transferred the holiday spending money from the joint account to my personal account. He wasn't very happy about it.'

My stomach chose that moment to noisily rumble. It had been a long time since I'd eaten any proper food, and whilst the complimentary biscuits had been nice, they weren't satisfying. Frankly I was amazed my tummy even wanted

181

food when my emotions were all over the place.

'I know you missed breakfast,' said Luca, walking over to the still open door. 'But I would strongly advise you not to skip meals. The last thing I want is one of my guests keeling over because their blood sugar has dropped. If you're doing battle with George, both your mind and body need fuel. Listen' – he glanced at his watch – 'I must go to Amalfi later this afternoon to see my solicitor, but first need some lunch. Why don't you let me drive you into Maiori and we'll eat together. Then, when I head off, you can explore the promenade. I'm sure you'll be able to find your way back to *Il Castello* afterwards. Does that suit?'

'It does,' I said, feeling a small ray of joy seeping into my soul. 'That's very kind of you,' I added.

Oooh, lunch with the Adonis, Sophie. Well done!

It's *lunch*, I retorted, mentally rolling my eyes. You make it sound like a date.

Well, once you've annulled your marriage to Grey George, you'll start dating again, so you might as well try it for size with Luca.

I will never date again, I protested. Been there, done that.

'Good,' said Luca, interrupting my inner argument. 'That's a date.'

A date! You see!

'Make sure' – he continued – 'to bring a floppy hat. The sun, particularly at this time of day, can be deceptively strong.'

'Sure,' I said, touched at his concern.

He's just being nice, said my inner voice.

I know, but I appreciate it nonetheless.

'You can now start to enjoy your holiday properly. On the way to the restaurant, I'll show you which beach belongs to *Il Castello*.'

'It has a private beach?' I asked in surprise.

I'd assumed the whole sandy stretch was for the public.

'All the hotels have their own area,' Luca explained. 'I'll introduce you to Floriana – she mans the kiosk – and tell her you're a VIP guest and exempt from paying for a sunbed throughout your stay.'

'You have to *pay* for a sunbed?' I said in astonishment. Sue and Charlie always splashed on fancy all-inclusive holidays abroad and had never paid a penny for sunbeds. I'd wrongly presumed that to be the norm anywhere in the world. 'How much?'

'Depends where you sit on the beach,' Luca explained. 'It's thirty euros for the first two rows, twenty-five for the next two, but only fifteen – an absolute bargain' – he gave a deprecating laugh – 'for the last couple of rows at the back.'

'B-But' – I spluttered – 'that's outrageous.' I did some mental maths. 'For two people, even the cheapest sunbeds for a week would be around two hundred euros.'

'Yes,' he said lightly. 'But the hotel has certain costs to pay.'

'Oh, you mean like staff to clean the beach and a couple of dudes to stack the sunbeds at the end of the day.'

'Um, something like that,' he said vaguely. 'This is Italy, Sophie.' He gave me a meaningful look. 'If you catch my

183

drift.'

My eyes widened.

'I'll leave you to get ready. See you downstairs in a few minutes.'

'Yes,' I said breathlessly.

Luca turned on his heel. I clung on to the doorframe, momentarily watching him walk along the corridor. Then, feeling like an extra in *Miami Twice*, I quickly shut the door lest Del Boy's Don Occhetti happened to be lurking.

Chapter Thirty-Four

I swung out of my room ten minutes later, straw hat in one hand, tote bag in the other, a pair of sunglasses perched jauntily upon my head.

Never had I dressed so speedily or applied lippy and mascara so swiftly. I'd stopped short of dousing myself in perfume – didn't want a swarm of bees after me – and hastily slipped on a halter neck sundress, then threaded dangly earrings through my earlobes in a nod to casual glamour.

I fairly skipped down the four flights of stairs to reception.

Steady, Sophie. You're a married woman. Don't let the sap rise.

Oh, do shut up, I silently tutted. I'm on my honeymoon.

I know but try and remember that Luca Lamagna isn't your husband.

Give me a break. What do you think I'm going to do? Ravish him in the restaurant?

I'm just reminding you to behave.

I'm fifty years old. Hardly a juvenile delinquent.

Okay, okay. Don't get irate. Just make sure you stay off the vino. You don't want to say anything stupid or make a fool of yourself.

Bit late for that. I made a clown of myself in Little Waterlow when I married George. Remember?

How could anyone forget?

'Sophie,' said Luca, as I bounced into reception. 'Mind the–'

'Argh,' I shrieked, as my rubber flip-flops suddenly became a pair of ice-skates.

'–the wet floor,' Luca concluded as I morphed into Jane Torvill, glided across the foyer, and crashed into the chaise longue.

'Ooof,' I said, grabbing hold of the couch to right my balance. My sunglasses slid down my nose, landing at a skewwhiff angle.

'Please don't sue me,' said Luca, hastening over. He pointed to a yellow portable sign on which was written *Pavimento Bagnato* with an accompanying mop-and-bucket symbol. 'There was a warning.'

'Must have missed it,' I gasped, as he hauled me upright.

His touch sent several hundred electric shocks zinging up my spine. I nearly whooshed across the floor again.

'Okay?' he asked.

'Yes,' I panted. 'No harm done.'

I shoved the sunnies back on my head, feeling both embarrassed and confused. Why did I keep getting zingers every time he inadvertently touched me?

Because–

I wasn't asking you, I snapped, immediately cutting off the inner voice.

'Right,' said Luca, releasing me. 'Let's head off.' As he

186

strode past the reception desk, he addressed a woman I'd not noticed until now. 'I'll be back around six o'clock, Vittoria.'

She glanced at me curiously as I scampered after Luca.

Outside, the heat of the afternoon took me by surprise. The sun on my bare arms was like a warm caress.

My eyes were instantly drawn to the view across the narrow road. To the left, the sea seemed to stretch to infinity but to the right its glittering waves met the longest beach I'd ever seen, smothered in various parasols of either blue, yellow, or white. Unlike other beaches I'd visited when on holiday, not all these sunbeds were in use. In fact, many seemed to be empty. Hardly surprising at those prices.

I was so busy looking at the view instead of where I was going, that when Luca stopped by a car, I cannoned straight into the back of him.

'Ooof,' I said for the second time in as many minutes. 'The seascape distracted me.' I then stood on his foot. 'Oops, terribly sorry.'

'No worries,' he winced.

'Sorry,' I said again, turning scarlet.

Why are you suddenly so clumsy?

Don't know. And stop talking to me. It's annoying.

'In you get,' said Luca, opening the passenger door of an open-top sportscar.

'Thanks,' I said, limbo dancing into the low bucket seat.

Oh, very nice, Luca. Very nice indeed. Quite a crumpet catcher.

I leant back and idly wondered if Luca had already caught crumpet, so to speak. The dark-haired lady on reception had looked rather proprietorial. Was she possibly his *interesse romantico*?

'Buckle up,' said Luca, as the engine roared into life.

He checked the rear-view mirror and suddenly we were shooting backwards. There was an abrupt change of gear and then the sportscar whooshed forwards, tyres squealing on the tarmac of the narrow road.

'Sorry,' he apologised. 'That was a bit of a blind bend, and one can't hang about.'

'Quite,' I muttered, waiting for my tonsils to realign with my throat. 'What sort of car is this?' I glanced around the interior.

'An Alfa Romeo Spider. Are you a bit of a petrolhead?'

'Oh yes,' I lied. 'I love fast cars.'

Subtly, I let my tote bag slide from my lap to the floor, then clamped my fingers around the sides of the seat. My knuckles instantly turned the same colour as a couple of clouds chugging through the sky. It didn't help that I was sitting in a lefthand drive vehicle while being chauffeured on the wrong side of the road.

It's the right side of the road here, Sophie.

I'm used to UK driving, okay?

Luca dropped a gear as the car whizzed round a bend, before levelling out to the main promenade. A bus barged out from a side turning, forcing Luca to slow down.

'I'll have to take you for a proper spin,' he said.

'Lovely,' I replied.

I tried not to visibly sigh with relief now that we were pootling along.

'I'll take you to Tramonti,' he said. 'The literal translation for that name is *in the mountains*.'

Oh God. Not those horrendous, hairpin bends again?

'The roads meander up and then double-back on themselves,' he explained. 'A car like this grips the road like a Dyson vacuum cleaner refusing to let go of a loose carpet.'

'Sounds amazing,' I warbled. 'And, er, does Vittoria like your car?'

'Yes, she loves it.'

Oh.

'And, um, her family?'

'They haven't seen it.'

'Why not?'

'They live in Florence. That's over three hundred miles away.'

'That's a shame. Don't you ever drive to Florence?'

'Whatever for?'

'Well, to see your in-laws.'

Luca looked puzzled.

'I don't have any in-laws. I'm not married.'

'O-Oh, but surely Vittoria's parents are as good as your in-laws. Aren't they?'

Luca laughed.

'Not at all. Vittoria is a member of staff. Our relationship is purely professional.'

I gave a sigh of relief as Luca glanced curiously at me. I quickly turned the sigh into some extensive throat clearing, then made a show of studying the people dotted along the promenade.

Retired locals were sitting on various benches, passing the time of day as they chatted together. The seats were strategically placed in the shade of pretty trees. Other folks were simply enjoying the sunshine and watching life go by – young mothers pushing strollers towards a playground a little way ahead – while others were taking advantage of the pavement cafés.

My head swivelled to take in a group of men playing cards and enjoying a cool beer, while their wives gossiped together, all the while gesturing with their hands.

Ahead, the bus belched diesel fumes into the air. Luca indicated right and suddenly we were scooting up a side street, then through an aperture so narrow I found myself breathing in.

'Private car park,' he explained. 'For patrons only. Let's eat. I'm starving.'

'Me too,' I said, quickly unbuckling.

Walking out of the car park, I smiled to myself. Vittoria wasn't Luca's girlfriend. I had no idea why that should make my heart sing but, as I followed my lunch date into the restaurant's cool interior, I had a sense that – right now – all was well in my world.

Chapter Thirty-Five

'So how are you feeling this afternoon, Sophie?' asked Luca.

We were now seated at a window table, overlooking the promenade. A waiter had already been over. Pizza had been ordered. Meanwhile Luca was sipping a cold beer while I cradled a glass of chilled white wine. I twirled the stem thoughtfully before answering.

'I'm a whole lot better than yesterday,' I said honestly. I gazed through the window for a moment. 'Bizarrely, the whole episode seems like it happened to someone else.'

'Probably a coping mechanism.'

'Yes, I did wonder that and suspect you're right. I shall spend the next week licking my wounds and mentally recuperating. Then I shall return home and do the necessary. Get the marriage annulled.'

'Well, I hope Maiori – indeed the Amalfi Coast – helps to heal your heartbreak.'

'Me too,' I said, before taking a sip of wine. 'This is delicious by the way.'

'Good.'

'I just feel such an idiot. This is the second time I've fluffed up. I loved Teddy – my first husband – to bits. I'm still very fond of him. However, he was a serial philanderer.'

'This is the first gentleman who called you.'

'Yes, him. He sweetly offered to drop everything and fly out to rescue me.'

'Ah, a knight in shining armour,' Luca smiled, before taking a glug of his beer.

'Teddy is definitely that sort of guy,' I laughed. 'A smooth operator.'

'As opposed to George.'

'I belatedly discovered that George is just plain devious. He certainly has none of Teddy's charm. I don't know how I managed to be so taken in,' I sighed. I stared at my wine, as if the pale liquid might somehow hold the answer.

'Put the whole episode down to one of life's experiences.'

'One hell of a lesson,' I said gloomily.

'But we all have them.'

I looked up at him curiously.

'Has something like this happened to you?'

Luca inclined his head.

'I have a failed marriage under my belt.'

'Really?'

'Yup. I married very young and, well' – he shrugged – 'it didn't work out.'

Thanks to an empty stomach, the wine was hitting its spot. I was starting to feel pleasantly relaxed.

'How young?' I asked nosily.

'Nineteen,' he said, looking sheepish.

'*Nineteen*?' I gasped. 'A teenager!'

'Indeed, and a know-it-all teenager at that, as was Jilly,

my young wife.'

'Tell me about her.'

'Not much to tell really. We went to school together. Childhood sweethearts.'

'How romantic,' I sighed, putting one elbow on the table, and cupping my chin in my hand.

'Oh, it was very romantic,' Luca agreed. 'From the age of twelve to nineteen, Jilly was my girl. We only had eyes for each other. Our parents warned us not to rush into marriage, but we ignored them. Our families were convinced it wouldn't last.'

'It might have done,' I said indignantly.

'Certainly, I thought it would,' he said quietly. 'And on that premise, we went ahead and married at the local registry office. My bride wore a white dress bought for ninety-nine pence off eBay while I was suited and booted in an outfit that cost a fiver from a local charity shop. Afterwards we went to McDonalds with a bunch of old schoolfriends and celebrated with Happy Meals.'

'Nothing wrong with a Happy Meal,' I said staunchly.

'Except, directly afterwards, my new wife locked eyes with the store manager. Instead of honeymooning for one night in a Premier Inn, I found myself back home with my mum and dad listening to an endless rant that always seemed to end in *I told you so*.'

I sat up straight as something occurred to me.

'So your marriage lasted less than twenty-four hours too,' I said in astonishment.

'Well, no, that's not strictly true. You see, my wife

eventually dumped the store manager and asked me to forgive her.'

'And did you?'

'Yes. Except it happened again. Different person. Same outcome. She went off with another man.'

'Ah, and then you divorced.'

'No.' Luca shook his head and looked faintly embarrassed. 'Stupidly, I forgave her again. And again. I told myself that money – or the lack of it – was the reason why she went off with other guys. After all, we hardly had two spare pennies to rub together, and hardship can cause a lot of resentment and friction between couples. I also told myself that she'd never had the chance to, as we say, *play the field*. I hoped that if she had dalliances with other guys, eventually she'd get it out of her system and properly settle down with me.'

'I see. And did you play the field too?'

'Not at the time,' he said sadly. 'I didn't want to. I was holding out for Jilly changing back into the girl I fell in love with. But after two years, it was an established pattern, and I knew there was no going back. So, I finally cut my losses. And then I played the field,' he added with a wicked laugh.

I privately concluded that Jilly was nuts to have walked away from such a smitten and forgiving Adonis.

'Have you never settled down with anyone else?' I asked.

'Nope.'

'Why not?'

He shrugged.

'I've never been short of female company but, so far, the

one who makes my heart sing has evaded me.'

'She's out there somewhere.'

Luca smiled.

'That's a very romantic thought for someone who has so recently had her heart broken. Do you think your soulmate is out there too?'

'I'm probably the wrong person to be dishing out advice when my own personal life has been such a disaster,' I sighed. 'Do you still see your ex around these parts?'

'Oh, no. My marriage drama took place in England. That's where I was born and raised, hence my British accent. My father was Italian and my mother English. They live in Hertfordshire. As for Jilly, I haven't seen her for years. Many moons ago, she met an Australian guy and eventually took off to the Gold Coast. As far as I'm aware, she's still there.

'So, what made you decide to live in Italy?'

'Good question,' he grinned. 'I had an uncle on my father's side, who never married, never had any children, and happened to own a hotel. *Il Castello.* He died earlier this year, and I was his sole beneficiary.'

My eyes widened.

'Wow, what an amazing inheritance.'

'It is,' he agreed. 'Except you don't need to scratch the surface too hard to note the place is falling apart. It's a money pit. I'm here for now, trying to decide whether to make a go of it, or sell it.'

'Have you made any decision yet?'

'Nothing is set in stone,' he sighed. 'But more particularly, I've fallen in love with Maiori. I'm not sure I *can* leave this place. You'll see what I mean as you settle in over the next few days. Maiori will work its magic on you too.'

'I hope so,' I said, gazing through the window at the sparkling sea beyond.

The water glittered and twinkled under the afternoon sun, and I was reminded of something someone had once said. You can't stop the waves, but you can learn to surf. What very wise words.

Chapter Thirty-Six

By the time the waiter had served our pizzas, a good half hour had elapsed since we'd first sat down, and I caught Luca discreetly looking at his wristwatch.

'What time is your appointment with the solicitor?' I asked, picking up my knife and fork. Mm. This food smelt so good, and my mouth watered in anticipation.

'It's okay, I don't have to rush,' Luca assured. 'I'm simply keeping an eye on the time. After I've gone, will you be okay on your own?'

'Of course,' I said, tucking in. 'Anyway' − I tried and failed not to speak with my mouth full − 'I made the decision to come here alone, so shall explore the sights alone too.'

'You don't have to be Sophie-No-Mates,' Luca grinned, picking up his own knife and fork. 'I'm sure you'll make friends here, plus I'm happy to show you around.'

'You have a hotel to run.'

'True, but I also have staff. Likewise, as their boss, I'm the one that gives the orders.'

'Said like a man who cracks the whip,' I teased.

'Not at all,' he grinned. 'I'm firm, but fair. Everyone is aware of your, er, wedding *disappointment*, Sophie.'

'How embarrassing,' I muttered.

I quickly looked away and concentrated on cutting up another segment of pizza.

'On the contrary,' Luca said. 'Everyone feels sorry for you.'

My head shot up.

'I'm not a victim,' I protested.

'Nobody said you were, Sophie, but equally you're a woman alone in a foreign country. My staff are hugely sympathetic to your situation. So, if they see the boss occasionally disappearing to show you around, they will be both pleased and delighted to know you're in safe hands and being looked after.'

'I didn't mean to sound ungracious.'

'You didn't. Just… a little prickly.'

'Sorry,' I said. 'Anyway, I wouldn't dream of impinging on your time, especially when you're trying to make things work at the hotel. There must be a million things to do.'

'There are, and those million things cost money – and I don't have all the readies right now. The first thing is to get the lift operational. That's in hand but I'm still waiting for the engineer to turn up. Second, the swimming pool. Third, a revamp. The latter is the biggest cost and will have to wait until more paying guests have found their way here, although I have splurged on the roof terrace. That was a priority. Defunct swimming pool aside, the terrace looks good. If you like, I'll take you up there for a drink this evening, before you go out to dinner. Unless, of course, you'd prefer to be left alone,' he added.

'N–No,' I said quickly.

What? Turn down the chance to spend some time with this gorgeous looking guy? Not that I was interested in him. Not like that, anyway. And even if I was, it wasn't like he was interested in *me*. After all, I was a knackered fifty-year-old and down on my marital luck, whereas he was a handsome footloose and fancy-free forty-something. However, there was no harm in taking advantage of a free guide who just happened to be extremely easy on the eye.

'How old are you?' I blurted.

'Forty-four. Why?'

'Just wondered,' I mumbled.

Wow. Six years younger than me. Not a huge age gap in the grand scheme of things.

Why is Luca's age of interest to you? asked my inner voice.

It isn't, I quickly replied.

'Um' – I cleared my throat – 'I'd love to have that drink on the roof terrace and admire the view.' I took another bite of pizza. 'This is so good. I can't imagine being hungry again this evening after eating such a huge meal.'

'You will be,' Luca assured. 'If you're planning on exploring, you'll burn calories like nobody's business. Anyway, it would be a sin to come to this country and not enjoy the food.'

'True,' I said, putting my knife and fork together. 'That was a piece of heaven. Anyway, I think I'll spend the rest of the afternoon checking out the entire length of the promenade.'

Luca put his own knife and fork together.

'Coffee?' he asked.

'Yes, please.'

He signalled the waiter. There was a pause in the conversation while Luca ordered two cappuccinos and asked for the bill, before being interrupted by an incoming phone call.

'Sorry,' he murmured, momentarily putting one hand over the microphone.

'Go ahead,' I whispered back.

His conversation took place in Italian, so I had no idea what he was talking about, or to whom. A waiter appeared with a card machine and Luca tapped it with his bank card. I made a mental note to ask how much I owed him, then plucked my own mobile from my handbag and checked it. Oh, a text from Sue. I hadn't heard my phone ding.

Are you okay, Soph? George turned up on our doorstep about five minutes ago.

Oh, so my arrogant ex-to-be had eventually remembered where my bestie lived.

He was in a foul mood. Accused me and Charlie of aiding and abetting your escape to Italy, then asked if we had a spare key to Catkin Cottage.

I paled. There *was* a spare key to Catkin Cottage, but it wasn't with Sue and Charlie. Instead, it was tucked away in the back garden under one of the many plant pots. Nobody knew of it, and most certainly not George. I silently thanked God that I'd never told him. The last thing I needed was George letting himself into my house, retrieving his passport and then turning up here.

Don't panic, Sue texted. *We said that nobody had a spare key to your place. Charlie then told George to sod off. George huffed and puffed for a bit. Eventually he got in his car and roared off, tyres screeching. Let me know all is well xx*

I tapped out a quick reply.

All good. Will FaceTime you later xx

Luca ended his call just as the waiter appeared with our coffees.

'Sorry about that,' said Luca, stirring sugar into his cappuccino.

'How much do I owe you?'

'Nothing.'

'Don't be silly, Luca.'

'If it bothers you so much, you can get the next one.'

'Um, okay.'

Oooh! The promise of another lunch together.

My heart has gone all fluttery.

That's because I'm doing a happy dance under your ribs.

Could you stop. It's making me feel a bit peculiar.

'Where were we?' asked Luca. 'Oh, yes. You said you were going to check out the promenade.'

'Most definitely.' I picked up my own cup and sipped the frothy liquid. 'I also want to take a closer look at that beautiful building high above the marina.'

'The promenade has *two* amazing landmarks. Between them, they make a lovely start and end point for your walk.' Luca put down his cup and pointed in the direction of the harbour. 'There's the building you just mentioned, perched

201

right on the top of that tall cliff. It's called *Castello Mezzacapo.* Its pointy turrets make it look like it's jumped straight off the page of a fairy tale. Once it was a fully-fledged castle, but now it contains luxurious apartments. Make sure you work your way back to the other end of the promenade and check out *Norman Tower.* It's awesome, and now used as an elegant location for events like weddings or a special dinner. That said, if you want to sightsee, the truly eye-popping views are those seen from the water.'

'I plan on taking water buses everywhere,' I nodded.

'Then I shall look forward to travelling with you.'

'Honestly, I really don't expect–'

Luca raised a hand to cut off my fresh protest.

'It will be my pleasure. And now, Sophie' – he drained his cup – 'you must forgive me, but I have to go. Enjoy the rest of your afternoon and pop up to the roof terrace about seven o'clock.'

'Okay,' I said happily.

After he'd gone, I sat for a little while longer, eking out the last of my frothy coffee and counting my blessings. Well, just the one. I'd made a friend in Italy. Actually, no. Scrub that. I'd made *two* friends. Luca, and also little Bella, the calico kitten. Talking of which, I had cat food to buy.

I drank the last of my cappuccino and stood up.

Chapter Thirty-Seven

Upon leaving the restaurant I paused under the overhead awning, taking a moment to get my bearings.

The promenade, with its decorative fantail brickwork, stretched out to both right and left. I realised I was standing roughly in the middle.

Ramming my sunhat on my head, I set off towards the marina but, as the sun beat down on me, realised within seconds that it would be prudent to buy a bottle of water.

Taking a right turn, I found myself in a side street. There was an eclectic mix of shops, the first of which was an old-fashioned greengrocer. Outside its frontage, stacks of crates were artfully arranged, showing off fresh produce.

My eyes widened at the largest tomatoes I'd ever seen. There were also shiny red apples, soft velvety peaches, long-stemmed scarlet chillies, and lemons so huge they looked like they'd been on steroids.

I pushed through the shop's plastic-strip curtain, my eyes taking a second to adjust to the dim interior within. Locating the chiller cabinet, I helped myself to a bottle of water and, for later, grabbed a ready-made mozzarella and tomato roll. Okay, the cheese might sweat a bit in this heat, but it wouldn't go off.

Despite Luca telling me I'd be hungry again this evening, the reality was that I didn't fancy going out on my own later. Not on this first day. As a sort-of-singleton, I didn't feel brave enough to venture into a restaurant by myself, not when everyone else would be coupled up over candlelight, sharing a bottle of wine.

No, I couldn't do it. Not yet anyway. Instead, I'd go back to my room and have my snack with a cuppa before later going up to the roof terrace for that drink.

You had a margarita pizza for lunch, Sophie. Do you really want more bread, cheese, and tomato for your evening meal?

What's wrong with that?

Isn't it a tad boring?

Fair point. I'll add some fruit.

I went outside again and selected a peach and an apple as a casual nod towards one's *five a day*. Right, cat food next.

I once again swished through the plastic curtain, then cast about for the pet food section. Ah, there it was. I wouldn't buy any tins. Didn't want to cart a heavy tote bag around in this heat. Instead, I selected half a dozen pouches of kitten food – nice and light – and then found the checkout.

'*Turistica?*' asked the smiley lady manning the cash till.

'Sorry, I don't speak Italian,' I apologised.

'*Ah, inglese,*' she nodded. 'I asked if you were a tourist,' she said in impeccable English.

'Yes,' I said shyly.

'You're very pale' – she indicated my white arms as she

deftly weighed the fruit – 'so it must be your first day.'

'It is. I'm hoping to go to the beach tomorrow.'

'Don't get burnt,' she warned, popping my shopping into a paper carrier bag. 'Take lots of water and plenty of suncream, otherwise you'll end up looking like a piece of rhubarb in your bikini.'

I laughed.

'That reminds me. I want to buy a new bikini. Can you recommend where to go?'

'Sure,' she said, holding out the terminal for me to tap my card. 'Carry on along this street, look to your left for my sister's shop, *La Moda di Isabella*. Izzy has gorgeous bikinis and beachwear, not to mention beautiful dresses. Tell her Daria sent you and she will give you a discount.'

'That's very kind,' I said.

'I always like to be on first name terms with my customers,' said Daria. 'And you are?'

'Sophie,' I said.

'Well, it's been a pleasure to meet you, Sophie, and I hope to see you again.'

'You will, Daria,' I smiled, taking my shopping from her.

I left the shop with a spring in my step. What a nice lady. What a pleasant shopping experience. So much better than back home.

My mind briefly rose, soared upwards, zoomed northwards across Italy, took a left over France, zipped across the English Channel and then landed in my local supermarket. I tried to imagine a similar scene of camaraderie at the checkout.

205

'*Would you like to be on first name terms with me?*'

'*No. Anyway, I already know your name. It's Weirdo...*'

Yes, Italy was proving a very different experience to good old Blighty.

I set off, looking around with interest at the different shops. There were cafés, *gelato* parlours, shoe shops, an optician, and a chemist, but most were souvenir shops. Many displayed ceramics, tea towels, and postcards and all depicted the many regional lemon groves and local scenery.

I walked on, passing a pale blue Vespa. Its owner had propped it against a cream-coloured wall upon which a small mural was painted. It created the tranquil illusion of the pop-pop residing under leafy boughs and pink frothy blossom.

Every shop sold punnet upon punnet of locally grown lemons. There was no getting away from the fruit. Souvenir wicker baskets were stacked with beribboned bottles of limoncello, lemon curd, even lemon shortbread, all gifts to take home from Italy.

Most of the shops had overhead living accommodation. Shuttered windows kept out the heat. The louvres were vivid in colour – emerald-green here, azure-blue over there.

Nearly every balcony was edged in elaborate wrought ironwork. Most displayed troughs of vibrant plants and flowers. The pots contrasted perfectly with buildings' peeling paint, exposed brickwork, and terracotta-tiled rooftops.

Every now and again I glimpsed an alleyway. The gaps were narrow and more like stone-stepped corridors. Each were armed with pewter coloured handrails firmly screwed into the brickwork. And no wonder, for the ascent was steep.

It seemed that, upon leaving the promenade, there was no avoiding the gradient.

I had no trouble finding Izzy's shop. It was typically Italian. Outside were several rails of clothes under a huge canvas awning. A handful of headless mannequins graced the pavement, showing off this season's must-haves – tasselled beach garments or dresses designed to show off both bust and legs.

I spotted Izzy immediately. She was a dead ringer for her sister. She was setting up a footwear display on a central island, but glanced up as I approached her.

'Hello,' I smiled. 'Daria suggested I pay you a visit.'

'Any friend of Daria's is a friend of mine,' said Izzy warmly. 'Tell me your name and how I can help.'

Half an hour later, I'd possibly tried on every bikini in Izzy's shop, but one was particularly flattering. The top wasn't skimpy, rather a balcony-bra affair. It lifted my boobs that, of late, had been cosying up with the navel.

The bottoms were well cut and gave the illusion of a longer leg – which I was all for – and thanks to the material being comparable to reinforced concrete, it lifted the butt.

I wiggled sideways and peered at the dressing room mirror to consider my derriere. Yes, it had definitely elevated. Hopefully, when going into the sea, the material wouldn't bag and cause various bits of me to collapse. Time would tell.

'Where are you staying?' asked Izzy conversationally, as she wrapped the revered bikini.

'*Il Castello*,' I replied.

'I know it,' she nodded. 'Have you met the owner, Luca Lamagna?'

'I have.'

She rolled her eyes in ecstasy, as if savouring something delicious.

'He's gorgeous.' She lowered her voice, sharing a confidence. 'Luca is also the most eligible man in Maiori.'

'Really?' I said casually. For some strange reason my heart was starting to go thumpity-thump. 'Does he have a girlfriend?'

'He always has a girlfriend,' she laughed.

Oh. Having ruled out Vittoria as his romantic interest, I'd rather assumed Luca was untaken.

I thought you weren't interested in him? piped up my inner voice.

I'm not! I'm just… curious.

'Possibly he's between girlfriends,' Izzy continued. 'I heard a rumour that Ariana, his most recent *fidanzata* was pushing for marriage, prompting Luca to run a mile in the opposite direction.'

'He's kindly taking me for a drink on his roof terrace this evening.'

'Is he now?' said Izzy, her eyes widening. 'Let's hope Ariana doesn't find out.'

'She has nothing to fear,' I laughed. 'First, I'm way older than Luca.'

'You don't look it.'

'Thanks.' I instantly shrugged off the compliment. 'Second, I'm already married.'

'So, where's your wedding ring?' she enquired, not missing a beat.

'Ah.' I followed Izzy's gaze to my bare fingers. 'I recently separated.'

I wasn't going to admit how recently.

'I see,' said Izzy. 'Well, be careful, Sophie. Despite your protests, you are a very pretty lady. And Luca does love a pretty lady.'

Upon leaving Izzy's shop, I noticed the shadows were lengthening. I decided to head back to *Il Castello*. As I walked up the winding hill towards the hotel, I could see the second landmark that Luca had mentioned.

Norman Tower – known locally as *Torre Normanna* – was jutting up and over the rocks below. Luca had elaborated, during our lunch, about its watchtower history. I gazed at the considerable structure, not quite managing to get my head around the fact that it had been built somewhere between 1250 and 1300. How incredible was *that*!

Its image had been splashed over tea towels in Maiori, along with several vast canvasses depicting local artists' impressions. Luca had also told me that the tower had once been used as a location for Roberto Rossellini's movie *Paisan*, and that Ingrid Bergman had spent time with him there.

Perhaps I'd check it out properly at some point. Not right now though. I wanted to get back to my room and see if Bella had returned, before having a leisurely shower and reapplying my makeup.

Ah, the "pretty lady" wants to look her best for Mr

Lamagna, eh? enquired my inner voice.

Oh, hello again. Don't you get fed up goading me?

Nope. There's nothing wrong in having a holiday romance.

Seriously, you are unbelievable. First, the guy isn't interested. Second, neither am I – or in any man, for that matter.

Not sure I believe you.

Leave me alone, eh! I'm licking my wounds, remember?

So long as that's the only thing you're planning on licking.

I can't believe you just said that, I mentally gasped.

I strode into *Il Castello*, said hello to Vittoria – no sign of Luca – and puffed my way up to the fourth floor. Walking into the room, I was delighted to see Bella was already in the garden. She'd curled up in the shade of a vast pot of flowering *Oleander*. Sensing movement, she opened her eyes.

Taking care not to frighten her, I gently creaked open the patio door, then waved the packet of kitten food at her. Bella was on her tiny feet in a trice. Making strange *breeping* noises, she weaved her small body around my ankles, then began purring.

'Mummy has bought you something nice, oh yes she has.'

I felt faintly ridiculous for speaking in a babylike way. Sadly, I'd never been a mother, but it felt wonderful describing myself as such to this teeny creature. I wondered where her real mum was, and whether there were any sibling kittens hiding in various places about the hotel.

I ripped open the packet, tipped the contents on to a saucer, then watched with satisfaction as Bella tucked in. Slowly, I squatted down – knees cracking alarmingly – and gently stroked her head. The purring grew louder.

Emboldened by her fearlessness, I let my fingers gently trace the markings along her spine. What a poppet. As I smiled indulgently at my four-legged "daughter", my stomach chose that moment to rumble. Good heavens, Luca had been right. I was hungry again.

I went into the tiny kitchenette, made myself a coffee, then took my cheese roll out to the garden. Sinking down on one of the patio chairs, I gazed out at the sea's horizon and sighed contentedly. This was the life. Snack in one hand. Drink in the other. What a glorious mood elevator.

Are you sure it's not your sap rising?

Can't you give me a break?

No.

What shall I wear this evening?

A chastity belt?

Do you have any idea how ridiculous you sound?

Stuffing the last of the roll in my mouth, I reached for my mobile and decided to FaceTime Sue and bring her up to date. I also wanted to check that George hadn't revisited her and made a nuisance of himself.

As I waited for Sue to answer, I reminded myself not to spend too long on the phone. I hadn't yet showered.

Or titivated with makeup.

I rolled my eyes, trying to ignore the fact that a tiny part of me – we're talking weeny – reluctantly knew that my inner voice was speaking the truth.

Chapter Thirty-Eight

At five minutes to seven, I left Bella snoozing at the end of my bed and quietly let myself out of the room. I'd left the balcony door cracked open so the kitten could let herself out when she wanted to go.

As the lift was still out of action, it meant walking up to the roof terrace. Thankfully it was only a couple of floors up.

As I teetered in precariously high heels up two flights of stairs, I mentally ran through the earlier FaceTime conversation with Sue.

With gusty sighs of relief on both sides, she'd informed me that George hadn't been back with further demands for entry to Catkin Cottage. Sue had then oohed and aahed as I'd held the phone aloft and shown her the view from my room. She'd also exclaimed in delight at my feline friend before asking why I was wearing a dressing gown so early in the evening.

'I thought you said you weren't going to hide away in the hotel,' she'd chided.

'I've just stepped out of the shower,' I'd quickly answered.

'Hm' − she'd given me a beady look − 'is that why you're looking so glowy, or is there another reason?'

'It's probably a combination of the hot water jet and some Italian sunshine,' I'd said dismissively.'

I'd skipped mentioning the impromptu pizza with an extremely good-looking lunch companion who just happened to own the hotel I was staying in, otherwise Sue would have quizzed me endlessly.

'Okay,' she'd relented. 'Just so long as you promise not to stay holed up in your room, lovely though it is.' She'd waggled a finger at me.

'I won't,' I'd assured.

Ringing off, I'd then zipped myself into a new dress bought exclusively to wear for an evening out with George. It was probably a bit over the top for a rooftop terrace rendezvous. A bit too dressy. However, having spent a small fortune on clothes for this trip, I wasn't going to leave them hanging in the wardrobe just because my new husband wasn't by my side.

As I pushed through the top floor's door, my eyes widened in surprise. Unlike the rest of the hotel, which was scruffy and neglected, it was clear that a lot of money had been spent revamping this area.

Plump white sofas covered in blue scatter cushions nestled alongside several low coffee tables, all of which were strategically placed upon the terrace's golden floorboards. A plethora of matching lamps added soft mood lighting.

At one end, a large gazebo played host to an abundance of potted plants and enormous terracotta urns full of young olive trees. At the other, there was a dining area screened with bi-fold doors. These were currently folded back on themselves allowing the evening air to caress any exposed arms and legs.

The terrace's perimeter was edged in a tough but transparent safety barrier. It gave the illusion that one could step straight off the side and plunge down to the rocks far below.

'Sophie,' said a voice behind me.

I turned to see Luca sitting on a tall stool at a bar. He was talking to a member of his staff. This part of the terrace had initially evaded me due to a large trellis screen acting as a room divider.

'Hey,' I said, walking over.

My heart was suddenly leaping about like a salmon swimming upstream.

'What would you like to drink?' he asked.

'Prosecco, please.'

Luca turned to the barman.

'Prosecco for the lady, please, Giuseppe.' The barman gave me a brief smile — one that told me he was familiar with this scenario — before turning away. 'You look lovely, by the way,' Luca added, flashing a smile.

'Thank you,' I said, nearly returning the compliment but stopping myself in the nick of time.

He looked divine. We're talking ravishing. A midnight blue shirt was undone enough for me to glimpse a smattering of dark chest hair. Nice. Much nicer than George's which, naturally, had been grey. Instead, I complimented Luca on the roof terrace.

'It looks amazing up here. You've done a fabulous job.'

'Thanks. It's just the pool that needs sorting. It's currently empty and hiding out of sight behind the gazebo. Anyway, how did you get on exploring the promenade?'

'I didn't even begin to cover it,' I confessed. 'However, I did make two new friends.'

'Oh?'

'Daria and Izzy. I bought some things from their shops.'

'I know them well,' Luca nodded. 'They're sisters. Daria is the eldest and like a mother hen. She clucks and fusses over everyone, including me. I also suspect she'd like to see me married off to Izzy.'

I smiled, just as Giuseppe returned with a flute of wine. He set it down on a little coaster mat in front of me.

'Daria did mention you.'

'Ah, that explains why my ears were burning earlier.'

'She confided that you're the most eligible man in Maiori.'

Luca threw back his head and roared with laughter.

'That's because I'm a little younger than the average age of a Maiori male and happen to be a bachelor. You know, Sophie, any single man of my age would be eligible in a place like this which is, essentially, a sleepy seaside village. It's where people come to retire. There isn't a glut of young, unmarried men about, hence the likes of Izzy having to travel further afield to meet someone. Anyway, Daria shouldn't worry so much about her sister's single status. The last time I saw Izzy, she was swiping right on a dating app. These days, most people seem to meet that way.'

'Is that how you met Ariana?' I blurted.

216

Luca looked momentarily startled.

'My goodness, the tongues *have* been wagging.'

I took a sip of my wine before answering.

'Maiori reminds me of Little Waterlow. That's the name of the village where I live. You can't hiccup without someone commenting upon it.'

'Would I be right in presuming that, back home, everyone will be gossiping about your marriage-that-was-but-then-wasn't?'

'You would,' I confirmed, taking another greedy glug of the deliciously ice-cold prosecco.

Go easy on that. You haven't had much to eat this evening.

Leave me alone, I silently retorted. I'm enjoying myself.

Luca stood up, indicating that I should do so too.

'Let's take our drinks over there, Sophie. We can sit on one of the sofas and admire the bay. The view is stunning, and I want you to see it in all its glory.'

I followed him over to a corner, then sank down gratefully amongst the scatter cushions. Luca sat next to me, and I felt a momentary frisson of delight. Okay, he was just being friendly and keeping me company. *Under his wing* as he'd mentioned earlier. But nonetheless, his presence – coupled with some pleasant zingers – was cheering me up no end. I was so grateful to be distracted from being miserable about George.

'You can't buy that,' said Luca, gesturing with one hand.

Below, Maiori looked like one of the local artist's paintings come to life. The beach was now a dark strip edged

217

by the promenade's old-fashioned streetlamps. They cast a glow over the sidewalk.

Twin beams of headlights from passing traffic gave an illusion of mini comets against a backdrop of towering hills. The ascending gradient ledges were dotted with houses. Their lights added twinkles of orange and yellow. The colours seemed to shimmer like the flickering flames of a thousand candles. And all the while came the constant shush-shush of waves as they lapped the shore.

I sighed with contentment. Under the not-quite-dark sky, the sea was currently a beautiful deep cobalt blue. My eyes traced the shoreline, noting the land's rugged semi-circular arc before it abruptly stopped by the harbour.

'What's beyond the marina? I asked, pointing at the rocky formation where hundreds of boats bobbed about.

'That jagged peninsula turns back on itself. It becomes another bay, with its own beach which edges Maiori's sister town, Minori. It's another ancient seaside resort of the Roman high society, as evidenced by a patrician villa that dates back to the first century. Minori is very charming and particularly known for its culinary traditions. That's why it has a nickname – *the City of Taste*.'

'That sounds so aweshum,' I said, slurring slightly. Everything was pleasantly blurring. The lights below. My mood. Even the blood in my veins seemed to be sighing with pleasure. I realised I was a little squiffy. 'You certainly know your local history, and make it sound far more interesting than a guidebook.'

Luca laughed.

'I've simply picked up information as I've gone along, whether visiting as a sightseer or when going about my business at the hotel. The entire Amalfi Coast is like an open record book.' He paused and nodded at my glass. 'Another one, Sophie?'

I was surprised to see that I'd already finished my wine.

Say no. It's not wise to have a second glass. That earlier bread roll wasn't adequate "blotting paper".

Don't tell me what to do.

'I'd love you to give me one,' I said dreamily.

Omigod, I can't believe you just said that.

'Wine!' I gasped.

'Of course,' said Luca, looking faintly amused.

He stood up, taking our glasses with him.

Make it the last one.

You're sooo boring.

Better to be boring than a berk.

Luca returned a couple of minutes later.

'Thank you,' I said, taking the glass. I sipped, enjoying the haziness that had enveloped me. 'How did you get on at your solicitor's meeting?'

Luca settled down again. Was it my imagination or was he sitting a little closer?

'It went well. Most of the legal procedures have been navigated, but they were tricky and endlessly time consuming. However, it had to be done. Apparently, it will reduce stress levels for all involved if the hotel subsequently goes on the market.'

'Have you come to a decision about its sale?'

'Not as such. It was one of the discussions I had with my solicitor. I've already poured a lot of my own money into this place – this roof terrace for starters. Our conversation was primarily about whether the property is worth the effort. My solicitor thinks it is, and I'm inclined to agree. Initially, when I first came here, I just wanted to sort out the legal side of things. Inheritance tax. Dealing with the *Agenzia delle Entrate*. The property's title deed. Getting an official translation of the Will, and then an Affidavit to state I was the new owner by law. We also had to ascertain the hotel's market value and, of course, its debts. But, as I said to you earlier, Maiori has its own special magic, and currently I seem to be caught up in its spell.' His voice softened. 'This inheritance has unwittingly brought me into contact with a whole new network of people.' He gave me an unfathomable look. 'Strangely, in a very short space of time, some have become special to me.'

'How wonderful,' I murmured.

I wondered who had become very special to him.

Ariana, of course.

Oh, yeah. Bugger.

Don't swear.

'Anyway' – Luca continued – 'selling an inherited property is a Herculean task, especially in Italy. Technically, I could put the hotel on the market before I have probate, but obviously a sale can't go through until it is all finalised. And that takes time. A *lot* of time. So, here I am,' he shrugged, giving me a deprecating smile.

'Here you are,' I said, grinning back.

Try not to leer, Sophie.

'And here you are, too,' he said softly.

For a moment, neither of us said anything. The sound of the sea continued to swish away in the background. It mingled with the murmur of chit-chat from a handful of guests who'd since made their way up here.

I could smell the salt of the ocean and the scent of Luca's aftershave. The combination of the two combined with the prosecco was seducing my senses. Inside my head, a klaxon horn chose that moment to go off.

WARNING! WARNING! YOUR EYEBALLS HAVE DILATED TO THE SIZE OF BEACH PARASOLS.

I know, and I can't help it.

'Whereabouts are you exploring tomorrow?' asked Luca.

The question didn't exactly pour a bucket of cold water over me, but it did serve to remind that my imagination had taken a fanciful turn – one that wasn't in the same direction as Luca's.

'Well, now that you've piqued my curiosity about Minori, maybe I'll pay it a visit tomorrow.'

'I don't like the idea of you exploring alone, Sophie.'

'Why, isn't it safe to do so?' I asked, faintly alarmed.

Luca shook his head.

'This place is no dodgier than any other, but you do need your wits about you in busy areas. Pickpockets, and the like,' he added. 'After your horrific wedding day, then arriving here alone, and George deliberately wanting you to be left stranded without a penny, I think you deserve some light relief.' Was it my imagination, or was he suddenly looking a bit shy? 'So, er, that's why, um, I took the liberty of tweaking staff rotas for the next few days.'

'Whatever for?' I asked fuzzily.

'Because…' – the coyness prevailed – 'if it's okay with you, I'd like to keep you company when you go sightseeing. Be your personal guide, so to speak.'

'That is terribly kind' – I blinked rapidly – 'but absolutely not necessary.'

'If you'd rather I didn't join you' – he said hastily – 'then please don't be afraid to say so.'

'N–No, not at all,' I stammered. Hell's bells. This man – apparently the most eligible in Maiori – was offering to spend his afternoons with *me*? Wild horses wouldn't stop me from agreeing. 'I–I'd be delighted.'

'Well, so long as you're sure. If you want to tell me to clear off, I'll completely understand.'

'Really' – I grinned – 'I'm very grateful.'

'There's some beautiful places to sightsee which, if you don't have a guide, you might otherwise miss out on.'

'As long as it doesn't interfere with you running the hotel,' I said, sobering up slightly.

'Not at all. Can I suggest you spend the mornings on the beach and have lunch at one of the seafront cafes, and then I'll meet you downstairs in reception around two o'clock?'

'Perfect,' I beamed.

'And now' – he stood up – 'I must leave you.'

'Oh,' I said, trying not to show my disappointment.

'I need to pop downstairs and talk to Vittoria. Oversee a few things. Can I get you another drink before I go?'

222

I looked at my glass. Blimey, it was empty again. How had that happened?

'Oh, why not,' I sighed, sprawling out and looking up at the stars. 'After all, I am on my honeymoon.'

'I'll have Giuseppe bring another prosecco over. Meanwhile, have a good evening, Sophie, and I'll see you tomorrow afternoon.'

It was only after Luca had gone that I realised he'd never answered my question about how he'd met Ariana.

Chapter Thirty-Nine

When I returned to my room, Bella had gone. Before pulling the drapes together and shutting out the night, I left a saucer of water for her outside. I then fell into bed and, once again, slept like the proverbial dead.

I was aware that my brain was still processing not just a disastrous wedding day, but also the discovery that George wasn't the person I'd thought him to be.

I needed to heal, and the starting point in achieving that was through sleep. It was Mother Nature's way of giving the mind, body, and soul restorative *time out.*

However, I felt confident that, like a toddler learning to walk, I'd now taken that first wobbly step along the road of emotional recovery. Psychologically, it helped too that, currently, Little Waterlow was far away.

Right now, I didn't have to face people. To deal with embarrassment. Shame. Humiliation. There were no neighbours asking questions. No locals giving me pitying looks. No clients in Ruby's salon raising one eyebrow.

Indeed, I didn't have to worry about Ruby in turn fretting about *me.* I could see her now, in my mind's eye. Anxious about me having a concentration lapse. Mistaking a female client for Fred Plaistow and accidentally delivering a short back and sides.

It also helped that I'd made a friend in Luca. There was nothing quite like a handsome man to bolster the spirits of a heartbroken woman.

When Monday morning rolled around, I lay in my bed for a moment and stared at the shadows on the ceiling before cautiously testing my heart. Was it my imagination or did it feel a little less tender than two days ago?

The bruises were still there. Of *course* they were. But they felt different. Rather, as if a protective covering had gently been placed upon them.

I swung my legs out of bed and found my mobile. The screen's digital clock informed it was a little before eight in the morning. Pulling back the curtains, light flooded into the room. The sky was already forget-me-not blue with the promise of another beautiful day.

Bella stepped into the garden area and trotted over to the glass door, squeaking a greeting at me.

'Good morning,' I said, letting her into the room. 'I suppose you want some more of the kitty food I bought you.'

'Meow,' she confirmed.

'You are so utterly gorgeous,' I said, feeling my chest swell with love. 'Would you let me pick you up?'

I stooped and attempted to scoop her into my hands. Unnerved, she backed away.

'It's okay,' I cooed. 'Mummy won't do that again. I'll let you decide when you want to have a cuddle. Meanwhile, I'm going to the kitchen. Want to come with me?'

Bella trotted at my heels as I went into the cupboard room's confines. I ripped open a food sachet and tipped its contents onto a saucer. Leaving her to tuck in, I picked up the kettle and went to the bathroom for water.

By the time I'd had a wash and made a coffee, Bella had let herself out, no doubt to chase butterflies and insects or snooze in another balcony garden. I still couldn't work out how she managed to climb up to the fourth floor. I made a mental note to ask Luca.

Taking my coffee outside, I sat down to enjoy a few moments of doing nothing. Getting lost in nothingness. Some might call it *being present*. I was instantly reminded of a quote I'd read somewhere. *The quality of the present moment is what shapes your future.*

I gazed out at the twinkling sea and decided that if all my present moments were like this one, then the future was going to be sparkly, full of diamondlike beauty, and utterly joyful. My stomach rumbled, scattering my thoughts. Time for breakfast.

When I walked into the dining area of the roof terrace, it was impossible not to notice the half dozen couples already in situ, eating their breakfast together, chatting excitedly about their plans for the day ahead. One or two people looked up as I rather self-consciously crossed the floor. Alone.

I picked out a table for myself and sat down, deliberately concentrating on the menu. Two tables away, a couple kept looking my way, perhaps wondering if a husband or companion would be joining me. Or maybe they were simply hoping to catch my eye and make conversation. That was the bit I didn't want to go through. The questions. People wanting an answer to the *how-come-you're-travelling-alone* thing. It was bad enough that I'd have to eventually face questions when I went home to Little Waterlow. But right now, I didn't need it in Maiori too.

According to the menu, I could have a Full English for – how much? – an extra forty euros, or I could enjoy a complimentary breakfast of fruit, scrambled egg and a platter of locally sourced cheeses and meats.

Giuseppe materialised at my table. Good heavens. He couldn't have had much down time after getting off duty last night. I knew for a fact that the roof terrace's bar shut at midnight and the dining room opened for breakfast at seven.

'*Buongiorno,*' he said.

'Bon john-oh,' I replied, wincing at my terrible accent.

'*Quale colazione?*' he enquired. 'Which breakfast?' he clarified, upon seeing my confusion.

'The scrambled eggs, and, um, stuff,' I mumbled, as the lady at the next table turned to look at me with interest. She was so obviously wondering if I was ordering for one person or two. I sighed. It was no good trying to make out I was waiting for my other half. As the week progressed, everyone would realise I was on my own.

'The complimentary breakfast for one,' said Giuseppe scribbling away on his notepad.

Upon hearing his words, the lady turned back to her husband and murmured something, a smug look upon her face. I didn't need a hearing aid to work out that she'd said something along the lines of, "I told you so. She's on her

Jack Jones."

'Coffee or tea?' asked Giuseppe.

'Coffee, please.'

I then pulled out my phone and occupied myself by reading the news online. I might be on my own, but I was going to do my best to show I didn't care two hoots.

Chapter Forty

Half an hour later, I walked down the hill to the beach and located Floriana, the lady in charge of the sunbeds.

'Ah, Sophie,' she said, with a pronounced accent. 'I remember. Luca's frienda.'

'That's right,' I said, returning her smile.

Her English wasn't as perfect as Daria's and Izzy's, but it was good enough.

'VIP, eh?' she teased, leading me to a lounger so close to the water's edge the waves were almost reaching its legs. 'Howa come?'

'Oh, it's a long story,' I shrugged.

She waggled her finger playfully.

'You no tella Floriana the trutha. I thinka *Signore Lamagna* lika you.'

'Luca is just a friend,' I assured.

'A gooda frienda,' she winked. 'The secret is safe witha Floriana.'

'It's no secret, honest,' I protested, dumping my tote bag on the sun lounger along with my rolled-up towel.

'Believa me,' she paused, placing a hand on my forearm to get my full attention. 'You needa keepa the secret. If Ariana finda out' – she mimed a bomb going off – 'then bigga troubles.'

'There will be no bigga... I mean, big troubles,' I assured. 'Apart from anything else, I am married.' There. Despite my marital status currently being up in the air, sometimes it was helpful to fall upon those three little words. This moment was a classic example.

'I heara different,' she frowned. 'I heara the husbanda... he go offa elsewhere.'

Flipping heck. Was I really in Maiori or had I just teleported back to Little Waterlow? It wouldn't surprise me if, any minute now, Floriana morphed into Mabel Plaistow.

'My husbanda... husband... is away on business,' I said firmly.

'*Si*,' she grinned. 'The funny business.'

Oh, for heaven's sake. I watched as Floriana turned on her heel, her bare feet kicking up little puffs of sand as she made her way back to the kiosk.

Feeling a little self-conscious, I slipped off my sundress and slung it over one of the overhead parasol's spokes. I'd put on the new bikini earlier, before leaving my room. I'd also applied copious amounts of suncream too, even though most of it might now be stuck to the sundress. Never mind.

I reached into my bag for a scrunchie and gathered my hair into a messy up-do, then shook out my towel. It floated down over the lounger like a tablecloth. Rooting around in my tote again, I extracted my kindle. Perfect.

Lowering myself down gingerly, I settled back, ready to read a novel about a woman who was on the threshold of discovering her fiancé was a cheater. Ha! Who was it who'd famously declared that life sometimes imitated art? Oh yeah. Oscar Wilde. He'd certainly known a thing or two about having his private life made public.

Heaving a sigh, I began to read, wiggling my toes with pleasure as the overhead sun warmed my body. Bliss. In the background, the waves continually shush-shushed. Within seconds, I was fast asleep.

I was awoken by cold water dripping on my bare calves.

'Wha–?'

I sat up, squinting attractively at the towering silhouette blocking out the light.

'Rule number one,' said a familiar voice. 'Never nod off while sunbathing.'

'Oh no,' I said in dismay. 'Have I turned into a roasted beetroot?'

'I suspect, when you stand up, you may look a little like a sausage that's only seen one side of the pan.'

I flushed with embarrassment at Luca's description. The last thing I'd reckoned upon was him seeing me in my bikini with wobbly bits on full display.

'A very attractive sausage,' he added, making me squirm with embarrassment over his attempt at damage limitation.

'What time is it?' I asked.

'Noon. I managed to get away a couple of hours earlier and thought I'd find you here. Fancy a swim?'

'Yes, okay,' I said, struggling to sit upright.

I got to my feet just as Luca whipped off his top. The sight of his naked torso nearly had me collapsing back down again on the sun lounger. For a peculiar moment, I felt like a

Victorian maiden having the vapours.

I quickly averted my gaze from his washboard stomach but not before glimpsing a golden-brown chest with a tantalising snail trail that disappeared inside his swim shorts.

'Phew,' I said, fanning myself.

'Are you hot?'

No, but you are.

'Come on.' Luca grabbed my hand. His touch caused so many zingers I nearly took off like a parachute flare. 'There's only one way to prepare for a swim in the sea, and that's to run into the water.'

And suddenly we were splashing our way into the waves, him bellowing in delight and me fretting that my bikini top wouldn't contain a pair of vigorously jostling bosoms.

As Luca let go of my hand, I belly-flopped forward, clutching my girls tightly to me. Luca immediately began a flashy front crawl, leaving me to sink below the waves and do some hasty rearranging.

Boobies in place, I set off after him doing – appropriately – breaststroke. I bobbed along, enjoying the sight of Luca zipping through the water, back muscles rippling, pumped arms windmilling. What a guy. What a body.

And then, instinctively, I felt someone staring our way. Turning my head, I spotted Floriana. She was standing on the sand, hands on hips, watching the two of us. Having caught my eye, she flashed a look. One that said *you might be married, but you don't fool me.*

Chapter Forty-One

Luca was an impressive swimmer, and I didn't even try to keep up with him. Eventually, he turned around and powered back to me. As we let our feet touch down on the seabed's sand and pebble floor, he threw back his head and shook salty water from his eyes.

'Refreshing, eh?' he grinned.

'Very.'

'Come on. Let's dry off and then we'll go to Amalfi.'

We waded out of the waves and back to the sun lounger. I gathered up my towel and gave myself a good rub down.

'I knew I'd forgotten something,' said Luca in dismay.

'Your towel? Don't worry. You can borrow mine.' I passed it to him. 'Although it's now a little damp.'

'Thanks,' he said, spreading it over the lounger. 'I'll let the sun dry me off.' He sat down on the towel, his sodden swim shorts instantly leaving a wet bum impression. 'Do you fancy a sandwich before we go?'

'Yes, but I'll buy them,' I quickly said. If Luca was going to show me around Amalfi, then the least I could do was buy him some lunch. I was also aware that he hadn't let me pay for any of my drinks last night. I didn't want him thinking I was a freeloader. 'You stay here. I won't be a mo.'

Five minutes later we were companionably sitting side by side on the lounger, devouring our cheese toasties and coffee as we watched a family frolicking in the waves.

'I meant to ask you something earlier,' I said, eyes on a young mum. She was holding a dear little tot whose upper arms were dwarfed by inflated water wings. What a sweetie. 'There's a little kitten that visits me at the hotel.'

'There are three cats,' said Luca. 'Two kittens and their mother. Mother Cat is completely feral. She's also a total hussy who regularly gets herself up the duff.'

'Why don't you neuter her?'

'I would if I could catch her,' said Luca. 'Every time I set a trap with a tasty tuna meal, either the trap fails, or she rejects the tuna and gives me a look which says, "You don't fool me." So, for now, all I can do is make sure she's fed and watered. She rewards me by catching lurking mice.' He caught my look of horror. 'Oh, yes. There's always a few of them wanting to raid the dustbins. Meanwhile, Mother Cat allows me to fuss her kittens who are considerably tamer than her. The offspring usually get rehomed, but for those that don't, Vittoria has a veterinary friend who kindly neuters them for free and then returns them to their habitat, so at least they don't add to the stray population.'

'That's good to know,' I said, glad to hear that the Italians were kinder to their strays than some countries. 'I've only seen one of the kittens. A little calico.'

'Ah, that's the female. I call her LM.'

'What does that stand for?'

'Little Madam. Her brother is called LS.'

I raised my eyebrows.

'Meaning?'

'Little Sod,' Luca grinned. 'He likes to decapitate the mice his mother catches and then leave the mess for me to clear up.'

'Oh. Well, I've renamed Little Madam. She's now called Bella and I am totally in love with her.'

'Are you feeding her?'

'No,' I lied. I had a feeling that it would be frowned upon to have pets in one's room.

'Because if you are' – Luca gave me a knowing look – 'there's really no need. As I said, they get fed and watered by the kitchen staff.'

'I mentioned her simply because I can't work out how she manages to get up to the fourth floor.'

'The hotel is built into the rocks. At the rear, there are lots of easily accessible ledges that meander up and around the building, right to the top floor.'

I paled at the thought of Bella clambering up so high.

'Don't fret,' Luca assured. 'Cats are very sure footed. Also, I suspect LM' – he caught my look of reproval – 'I mean, *Bella*, is staking out her territory, especially if you haven't seen LS in your garden.'

'I wish I could take her home,' I said wistfully.

Luca waved his hand at a seagull that had landed at our feet.

'Shoo,' he said.

The gull squawked an angry complaint at us not sharing our meal.

'No chance, matey,' said Luca, popping the last of the toastie in his mouth. 'That was delicious.'

'It was,' I agreed, rubbing crumbs from my hands.

'Ready to make tracks?' Luca enquired.

'If you don't mind, I'll just quickly pay a visit to Floriana's loo.'

'Sure,' he replied, swinging his legs up onto the lounger and stretching out on my towel. Oh, lucky, *lucky* towel. 'Take your time. I'll catch a few rays.'

My bikini was now completely dry, so I grabbed my sundress and popped it over my head. Picking up my tote bag, I headed off to the Ladies, hoping that I'd remembered to chuck some lip gloss in my bag before leaving the hotel.

Are you trying to impress a certain gentleman currently sprawled upon your towel?

I ignored my inner voice's taunt.

Pushing my way into the toilet cubicle, I had a quick rummage inside the tote. Success! I extracted the lippy and slicked it over my lips. Amazingly, I didn't look too bad. The sun had kissed my face. My skin was now a flattering shade of gold, which helped to conceal the eyebags.

I removed my hair scrunchie, releasing the messy up-do so that wavy tresses now tumbled down my back and over my shoulders. Better. A bit of casual beach glam.

Hovering over the loo – I never sat on public toilet seats – I emptied my bladder, then washed my hands. As I unexpectedly caught sight of my reflection in the mirror over the sink, I felt a frisson of shock. There was no sign of the heartbroken jilted bride who'd arrived in Italy two days ago.

Two *days* ago! Ridiculously, it was starting to feel like two lifetimes ago.

I adjusted the shoulder strap of my bag, then let myself out of the loo.

Chapter Forty-Two

'Bye, Luca,' said Floriana, as we walked past her kiosk. 'Should I tell Ariana I saw you?' she asked slyly.

'If you like,' said Luca affably.

Floriana gave me a cool look as Luca and I set off.

'Everywhere I go, I seem to hear Ariana's name,' I ventured.

'She's a friend of Floriana's.'

'Ah. And, er, I've heard she's a friend of yours too.'

'Yes,' Luca nodded, but didn't enlarge.

Flipping heck, trying to get him to talk about this woman was like drawing blood from a stone.

'A good friend?' I persisted.

'No.' He shook his head.

'It's just that, well, tell me to mind my own business, but earlier Floriana indicated that if Ariana knew you were keeping me company, she'd, um, not be very pleased.'

Luca sighed.

'Honestly, some of the women in this place make gossip a national pastime.'

It was no good. I had to ask.

'Is Ariana your girlfriend?'

'No,' said Luca emphatically. 'We went out to dinner,

just the once, and the locals in the restaurant were visibly nudging each as we worked our way through our carbonara. They put two and two together and came up with the proverbial five. I've had the likes of Daria and Floriana hinting at wedding bells. I won't deny that Ariana has hinted at being interested in me and, yes, it might raise her hackles if she knows I'm keeping you company. But that's her problem, not mine. I've never led her to believe that I'm romantically interested in her.'

'Right,' I said, inexplicably relieved. 'Perhaps she got the wrong impression because you asked her out to dinner.'

'I didn't ask her. She suggested it under the guise of a business meeting.'

'Oh, I see.'

I wondered what Ariana did. Was she a hotel owner too? Had she wanted to suggest some sort of merger? Or maybe she produced bedlinen, and wanted Luca to bulk-buy pillowcases. I could imagine them now. Crisp white cotton slips with monogrammed corners. *Il Castello* machine-embroidered on the left and, to the right, *Ariana loves Luca – hands off.*

I was just about to ask Luca another pertinent question when he paused by a ticket kiosk. The signage read *Tra Vel Mar.*

I fished inside my tote for my purse, but Luca put up a hand to stop me.

'I'll get these,' he said.

'Don't be silly,' I protested.

'Put your money away,' he insisted, touching my

239

forearm.

A zinger instantly whizzed up to my armpit, causing me to drop my purse. As I stooped to pick it up, I privately decided that having sex with him would be hell. If he touched me *there,* I'd probably light up like the Maiori streetlamps and cause a power outage.

Why are you thinking about going to bed with Luca?

I'm not, I mentally gasped, as a semi-pornographic image unexpectedly began to play out in my mind. Luca pushing me into my hotel room. His lips glued to mine. Perfect choreography as we moved together towards the bed. His warm hands lifting the hem of my sundress, whipping it over my head and–

You need help, said my inner voice. *Have you thought about some counselling?*

Instantly my mind veered off to a therapist's couch. There I was, lying down on a couch while a man noted down what I was saying.

'Ever since my last marriage failed, I keep having erotic thoughts about another man.'

'Tell me more.'

'We're on an uninhabited beach, and this man pulls me down on the sand under a sunset that's turning everything orange.'

'Sounds like a Fanta sea.'

I extracted a twenty euro note from my purse and waved it at Luca.

'You really must let me pay my way,' I insisted.

'Hush,' he grinned. 'If it bothers you so much' – he

240

pocketed the tickets – 'you can buy us both an Aperol spritz in Amalfi.'

'Deal,' I said, tucking the note away. 'I don't think I've ever tried one of those before.'

We resumed our walk towards the marina.

'An Aperol spritz is a Venetian wine-based cocktail,' said Luca. 'And a very pretty orange colour.'

Orange? I'd literally just been thinking about the colour. Had he somehow tapped into my earlier thoughts?

Don't be silly, Sophie.

'The drink is commonly served as an aperitif in Italy,' Luca continued. 'It consists of prosecco, digestive bitters and soda water.'

Personally, I liked my prosecco left alone, but I was game to try something new – especially if it meant sharing the experience with Luca.

Yeah, just make sure the experience with Luca is cocktails and doesn't have that last syllable left off.

Dear God but you are outrageous, I silently declared.

Just flagging up your thought processes.

Well please don't.

We circumnavigated a large stone walkway where hundreds of boats were moored side by side. I ran my eye over them. Blue and white fishing vessels. Inflatable dinghies. Deck boats. A handful of catamarans. Several cubby cabins. Trawlers. There were also lots and lots of expensive looking cruisers.

'Nice, eh?' said Luca, nodding at one of the latter. On the boat's side was elegant script. *Fortunata Signora.* 'Lucky

Lady,' he translated.

'She's beautiful,' I sighed.

'Meanwhile' – Luca nodded at a vast double decker affair that was chugging into the bay – 'here's our lift.'

We joined the queue. Bit by bit we shuffled forward, eventually bouncing over the narrow ramp and into the shadows of the cabin area.

'Do you want to go up to the top deck?' Luca asked.

'Would you mind if I sit in the shade?' I asked, fanning myself with one hand. 'I need to cool down, but if you want to go upstairs, don't let me stop you.'

'Downstairs it is,' said Luca, guiding me over to a window seat.

I flopped down on the upholstery and stared through an open window at the blue waters beyond. Maiori was spread out in front of us. To the right, almost on the horizon, I could see *Il Castello* jutting out of the rocks.

The boat began to quickly fill up with a mixture of tourists and locals. I did some discreet people watching, regarding them as they hastened across the walkway before filtering off to different areas in the boat.

Upstairs was the perfect place to top up the tan, but my shoulders were a little pink after falling asleep in the sun.

'We're off,' said Luca.

I watched in fascination as one of the crew pressed a button. The footbridge began to rise. Yards and yards of chain began to clatter and whirr as it reeled itself in.

I placed my hands on the window ledge, using them as a chin rest as I lowered my head. The breeze carried in a belch of diesel fumes. Seconds later, it was replaced by the smell of salty sea spray. I closed my eyes for a moment, enjoying the lullaby effect of the ferry's rocking.

Within a minute or two, we were far enough away to appreciate the full picture of the coast. I was amazed that such a hot country could be so verdant. Wherever I looked, the hills were covered in huge swathes of green. I now knew these to be thousands of lemon groves.

From here shops, hotels, houses, and villas looked like they'd been precariously stacked upon the land's rocky ledges, adding colours of white, cream, peach, and terracotta-orange to a granite backdrop. The whole thing was set off by a clear blue sky and golden sun, its rays beating down on the water, turning the sea to a shimmering expanse of sapphires and diamonds.

I closed my eyes again, loving the throaty roar of the engine, the constant swish of waves slapping the boat's sides, and the fine spray cooling my face.

A sudden whoop of joy had me swivelling my head to the right. The boat's propellers were generating a wide trail of churning white froth. A couple of jet skiers had appeared from nowhere, taking advantage of the rough surf.

I watched in amazement as they bounced over the huge swells, arms taut as they grimly hung on to their machines, no doubt loving the adrenalin rush – until one of the guys nearly lost control. Laughing uproariously, they changed direction, heading off to a beach I'd not seen before.

'That's Minori,' said Luca, pointing.

I screwed up my eyes to focus better on a small cove

with overhanging structures that looked like they could topple straight down into the turquoise waters below. Nearly every building sported window boxes, and all were stuffed with a floral explosion of colour.

I could make out red and white geraniums, and hot pink Vicenza. Many awned porches sported huge tubs of olive trees. Nearly all the houses had swathes of deep purple bougainvillea climbing up paint-peeled walls.

The jet skiers were now gently chugging past swimmers and families paddling in the shallows. Dismounting, they waded towards a guy who'd presumably hired out the machines. Nearby was a small jetty. A canvas advertisement stated that this was the spot to visit for renting a boat or anything related to water sports.

A pile of colourful surfboards was stacked next to a neat row of dinghies. I couldn't help noticing the many empty sun loungers, with people opting instead to place their towels on the sand.

The ferry chugged on, circumnavigating another rocky peninsula and within seconds Minori had disappeared.

Chapter Forty-Three

'Did you enjoy that?' asked Luca, as we disembarked.

'It was terrific,' I grinned.

Looking around the jetty, I drank in our new surroundings. Wow, Amalfi was far busier than sleepy Maiori. Sandwiched between the water and the mountains, it had the typical appearance of towns in the area – mostly vertical, filling in whatever space was available as defined by the geography of the land. From here, I could see a row of distinctive cypress trees, colourful houses and – higher up, peeking over it all – a church tower's bell.

'Was the ferry ride better than travelling in my Alfa Romeo Spider?' Luca teased.

'Your sportscar is lovely,' I said carefully. No point in ruffling male pride. 'But the boat was peaceful, not to mention magically scenic.'

'It's picturesque on the coastal road too,' Luca protested. 'The *Strada Statale 163 Amalfitana* has terrific views over the sea. Obviously, the hairpin bends, zigzags, and general narrowness isn't for the fainthearted.'

'Quite,' I said, keeping my tone deliberately vague.

I now regretted previously telling Luca that I loved fast cars. I'd made out that I was some sort of petrolhead girl racer. He'd been delighted. So much so he'd offered to take me somewhere. The details evaded me. Hopefully he'd forgotten about it.

'I can't wait to drive you to Tramonti in the Spider,' he said, grinning from ear to ear.

Bugger. He'd remembered.

'In fact' – he continued – 'instead of taking the ferry back, let's take the bus. That will give you a taste of some high jinks when a huge vehicle nearly swings off the road as it passes a car from the opposite direction.'

'Can't wait,' I said faintly.

'All good fun,' he said. 'Come on, this way.'

'Amalfi is so pretty,' I said, as we darted across a road and entered an alley.

'It is,' Luca agreed. 'It has fabulous history too. The town is medieval in origin. It saw a time of splendour back in the tenth and eleventh century. That was when the place dominated the trade routes of the Mediterranean with powerful fleets. It's also where it gets its landmarks and architecture from. Your first impression might be that this is simply a tourist trap with loads of people milling about, but there are a few things to see here. Let me show you.'

We entered a square, heaving with individuals and noisy with the chatter of so many tourists. To the left was a restaurant so full its clientele had spilt out into the piazza, filling some fifty or sixty extra tables. Pigeons were everywhere, weaving around diners' legs, pecking up dropped crumbs and squabbling with each other over the spoils.

Ahead, the piazza dramatically narrowed, but to the right, high above us, was a sight that momentarily took my breath away.

'Oh, my goodness,' I gasped, looking up at an enormous structure with imposing staircase. It was like a giant protective angel crouched over the square. 'What a beautiful building.'

'That's Amalfi Cathedral. It's also known as *Duomo di Amalfi* and *Cattedrale di Sant'Andrea*. The latter name came about because the relics of apostle Saint Andrew are here.'

The crowd milled around, jostling, and pushing. One particularly frustrated tourist shoved his way past, instantly separating us. Luca lunged forward and grabbed my hand.

'Stay close,' he said, pulling me towards him.

'Doing my best,' I squeaked as several zingers set my fingers tingling.

Oooh, the two of you are holding hands! piped up my inner voice.

I know, and it's so lovely.

Doesn't mean anything though.

Thank you for reminding me.

You're welcome.

'This way,' said Luca.

We moved with the throng, taking shuffling mini steps, side-stepping here and there, then broke through the main crowd to stand at the bottom of an impressive but very steep staircase that led up to the cathedral.

'I don't think I've ever seen such an attractive church,' I said, noting its gothic windows, three vast archways and vivid painted illustrations. 'The colours are incredible.'

'It's been redecorated several times over the centuries – Arab-Norman, Gothic, Renaissance, Baroque and finally a nineteenth century Norman-Arab-Byzantine façade.'

I looked down at the first step we were currently standing upon.

'It feels like a staircase to Heaven,' I said in awe.

'There are sixty-two steps to the top. As there are still plenty of people going up and down, hang on to the safety rail and hold on to me too.'

'I will,' I replied nervously.

Slowly, steadily, we started to climb. I wasn't sure I liked this. It was a bit giddy-making. A group of excited teenagers charged towards us, gabbling away in Italian. Surefooted and untroubled by the height, they brushed past, accidentally breaking my contact with the rail. Panicking slightly, I tightly gripped Luca's hand.

'Well done,' he said, as we finally stepped onto the upper walkway.

Many beautiful mosaics decorated the church's exterior and, oh my goodness, just look at that door! Luca caught my gaze.

'Amazing, eh? It's bronze and was crafted in 1066.'

'I can't get my head around that bit of information,' I confessed.

How could I be looking at something in the here and now that dated so far back to the past? It made my brain boggle.

'Can we go inside?' I asked.

'Absolutely.'

Luca was still holding my hand and guided me through the magnificent bronze door.

'Wow,' I whispered.

My gaze took in the interior's plethora of marble ornaments, soaring columns and pillars, and a coffered ceiling. The latter was smothered in paintings that, presumably, told the story of Saint Andrew. For a few minutes we said nothing, instead quietly moving around, admiring ancient artefacts, taking in the lingering smell of incense, and absorbing the peace.

'Oh, look,' I pointed. 'Far corner to the left of the altar. People are lighting candles.'

I began to gravitate towards the tiny flames, like a moth on a mission, pulling Luca along with me.

'Do you want to light one too?' he asked.

'If you don't mind.'

'Not at all,' he said in bemusement.

I didn't often go to church, and I wasn't particularly religious, although I did believe in God. But if I *did* happen to find myself in a house of worship, I liked to honour and remember those who had passed away. Somehow it provided comfort amid the grief which, though now a long time ago, was never far away.

I released Luca's hand and reached for three white taper candles.

'Three?' he asked, as the flames came to life.

For a moment I was unable to speak, so simply nodded. My eyes momentarily brimmed.

'It's for Mum, Dad and my sister, Carly.'

Luca looked momentarily shocked.

'Did you lose your family all at the same time?'

I nodded again.

'Yes.'

'How?' he asked, looking appalled.

'In a car accident.' I turned to look up at him, a lone tear running down my cheek. 'And I was the driver.'

Chapter Forty-Four

'Sophie…' Luca stared at me for a moment, aghast at my revelation. 'There are no words.'

'Oh, I don't know,' I quavered. 'I managed to find quite a few when I woke up in Intensive Care and discovered the enormity of what I'd done. There was a lot of vile verbal invective, naturally directed at myself.'

Suddenly Luca's arms were around me, and I was being pulled into a tight embrace.

'Don't,' he whispered into my hair. 'It was clearly an accident.'

'Yes,' I sobbed. 'But all these years later, I still can't help blaming myself.'

'And to think I suggested we bus back to Maiori later, so you could experience the thrill of adrenalin and fear whilst travelling along twisting coastal roads. I could kick myself for being so insensitive.'

'You weren't to know,' I protested.

'But surely our Neapolitan roads must trigger you? Come on' – he didn't wait for my reply – 'I don't know about you, but now might be the time for that Aperol spritz.'

He led me by the hand, out of the cathedral and down the steep steps. His fingers remained firmly entwined with mine as we once again jostled through the heaving crowd. Moments later we were ducking down a side alley.

'This place might seem like a maze' – Luca said as we bowled along – 'but you can't really get lost. It's a series of squares connected by pedestrian streets.'

I scampered alongside him. All the narrow walkways were home to restaurants, jewellers, and souvenir shops, the latter once again selling plenty of the famous limoncello.

'Here we are,' he said, leading me up a series of stone steps into the cool depths of a wine-bar-cum-restaurant. 'One of Vittoria's cousins runs this place and the food here is amazing.' Luca stopped by a table for two and pulled out a chair for me. 'Do you fancy something to eat?'

I shook my head and flopped down on the seat.

'Thanks, but not just yet.'

'Heyyy,' said a man's booming voice.

I was immediately reminded of Graham Rollinson, Jackie's cuckolded husband. Dear God. Had George somehow managed to persuade Graham to come to Italy and drag me home on his behalf?

I glanced up fearfully, but any similarity to Graham ended at the voice. The chap standing before us looked like an Italian version of Tom Jones from the eighties. His shirt was unbuttoned to the navel revealing the hairiest chest I'd ever seen. Around his neck was a thick rope chain from which dangled a gold sovereign.

'*Il mio amico*,' the guy grinned, high-fiving Luca.

'Mario! It's good to see you,' said Luca. The two of them man-hugged, with lots of back slapping, as only men do. 'How's business?'

'Busy, but I no complaina.' Mario looked at me. 'And Luca bringa pretty lady.' He kissed his fingers. 'He hava the gooda tasta,' he smiled before belatedly clocking my red eyes, matching nose, and tear-stained cheeks. 'Don'ta worry. He lova you!'

Oh no, how embarrassing. He thought I was Luca's girlfriend and that we'd had some sort of lover's tiff.

'This is Sophie,' said Luca. 'She, um, had a bad experience earlier, so we thought we'd chill for a bit with a drink.'

'Of coursa,' Mario agreed expansively. '*Mario's* is the place for the beeg chilla.'

'We'll have two Aperol spritzes, please,' said Luca.

'Coming uppa,' he promised.

As Mario walked away, Luca turned to me.

'Sorry about him thinking you're my girlfriend. He's another one who'd like to see me married off. He's probably now telling all his kitchen staff that you're my fiancée.'

I gave Luca a wan smile.

'It's fine. Really.'

'Are you feeling better now?'

'Yes,' I sighed. 'Sorry to weep all over you.'

'Do you want to tell me about it?' he asked gently.

Mario chose that moment to return with the drinks.

'Enjoya,' he said. 'Anda remember' – he waggled a finger – 'he stilla lova you.'

A woman at the next table, who'd clearly been earwigging, looked my way and grinned.

'Men, eh?' she said in her London accent, while her husband rolled his eyes. 'Whatever he has done wrong' – she jerked her head at Luca – 'you give 'im hell, love. Make 'im buy you half a dozen of those pretty drinks and then a nice fillet steak with some cheesecake for dessert.'

Flipping heck. Did everybody get the wrong end of the stick in Amalfi?

'Drink up, darling,' said Luca, playing along. He reached across the table and took my hand in his. 'See? She's now forgiven me.'

Chapter Forty-Five

'So, tell me about it,' said Luca.

Despite the nosy woman at the next table having turned her attention back to her husband, Luca continued holding my hand. His thumb was currently rubbing over my knuckles. I had no idea if he was aware of what he was doing, but what with the gentle zingers pulsing around my wrist, to me it felt faintly erotic.

He's just being kind and comforting you, said my inner voice.

I didn't presume it to be anything else, I silently retorted.

You mentioned the word "erotic".

I was talking to myself, not you!

But I am you.

Please go away.

'When did the accident happen?' Luca prompted.

'Thirty years ago.' I shook my head. 'I don't know where time goes. A part of that terrible day seems, oh, I don't know, like last week. They say time heals. I'm not sure it does. It's more… a coming to terms with the situation. But the anger… the grief… it's never far away.'

'Thirty years is indeed a long time,' he said gently. 'But I totally get how it can also seem like yesterday. It's almost as if our own personal timeline shifts and blurs, taking us back to the moment when something pivotal occurred.'

'You're so right.'

'So… what happened before you woke up in Intensive Care?' he asked.

I gazed at a spot on the wall, high above Luca's head, and took a deep breath.

'I'd not long since passed my driving test. I passed first time, too,' I said proudly, aware that I was also defending myself. See! I was a *good* driver! 'My dad ripped up my L-plates, then took me to a local dealer in search of a suitable car. I'd been saving long before I took my test, anticipating this very moment. My parents kindly made up the financial shortfall on a second-hand Ford Fiesta. I was over the moon. It was bright red, and Carly was so jealous – in the nicest possible way.'

I smiled at the memory of my sister running one hand over the car's shiny bonnet. She'd smiled and said she couldn't wait to get her own car when she, too, had passed her test.

'Anyway' – a shadow passed over my face – 'Mum and Dad were booked to go to Majorca for a week. As Carly and I weren't little kids, our parents were happy to leave us at home alone. Holding the fort, so to speak. Dad asked if I'd drive them both to the airport…'

I paused to take a shuddering breath.

'You don't have to continue with this story,' Luca murmured.

'I want to,' I said firmly, mentally squaring my shoulders.

'So, we set off. Everything was fine. Great weather. Good driving conditions. No problems with visibility. Eventually we were cruising along the motorway. On the left were the usual intermittent slip roads. You know, exit points. I'd failed to see, as we passed one such slip road, that an international lorry driver had gotten himself into big trouble. Obviously, in the UK, we drive on the left side of the road. Other countries drive on the right. Later, witnesses said they saw the lorry incorrectly negotiating a roundabout before taking a one-way slip road – also in the wrong direction.' I gulped. 'Vehicles, back then, weren't equipped with modern-day satellite systems warning you when to make a U-turn. Instead, he accelerated on to the motorway, heading straight towards me. There was no time to take evasive action... no split-second chance to swerve left or right. However, I do remember my foot pumping the brake pedal as my eyes locked on his. I'll never forget them. Bright blue. Wide open. Filled with horror. Then... sound. Terrible, terrible sound. Just seconds earlier we'd all been chatting, laughing, and in high spirits. In a matter of moments, everything changed to blackness.

When I woke up in hospital, I was told that I was incredibly lucky to be alive. Unlike my family. They died at the scene. The lorry driver also died. His vehicle swerved off the road, then down an embankment. He went through the windscreen. Despite seat belt laws being in place back then, he wasn't buckled up. Mercifully, my family wouldn't have known much about it.'

'That is a harrowing experience. Do you mind me

asking' – Luca looked awkward for a moment – 'have you had counselling?'

'Oh, yes, lots and lots of lovely counselling.' The last two words came out sarcastically. 'Sorry, I don't mean to sound so cynical.'

'Maybe you haven't had the right sort of therapy,' he suggested.

'I've tried it all. Talking face to face. Talking on the phone. Being analysed. Taking pills–'

Luca looked alarmed, and I caught the meaning behind his expression.

'No, not that.' I shook my head. 'Anti-depressants. They stop you... *feeling*. Well, to a degree. However, ultimately, they didn't help either. You see, I *wanted* to feel. Otherwise, it was as though my family had never existed to me. I can't really describe it. Eventually I flushed the pills down the loo, and then booked myself in for something called EMDR therapy – eye movement desensitisation and reprocessing. That helped a bit. And then I discovered meditation.'

I gave Luca a direct look. Sometimes that last word had people thinking you were a bit, you know, nuts.

'Did it help?'

'More than anything else,' I said quietly. 'I still like to close my eyes and, as they say, sit with myself. It's very calming. Meanwhile, life goes on, and all those other crap clichés.'

'You've certainly had some trials and tribulations in your life, Sophie. What with losing your family and–'

'Losing my new husband to another woman.' I finished

the sentence for him. 'Believe me, Luca, the latter is nothing. Not compared to the former. If anything, the loss of my family gave me the gift of an emotional barometer. I use that gauge whenever dealing with grief or upset. I mean, it hurt when I divorced my first husband, but I didn't curl up in a ball and want to die. I coped with it. Got on with life. And Teddy and I are still friends, which is nice. Despite him not being able to keep his trouser zip up, he's actually a very sweet guy. And, yes, it's been devastating to remarry only to immediately discover I'd got it wrong again. But I'll get through it. The pain isn't all-consuming. It's not like when I lost my family.'

'Can I ask… why *did* you marry George?'

'Honestly?' I blew out my cheeks. 'I'd recently turned fifty. The number seemed, somehow, very defining. A moment to take stock. A reminder that the autumn years were approaching and maybe it would be nice to have a companion to grow old with.'

'Sophie, first of all, can I say you look nowhere near fifty. Second, I can't believe you were thinking about growing old *at* fifty! I'm only a handful of years behind you, and never think about aging. I know I'm not twenty-one anymore – even though my heart still feels that way – but I have a lot more living to do and I want it to be fun.'

'Is that why you bought your Spider?'

'Partly,' Luca acknowledged, before pausing. He gave me a curious look. 'How do you cope with driving – that is, assuming you still get behind the wheel of a car?'

'I do,' I confirmed. 'Although I'm not too keen on

motorways but, believe it or not, they aren't a major issue. Nor are these twisty roads. Sometimes you must face your fears. I *made* myself face mine. Still do.' I took a sip of my spritz, then gave Luca a matter-of-fact look. 'So, if the offer of returning to Maiori on the bus still stands, then that's what I'd like to do.'

Chapter Forty-Six

Later, *much* later, we left the restaurant, our appetites sated by Mario's delicious food.

There had been so much choice. *Scialatielli cozze vongole e pomodorini* – a local pasta with mussels, clams, and fresh cherry tomatoes. *Ndunderi* – an ancient pasta originally from nearby Minori and reminiscent, in shape, of gnocchi. *Spaghetti al limone* – spaghetti using the famous local lemons as a delicate pasta sauce. *Colatura di alici* – anchovies from nearby Cetara. *Pezzogna all'acqua passa* – fish with fresh tomatoes, garlic and parsley; and then, for dessert *pastarella amalfitane* – small pastries filled with lemon cream, followed by *limoncello,* the famous lemon-based liquor and *digestif* from Amalfi itself.

'I can hardly move,' I said, almost waddling out of the restaurant.

For a moment we paused in one of the narrow pedestrian streets, getting our bearings. It was dark now. All the shops and restaurants were lit up, their lights softly twinkling. Overhead, a shiny full moon lent a magical air to the evening.

'We can't get on that bus until we've digested our food,' said Luca. 'We don't want to embarrass ourselves.' He gave me a look. 'I'm not joking either.'

'Then let's walk around for a while,' I suggested.

'Good idea. Come on, let me show you Amalfi's famous fountain.'

We retraced our steps, walking along several of the smaller, covered alleyways. The maze-like streets and narrow passageways were full of balconies and hidden corners. They were all incredibly pretty but also confusing, although Luca seemed to know them like the back of his hand.

Eventually, we were back in the main piazza and, from there, located the fountain. Standing side by side, I gazed up at an elaborate marble sculpture of Saint Andrew standing on a plinth while cherubs frolicked at his feet.

'Beautiful, eh?' murmured Luca.

'Very. It looks incredibly old.'

'It is,' he agreed. 'I read somewhere that it was carved in 1760.'

I tried not to giggle at one of the nymphs who had water arcing out of a nipple.

'Can you drink from the fountain?'

'Yes, and it tastes good. Locals and tourists often fill up their water bottles here. Want to try some?'

Luca put his hand in the water. Palm dripping, he held it out to me, but I shook my head.

'Thanks, but I'll pass.'

My stomach was feeling more comfortable now. However, I didn't want any liquid sloshing around my insides when the time came to board the bus.

'Ready to head back to Maiori?' he asked.

'As ready as I'll ever be.'

'Attagirl.' He proffered his elbow. 'Would the *signora* like to link arms with the *signore*?'

I smiled.

'She would.'

It seemed like the most natural thing in the world to loop my arm through his as we walked out of the square and headed off to the bus stop.

Once there, we stood at the side of the main road with a crowd of chattering locals and tourists. A few minutes later, the bus turned up in a blaze of headlights and hissing brakes.

The doors slapped open, and everyone piled in. Bagging a couple of seats, I told myself to relax. I also offered up a silent prayer of thanks that the darkness would blot out views of any stomach-churning sheer drops along the unlit coastal road.

'Okay?' asked Luca, as the bus set off.

'I'm good,' I said realising that, strangely, I was. If this bus *did* plunge off the road and take everyone to their maker, then at least I would die reasonably happy. First, I'd never have to return to Little Waterlow with red-faced embarrassment over the wedding fiasco. Second, I'd float off into the ether with a handsome buddy by my side.

We'd dropped the arm linking once at the bus stop, but it had felt so nice. I knew it had only been companionship, and totally innocent. However, another part of me had acknowledged something else. A sense of belonging. Of being one half of a couple. It had felt very... right. And absolutely nothing like being with George. Nor Teddy

263

either, if I was honest. I wondered why that should be, then put it down to fanciful imagination.

I jumped as the lurching bus gave a series of long warning honks. We were approaching a hideously sharp zigzag. A sweep of headlights from the opposite direction confirmed the approach of another vehicle, but the bus wasn't slowing down, nor making any allowances for other drivers. I glanced through the window and saw that the vehicle's sides were almost grazing the wall of a house that abutted the road.

The front section of the bus bobbed heavily downwards as the driver floored the brake. The circulating compressed air once again spat, this time with every pump of the pedal as the driver inched his vehicle past a line of cars that had tailgated one another.

All the passengers seemed unperturbed, chatting, and laughing away, but when I looked to the right again, I nearly swallowed my tonsils. Even though it was dark, the silver moon had come out from behind a bank of clouds and was now acting as a torchlight.

I could see the coach's sides only millimetres from a dwarf wall. Surely those bricks were as good as useless against a vehicle of this height. How easy would it be to tip over and tumble into those black waters currently shimmering with moonbeams?

'No need to be anxious,' said Luca, as if reading my thoughts.

'I know,' I answered, giving him my best I'm-totally-okay-with-this smile.

I was aware that many barriers had come down between us this evening. Inexplicably, even though I'd only known this man for five minutes, somehow it seemed like a lifetime.

Weird.

Chapter Forty-Seven

The bus dropped us off at the promenade and, once again, Luca offered his arm as we walked back to the hotel.

Every now and again, fireworks went off in the sky. They were coming from the direction of the Norman Tower.

'What's the occasion?' I asked, as we paused for a moment to admire the pyrotechnics.

'Fireworks mark a celebration,' Luca explained. 'Usually a marriage. In summer, fireworks go off almost every night, and if not here, then over in Minori and Amalfi. In this huge sweep of coastal sky, rockets and sparkles are visible for miles.'

'The acoustics of the bay make it extra noisy,' I said, as a cracker shot upwards with a series of squeals. Moments later, it exploded in a shower of pink, silver, and gold. 'I hope Bella is okay,' I added, suddenly worried about my little kitten. No animal likes sudden noises, especially bangs, and blasts as deafening as these.

'She'll have tucked herself away in a plant pot,' Luca assured.

'I hope you're right,' I said, as we resumed walking.

A few minutes later and we were back at *Il Castello*.

Luigi, the night receptionist, greeted Luca, before giving me a polite smile as he handed over the key to my room.

'So, what did you think of Amalfi?' asked Luca.

'It was stunning.' I fingered the key, suddenly feeling a little awkward. 'Thank you so much for showing me around, Luca. I really appreciated it.'

'The pleasure was all mine,' he said gallantly.

I was aware of Luigi suddenly busying himself, apparently engrossed in some all-important paperwork, but it was obvious he was earwigging. More and more I was reminded of Maiori being an Italian version of Little Waterlow.

'Meanwhile' – Luca continued – 'I checked my weather app earlier. The temperature is going to change tomorrow.'

'Oh no,' I said, trying not to feel disappointed.

'Heavy rain in the morning, but drying up around noon, although remaining overcast.'

'I guess it won't be a day for sunbathing.'

'On the other hand, it would be a perfect opportunity to enjoy a hike without suffering heatstroke. Would you like me to show you the lemon walk?'

'Yes, please,' I said eagerly.

You are so uncool, chimed my inner voice.

Don't care, I answered back.

'Do you have suitable footwear?'

'Will flip flops do?'

'I wouldn't recommend them, especially as there's something like four hundred steps on the walk.'

'In that case, I'll wear my trainers.'

From outside came a low rumbling noise which was nothing to do with fireworks.

'Thunder,' said Luca, just as the entire sky – like a giant camera flash – turned white.

I took a step back, trying not to cringe.

'I hate thunder and lightning,' I said.

The sky flickered again, followed by a crash that made me jump.

'You're perfectly safe,' Luca laughed. 'That's the only thing about this place. When it rains, it's torrential, and the heavens can be extremely noisy.'

'Thanks for the warning.'

'Right,' said Luca, shifting his weight from one foot to the other.

For a moment we were silent. It was time to say goodnight. I hovered uncertainly. What to do? Kiss him on the cheek, the way a child did with a parent before a bedtime story and lights out? We'd done quite a lot of handholding earlier, and extensive arm linking. Okay, a heaving crowd and being in tears about my family had instigated the former, whereas simple companionship had been responsible for the latter so... but maybe I should wait and see if Luca pecked me first?

Luigi was now apparently enthralled with a stapler. He picked it up, turned it over in his hands a few times, then opened it up. Deciding its contents needed replenishing, he rummaged in a drawer for refills. It seemed to me that his right ear was extending, cartoonlike, in our direction, so that he could catch whatever Luca was going to say next.

'Sleep tight,' Luca eventually said.

'You too,' I replied.

He gave me a smile that made my entire body sigh then, turning on his heel, went through a door to staff quarters. I watched him go, my mood instantly flattening.

Sensing Luigi's watchful eyes upon me, I took a deep breath and began the long climb to the fourth floor.

Chapter Forty-Eight

The thunder continued to rumble and crash. Initially anxious, I pulled the duvet over my head. Surprisingly, despite the noise, I slept well.

On Tuesday morning I opened the blinds to a very different sea view. A vast raincloud was hovering over the entirety of the promenade. A cloudburst was drenching everything. Indeed, water was falling so heavily it reminded me of being in a carwash. To say it was torrential was an understatement.

Outside, the garden balcony was sporting mini lakes. Sheets of rain were hitting the patio's paving slabs, the force sending the water bouncing upwards again.

A tri-coloured face peered around one of the plant pots. Bella! Oh, good heavens, she was soaked. She reminded me of a tiny porcupine with her ruffled fur standing up in wet spikes. I wrenched the door open.

'Come on, sweetie,' I called, hunkering down.

Extending one hand, I rubbed my fingers together to coax her inside. She didn't need much persuasion and shot into the room like a mini missile, tiny wet paw prints puddling on the floor. I left the door ajar in case she felt trapped and wanted to scoot out again.

For a moment I paused, breathing in the rain-soaked air. Despite the downpour, it was exceptionally mild out there.

Going into the bathroom, I grabbed the hand towel and then turned to Bella.

'Can Mummy dry you?'

The kitten initially shied away, but then decided that a gentle rubdown was rather nice. As I softly ran the towel over her body, she began to loudly purr.

After she'd had something to eat, we settled down together on the bed. I didn't feel at all hungry, so decided to skip breakfast. Bella curled up at my feet, leaving me to spend a pleasant morning drinking coffee, chatting to Sue on the phone, and then taking my online Scrabble moves with people I'd never met – and probably never would. What a peculiar place the virtual world sometimes was.

Meanwhile, in the real world, the rain eventually stopped. Bella opened her eyes, yawned, stretched, then took herself off.

Pulling the bed together, I found my trainers and sorted out what to wear for today's hike. Grabbing my tote bag, I popped in some Factor 20 – just in case the sun did deign to reappear – and also mosquito repellent. Mozzies loved damp weather, and I had a feeling there might be a few hovering amongst the lemon groves.

'Hey,' said Luca, as I skipped into the foyer.

He was standing behind the reception desk with Vittoria. I put up a hand to her in greeting and she waved back.

'Did the thunder keep you up?' Luca asked.

'Not really. Perversely, I found it quite comforting.'

Luca gathered up a rucksack from a nearby chair, then moved out from behind the desk.

'Are you ready to explore?'

'I am,' I beamed.

Luca turned to Vittoria.

'Any problems, I have my mobile.'

'*Sì* – she made shooing gestures with her hands – '*divertiti*.'

'What does that mean?' I whispered, as we walked out.

'Have fun,' he whispered back.

And you're certainly having that, said my inner voice. *You haven't had a troublesome thought about George in ages.*

Who's George?

Your husband.

Ex-husband. And anyway, he was never a proper husband. Not in the true sense of the word. Now would you mind shutting up and leaving me alone. I have exploring to do.

Bet you wouldn't mind exploring Luca.

You have a filthy mind. Bog off.

'Tell me about the lemon walk,' I said to Luca, as we headed down the hill to the promenade.

'It's known locally as the path of lemons where it produces the *Sfusato Amalfitano* – the Amalfi lemon. The trail connects Maiori to Minori.'

A light wind was blowing, carrying a salty scent. I breathed it in, my lungs relishing the sea air as I listened to Luca.

'Even before the construction of the *Amalfitana*' – he continued – 'the path was the only walkable route that connected the two towns. For centuries, the peasants used this path, weighed down with their bags of lemons which were then shipped off to Spain and other countries. The area has the highest concentration of terraces, which is where the *Sfusato Amalfitano* is cultivated. Eventually, when the main coastal road was built – the *Strada Statale 163* – the lemon path was abandoned. However, the farmers saved the plantations. It's only because of them that this path remains one of the most evocative on the Amalfi Coast.'

We were now walking along the promenade and, for a while, held a companionable silence. Occasionally it was broken by chit-chat about everything and nothing. Seagulls whirled over the sweep of beach, squawking shrilly as they kept their eyes peeled for fish.

Luca asked what I did for a living, and I told him all about Ruby Walker's little salon where I worked as a hairdresser. Every now and again, a passer-by would say hello to Luca. He seemed to know so many people but explained that knowing everyone was simply the way of life in Maiori. Once again, I was reminded of Little Waterlow.

Each time a local stopped to chat to him – in Italian – their eyes would stray to me. It was obvious they were curious. I could almost read the questions going through their minds: *who was this woman with the guy who owned the big hotel on the hill?*

I heard Luca repeatedly mention my name and concluded that, just like my village back home, the people here weren't backward in coming forward when it came to nosiness.

We took a right turn and continued walking until reaching a church.

'This is where the path starts' – Luca made a sweeping gesture with one hand – 'right alongside the collegiate church of *Santa Maria a Mare* and the stairs of *Via Vena*. This path will take us through the town. Have your mobile ready to take some pictures. There's lots of typically Italian ceramic domes along the way. The path will eventually open out and you'll see terraces of olive and lemon groves under their trademark arbours.'

'It sounds delightful,' I said, extracting my phone from my tote back. I switched it to camera mode. 'How long will the walk take?'

'There are a lot of steps, Sophie, so we'll take the shortest route through Torre. It will be about an hour, which doesn't sound particularly long, but the vertical climb is hard on the body. The last time I did this with someone, her legs shook afterwards, so I hope your thigh muscles are prepared.'

For a moment I wondered who he'd previously taken this walk with. He'd said *her*. Had he been referring to the elusive Ariana? One way or another, this woman was quite an enigma. Apparently, everyone in Maiori wanted to see Luca married off to her, despite him denying she was a girlfriend.

'My thigh muscles are in great shape,' I said glibly.

No they're not, said my inner voice.

Listen – I mentally snapped – I stand on my feet all day.

Therefore, my thigh muscles are fine.

I wonder what Luca's thigh muscles are like?

At the thought of Luca's thighs, I suddenly felt a bit peculiar.

'Are you sure you're up for this?' asked Luca, looking concerned.

'Yes,' I said, a trifle hoarsely. 'Now stop wasting time and show me your lemons.'

His mouth momentarily twitched.

'In which case, follow me.'

Chapter Forty-Nine

Luca hadn't been teasing when he'd mentioned thigh muscles. Within minutes, it became apparent that my leg trembles were nothing to do with the effect this man had on me and everything to do with being unfit.

'How are you feeling?' he asked, as we continued to climb.

'Yes, great,' I gasped.

Flipping heck. Each step was taking us up higher... and higher. My heart rate was increasing with the climb – and uncomfortably so. Right now, it felt like a fist was knocking on the underside of my ribs.

'Let me know when you want to pause and take a rest.'

'All good,' I wheezed. 'Keep going.'

It's only an hour's walk, I told myself.

Yeah, that's an hour for people who are fit, my inner voice pointed out.

I am fit!

You reckon? You should see your face. It looks like a Maiori tomato. Bright red.

For God's sake, stop annoying me and go away.

'You said the walk would take about an hour,' I puffed. 'What distance does it cover?'

'About three kilometres,' said Luca.

I tried not to whimper. Three kilometres? That was about two miles in *old money*. Two miles of steps. I'd never been a gym bunny, but I reckoned even the most devout fitness fanatic wouldn't use a plyometric box set at this height and for that length of time. Omigod, how was I going to get through this?

I stared at a ceramic street sign as if willing it to give me some answers. *Sentiero dei limoni* – Lemon trail. Or lemon *fail* in my case because I couldn't see myself completing this walk. In fact, if I could just stop and lie down under this pretty arbour, that would be perfect.

I could lay flat on my back. Admire the brick walls on either side of the path. Marvel at the lush plants sprouting from various cracks in the mortar. Gaze up at the overhead criss-crossed wooden poles. Note how the trees grew, their boughs full of lemons that dripped through the open gaps.

Maybe one of the fruits would fall and hit me on the head. Perhaps it would whisper in my ear: "Hello! Use me not for lemonade, but lemon-*aid*." Was I going mad? Was this relentless climb starting to affect my brain?

'Shall we stop for a bit?' asked Luca.

He was puffing slightly, but nothing like me. I couldn't even speak. Instead, I resorted to sign language and gave him a thumbs up.

'Let's have a drink,' he suggested.

Good idea, although I wasn't sure the contents of the bottle in my tote bag would be enough. A hosepipe connected to an infinite supply of water would be better.

Not just to drink from, but also to cool my face.

'You look a bit pink,' Luca commented.

I nodded. Speech was still a no-no. I swung my bag from my shoulder and tried to extract my water bottle but, embarrassingly, my hand was shaking like an alkie suffering withdrawal. In fact, my whole body seemed to be vibrating.

'Here, let me help you,' said Luca, taking my bag and rummaging within. 'Let's take five minutes to recover.'

Only five minutes? I needed about five *hours*. Preferably in a health clinic, gazing at surrounding green fields while drinking iced tea.

Luca unscrewed my water bottle.

'Sip,' he ordered.

I tried to take the bottle from him, but my entire arm was behaving as if strapped to a pneumatic drill.

'Oh dear,' he grinned. 'You're not as fit as you thought.'

Told you.

Get stuffed.

'Let me hold the bottle to your mouth. That's it. Now drink.'

I glugged and swallowed, slurped, and gulped, as water went partly in my mouth and mostly down my chin, dripping onto my t-shirt. My skin welcomed the coolness.

'Feeling better?' Luca asked, pulling the bottle away.

'Yes,' I gasped, and promptly let out a huge belch from all the air I'd inadvertently swallowed. 'Oops. Sorry about that.'

'Couldn't matter less,' Luca laughed. 'Ariana had an attack of the trembles when we walked this path together.'

I knew it, squealed my inner voice. *Are you sure she's not his girlfriend?*

Right now, I don't care if she's his girlfriend, fiancée, or flaming wife. I just want to stop shaking. In fact, I feel rather sick.

You should have had some breakfast before leaving.

'Did you have breakfast earlier?' asked Luca, peering at me.

I had a nasty feeling that my previously scarlet face had now turned chalk white laced with grey.

'No,' I shook my head. 'I didn't feel hungry.'

'Here.' He pulled a packet of biscuits from his rucksack. 'Have some of these. We'll have a proper meal when we get to Minori.'

'Thanks,' I said, taking a shortbread biscuit, and resisting the urge to cram the whole thing into my mouth at once. Suddenly I was ravenous.

'While we're having a break, admire the surroundings,' Luca suggested. 'Look over there,' he pointed.

We were currently in an area where one's gaze simply got lost in the sheer immensity of its landscape – an endless parade of flower and lemon gardens that seemed to fall away to the sea.

'Twenty years ago' – Luca continued – 'the lemons that fell from the trees to the street were declared public property, so anyone could pick them up. Back then, the doors of the gardens were always open. At the entrance, you'd find a small table set with fruit, wine, and lemonade. Anyone could take it.'

'I presume that now doesn't happen because of the vast number of tourists.'

'That's right,' said Luca sadly. He gave me an appraising look. 'Feeling better?'

'Yes, thank you. Sorry to have acted like a wimp.'

'Don't be hard on yourself. This walk isn't for the fainthearted. Many underestimate it.'

We continued along the path. Slowly. Steadily. Taking lots of rest breaks. Eventually we arrived at a ceramic sign set in a wall. It read *Belvedere Mortella.*

'How does that translate?' I asked.

'Basically, it's a lookout point,' Luca explained. 'Step over here and you'll see why.'

I moved closer to him and gasped with delight. Far, far below was a stunning panoramic view of a glittering sea and the Gulf of Salerno.

'And now' – his tone indicated that this was the highlight of the walk – 'we begin the descent to Minori.'

'Downhill?' I asked, trying, and failing to stop my whole face from lighting up.

'All the way,' he grinned.

Chapter Fifty

As we entered Minori, all traces of the earlier cloudburst had gone. The sun was shining and the sky was blue, although the air remained somewhat muggy.

We headed to the village's tiny beach, paddled in the sea, and watched weeny minnows darting back and forth in the shallows.

After drying off, we headed along a palm-lined boulevard, past pretty villas, then stopped at the first restaurant we came across.

'I've been here before and the food is great,' said Luca. 'I highly recommend the steak.'

A waiter greeted Luca as if a long-lost brother, all the while looking at me curiously as he talked in Italian to Luca. I heard Ariana's name mentioned. Blimey, was Minori like Maiori too, in that everyone knew everybody's business?

Luca eventually switched to speaking in English.

'This is my friend, Sophie,' he said to the waiter. 'She's staying at my hotel.'

The waiter gave Luca a sly smile.

'Nel tuo letto?'

'No!' said Luca emphatically.

The waiter gave me a wink before replying in heavily

accented English.

'How you say? Pulla the other one,' he chortled, clapping Luca on the back before leading us to a table.

We were presented with a couple of menus before the waiter swaggered off, whistling a jaunty tune that seemed to be directed at Luca. It sounded familiar and I realised I'd heard it before, blasting from the speakers of various beach cafés.

'What *is* that song?' I asked Luca.

He looked faintly embarrassed.

'*Storia d'Amore.*'

'What does that mean.'

'Love Story.'

I blinked. Why had the waiter been whistling the song, and why had he joked with Luca about pulling the other one? And whilst I'd not understood what he'd been talking about when we first came in, my ears had pricked up at the mention of a woman whose name had begun with A.

I didn't need to be Einstein to piece together the waiter's thoughts. He thought Ariana was Luca's girlfriend and that I was the bit on the side.

Luca made a show of studying the menu, even though he'd already recommended what to eat. I did likewise. Neither of us spoke. The waiter returned with a carafe of water and two glasses. He exchanged more nudge-nudge-wink-wink conversation with Luca, all in Italian, before taking our steak and side salad orders.

'So,' I chirped, after an interminable silence.

'So,' said Luca, putting his elbows on the table and

282

steepling his fingers together.

'I'm not going to beat about the bush, as us Brits say.'

'I sense you need to get something off your chest.'

'Yes, I do,' I nodded. 'Earlier, you mentioned you'd eaten here before. Who with?'

Luca looked at me for a moment, without saying anything.

'Does it matter who?' he eventually said.

'Yes, because I get the distinct feeling that our waiter' – I could feel myself reddening – is under the impression that I'm somehow romantically involved with you. Also, that a certain lady friend wouldn't be thrilled to know you're here with me.'

'I've already told you that the people round here are gossips. They have nothing better to talk about.'

'That doesn't answer my question.'

'Okay. Yes, I came here with Ariana.'

My nostrils flared. I'd never met this woman but, wherever we went, people seemed to think I was a threat to her. I didn't like that. Not after all the crap I'd been through regarding George and Jackie Rollinson. If a man was with another woman – no matter how tenuously – I didn't want to tread on anyone's toes. Even though no romance was going on between Luca and me, I didn't like that others seemed to think there was. Nor did I appreciate the insinuation that if Ariana found out there would be trouble.

'I suspect this lady means more to you than you're letting on,' I said, deciding to say what I was thinking.

After all, did it really matter if I offended Luca? Come

the weekend, I'd never see this man again. On Saturday I'd be on a flight back to England facing the music in my own complicated love life.

'You even' – I continued – 'revealed that you did the lemon walk with her. Are you sure she's not your girlfriend?'

'Quite sure. Look, when I first came to Maiori, it was Ariana who showed me around. The path of lemons was one of the places we visited. And yes, I suspect she has a crush on me, but it isn't reciprocated. And yes again, we had a meal together. Here. At this restaurant. I've already mentioned it was a business meeting.'

'Business,' I muttered. 'That old chestnut.'

'Sorry?'

'What sort of business is she in?' I challenged, horribly aware that I was starting to sound like a possessive girlfriend.

'Haven't you figured that out?' Luca asked.

And then he said something that took the wind right out of my billowing sails.

'Ariana is my solicitor.'

'Your solicitor?' I repeated stupidly.

'Yes. She's handling my affairs regarding the inheritance of *Il Castello.*'

'Oh,' I said. 'Right.'

'Does that answer your question?'

I sat there, scarlet in the face, feeling rather foolish.

'Er, yes. Yes, it does.'

'Good,' said Luca.

He gave me a look that I couldn't quite fathom. Unable to meet his eyes, I instead turned my attention to the other diners. The place was starting to fill up with early evening visitors. Tourists over there. Now some locals were coming over the threshold.

I watched as the waiter hastened over to the new arrivals. Arms extended. Expansive greetings. Handing out menus. Now hurrying over to Table Eight to take a couple's orders. I wondered how the occupants of that table were getting along. If their conversation was flowing. Or whether it was as awkward as the atmosphere here, at Table Two.

I studied my fingernails briefly before risking a peek at Luca. My stomach lurched as I realised he'd been staring at me all along.

'What?' I asked uncertainly.

His face was serious. His gaze unwavering.

'I think' – he said carefully – 'that your question gives rise to another question.'

'O-Oh?' I stammered.

'There's something going on here.'

'What do you mean?' I whispered, suddenly unable to tear my eyes away from his.

'Between us,' he said simply. 'Let's not – as you said earlier – *beat about the bush.* I think you have feelings for me, Sophie.'

Oh God. How cringemaking. I could feel my red face turning puce. My embarrassment was evident. As was the truth. He was right. Why else would I cross-examine him over Ariana? His personal life – whether business or private – was his affair. Nonetheless, it was mortifying to be called out.

'L-Look,' I stuttered, wondering how to backpedal, and

save face. 'I–'

'Sophie,' he interrupted. 'To coin another phrase, it's cards on the table time. I'll play the first hand.'

'Okay,' I muttered, wishing that a convenient crack would appear in the restaurant floor and swallow me whole.

'I can't explain why, and frankly I'm not even going to try.'

'About what?' I whispered.

Luca paused. His expression was earnest. Intense. Also tender. When he next spoke, his voice was barely audible.

'About how you've stolen my heart.'

Chapter Fifty-One

'W–What?' I spluttered.

'You heard,' said Luca softly. His eyes were still upon me.

'B–But it's not… I mean… we only met three days ago.'

'So?'

'This is crazy. We don't know each other.'

'I'm right, aren't I?' he said gently. 'You have feelings for me, just as I have feelings for you.'

The waiter interrupted the moment, by putting our steaks in front of us. I stared at the food helplessly. No way was I going to get through this when my stomach was churning with emotion.

'Wassa matter?' asked the waiter, clocking my stricken look. 'You too in lova to eata, eh?' He laughed uproariously before heading off to greet more tourists.

In love? Me? I couldn't possibly be. It was only last Friday I'd got married. How many men was it possible to love in such a short space of time?

Ah, but I don't think you were ever truly in love with George, said my inner voice.

I must have been – I retorted – after all, I let him put a ring on it!

I'm sure we've already had this conversation, Sophie, but let me remind you again. You turned fifty and panicked about being on your own for the rest of your life. Anyway, George is in the past. Okay, it's a very recent past, but it's still the past. It's time to concentrate on the future.

Like rebounding with Luca? Are you completely off your trolley?

If you want to rebound, then rebound. There's no one here to judge you, Sophie. This isn't Little Waterlow. And anyway, who cares what anyone else thinks? You've had half a century on this earth, girl. Haven't you learnt anything by now in this school of life? We make mistakes. Some of our decisions are flipping brilliant. Others are downright disasters. But we learn. We listen to our heart and see if it's resonating with the soul. Luca is right. You have feelings for him. So how are they resonating?

Nicely, as it happens. He makes me feel happy.

Bella makes you feel happy. This is LUCA we're talking about! So, answer my question properly.

You're flustering me. Let me think. I've said before that I feel like I've known him for such a long time. It's strange. I can't explain it.

As I said, it's called resonance. Carry on.

Also, despite my two failed marriages – one of which must surely qualify for the Guinness Book of Records – he makes me feel like that isn't so awful. I came to Italy believing myself a total failure, whereas Luca makes me believe that I was just unlucky. That my failed marriages aren't all my fault. In fact, he makes me feel ten feet tall, and

288

that it's Teddy and George who are the losers, rather than me.

Luca gives you confidence.

Yes, and that's very liberating.

So, explore the feelings you have for each other.

You mean... have a holiday romance?

As I said, there's nobody here to judge you apart from yourself. Isn't it about time you let go of the past, stopped worrying about the future, and started to simply BE?

Okay, I think I understand. Just be... right here. Now.

That's it!

This moment.

You're getting it!

All that matters is this moment.

Bingo. I'll leave you to enjoy your steak.

'Sophie?' Luca prompted.

I looked at him. Saw the hope in his eyes. And a light. It was kindness but... so much more.

'You're right,' I said, as joy bubbled up from within. I gave him a glowing smile. 'I feel exactly the same way.'

Chapter Fifty-Two

'But the thing is, Luca–'

'Shh,' he said. 'You don't need to say anything. Eat your meal. Afterwards, we'll go for a walk and talk where ears can't hear.' He jerked his head meaningfully at the waiter.

'Okay,' I grinned.

I picked up my knife and fork. Suddenly I was ravenous again.

We tucked in and conversation resumed, but not about us. Instead, Luca chatted about his family in Hertfordshire, and how they'd telephoned late last night for a catch up, keen to know if he'd made a final decision on whether to keep or sell *Il Castello*.

'And have you?' I asked.

For a moment he looked cagey.

'I'd like to make a go of the hotel. That said, I miss my family. England, too. I need a reason to stay here. One that goes beyond doing up a crumbling hotel.'

'And do you have a reason?'

'I have the germ of an idea.'

'What is it?'

'It's a little too early to say,' he said simply.

We finished the meal with a *limoncello digestif* and then

headed back out to the late afternoon sunshine.

'Let me show you Minori,' he said, slipping his hand into mine.

My fingers entwined with his. This time the handholding was nothing to do with being jostled or pulled apart. This time it was romantic.

I felt my spirits rising like the seagulls lifting off the dark sands of Minori's beach. I wondered if Luca might kiss me.

No, Sophie. Not here.

Why not?

Tourists are milling around. It might not be as busy as Amalfi, but the last thing you want is someone barging past just as lean in for that first lip lock.

Fair point.

Minori was a delightful mix of small streets and narrow alleyways that meandered up the mountain. Some of the roads and walkways were open to cars but the majority seemed to be pedestrianised, making it both perfect and safe for a stroll.

Once again, these routes were notoriously steep. I noticed that several benches were dotted around, possibly to sit upon while recovering one's breath.

We passed a patisserie, its windows full of glorious pastries and extravagant wedding cakes, then took a side alley so narrow it felt as if the buildings were leaning in to share secrets.

The air was heavy with the scent of orange blossom. I inhaled it appreciatively, at the same time noticing how bougainvillea cascaded from so many buildings. Overhead balconies were full of terracotta pots bursting with blooms.

We walked past a souvenir shop displaying a trellis upon which several hats were pinned. I admired both the straw and colourful felt fedoras, but my eye was drawn to a wide-brimmed affair in black with a trailing silver ribbon. It reminded me of a portrait of Georgiana Cavendish, Duchess of Devonshire. She'd been painted in the late seventeen hundreds by the artist Thomas Gainsborough. Georgiana had worn such a hat and subsequently made it fashionable.

Continuing, we walked up a stepped pedestrian avenue, this time passing ceramic shops. A cat slept peacefully in a sun puddle, and I smiled at the thought of Bella waiting for me back home.

Home.

Wow. Since when had *Il Castello* become *home*?

We turned into yet another passageway, and I exclaimed with delight at a peeling wall covered in huge photographic enlargements. All were sepia in colour and preserved against the elements.

'This is Minori *waaaay* back,' said Luca, as we paused to study the pictures.

Old-fashioned fishing boats edged the beach and there wasn't a car to be seen.

As we turned into yet another walkway, a beautiful bell tower dwarfed the far end.

'That's from the eighteenth century,' said Luca. 'Let me show you the basilica next door.'

We took a final turning and suddenly were standing in front of an impressive baroque church with a light-yellow façade.

'We are now in the centre of town,' said Luca. 'This is the *Basilica di Santa Trofimena.*'

'It's very elegant. Is it the same age as the bell tower?'

'No.' Luca shook his head. 'It was built around twelve hundred in the Romanesque style. However, over the years it has undergone many restorations, so now it's more neoclassical. Inside are the preserved relics of Saint Trofimeno, whose bones were found on the beach somewhere between the seventh and eighth centuries.'

I stared at the church in awe.

'It's so beautiful.'

Luca turned to face me.

'Just like you.'

Instantly I felt my cheeks flush with colour.

'I'm not beautiful,' I protested.

'Yes, you are,' he insisted.

I was suddenly aware that nobody was around. An unexpected shyness crept over me, covering me like a fine blanket, immobilising my body and tying up my tongue.

'So are you,' I mumbled. 'I mean… you know, handsome.'

He threw back his head and laughed.

'Sweet Sophie,' he chuckled, squeezing my hand. 'There is something so deliciously naïve about you. It's so refreshing to be with a woman who isn't constantly whipping out a compact mirror, checking her reflection, adding another layer of lipstick to her mouth and flicking her hair extensions about.'

I didn't ask which woman did that but had a feeling I knew who he might be talking about.

'I don't have hair extensions,' I assured. 'Look, Luca, regarding the earlier conversation in the restaurant.'

'Yes?'

'Do you think it's just the Italian sunshine talking? You know, the romance of the Amalfi Coast and the decaying splendour of *Il Castello?*

Not to mention the emotional support of a man whose kindness had melted me faster than a choc-ice on the beach and whose good looks and current proximity made a pulse flutter between my thighs.

Since when did you get so specific? spluttered my inner voice.

Since now, I retorted.

'No, I don't think it's that at all,' he said, looking faintly amused. 'Why, do you?'

I didn't say anything for a moment, instead noting his face. The sweep of his cheekbones. The colour of his skin. The tenderness in his eyes, that said it all.

'Me neither,' I conceded.

The light was starting to fade.

'I think we should head back, don't you?'

I sensed that the question held another question. Head back to *Il Castello* and… whatever might follow next between us? I gave a shiver of anticipation at the thought.

Because of the late hour, the water taxi was a chilly ride. As the light quickly faded, Luca draped an arm around me, and I snuggled into his warmth.

We looked like a couple, and it made me feel so happy. I realised that all my life I'd been searching to be one half of a whole. I thought I'd found it with Teddy, but his constantly wandering eye had proven that not to be the case. I'd then hoped to have found it with George, but now realised I'd never felt like part of a proper couple with him. Something had been missing from the start, and I'd simply chosen to ignore it.

I wasn't stupid enough to think that Luca was *the one*. After all, I'd known him for all of two minutes. However, if I took on board my inner voice's recent words of wisdom – about being in the moment – then right now I could bask in a sense of deep contentment.

Sighing with pleasure, I let my head rest upon Luca's shoulder. Bliss.

When the boat docked at Maiori Harbour, darkness had descended. A band was playing at a waterside wine bar. As the other passengers disembarked, we held back. Men, women, and children hurried off, heading towards Maiori's promenade, while we lingered, enjoying the melody.

The lead singer was crooning into the microphone. The song was hauntingly beautiful. A rash of goosebumps broke out over my arms. It was nothing to do with being cold but everything to do with the ballad. I had no idea how the words translated, but somehow it seemed terribly moving, so much so that tears momentarily pricked my eyes.

We were now standing alone on the empty quay, and completely in our own bubble. Luca took me in his arms, and we began to slowly dance. I wound my arms around his neck as we swayed. Right there. On the waterside. Two people. One couple. Lost in their own world. Dancing under the early evening stars. I knew with certainty that, whatever happened in the future, I would never forget this moment. Then Luca lowered his head to mine and gently kissed me.

And I was lost.

Chapter Fifty-Three

Hand in hand, we slowly walked to *Il Castello* under an inky black sky full of twinkling stars.

Once again, we crossed the threshold of the hotel's foyer, and once again we stood together in the reception area. However, unlike last night, there was no Luigi behind the desk, ears flapping while he pretended to busy himself with bits of paper or a stapler's empty barrel.

There was the sound of movement behind the staffroom door. My eyes flicked to its frosted glass. I could make out the vague shape of Luigi beyond. His outline suggested he was sitting down having a cup of something and not in any hurry to interrupt his break.

'So,' said Luca quietly, wrapping me in his arms. 'How would you like to conclude today?'

In bed with you, were the first words that came to mind.

Luca's question very much put the ball in my court – but I didn't feel brazen enough to voice such words aloud. What if he thought I was a shameless hussy? Instead, I gave a coy smile – hopefully sweetly suggestive and not a gleeful leer – and evaded answering directly.

'I'm easy,' I said.

Careful, Sophie, cautioned my inner voice. *Those two*

*words could be badly misconstrued. Do you really want to
have sex on the same day as your first kiss?*

Yes, please!

Luca's mouth twitched.

'I'd quite like to have a shower and change into some
fresh clothes,' he said. 'How about we both do that and then
meet on the roof terrace for a drink. I don't know about you,
but after such a magical day, I think we should have
champagne. And who knows' – he flashed a meaningful look
– 'what might follow?'

This was more like it. A positive signal. A definite green
light. Verbal foreplay!

Luca's words couldn't be clearer: Shower from top to
toe. Pay particular attention to all those deliciously important
places in between. Put on some seductive kit. Drink
champers under a canopy of stars. Then back to mine.

Well, something like that.

I had a sudden vision of us tossing an empty champagne
bottle to one side before thundering down six flights of stairs
to Luca's flat and ripping each other's clothes off. Bring it on.

'That sounds fab to me,' I said, letting a flirtatious smile
play around my mouth.

'Excellent,' he murmured. 'I'll see you up there in half
an hour.'

'Make it forty-five minutes,' I said hastily.

I might not be the sort of woman who – as Luca had
mentioned earlier – whipped out a mirror every so often to
add more lipstick but, in the privacy of my own room, I
quite liked to titivate. And tonight *definitely* called for some

serious titivation.

In my head I was already rifling through my makeup bag. In England I'd purchased a tube of glowy stuff that promised to give one the dewy complexion of youth. Let's face it, what fifty-year-old was going to turn down that offer?

I'd also previously purchased lots of honeymoon lingerie that was begging to be paraded. In the absence of a husband, who better to wear it for than my lover?

Steady, Sophie. You haven't even touched the champagne yet, and you're already sounding drunk.

I am, I mentally cackled. I'm totally intoxicated!

'Right,' said Luca, giving me a little squeeze. 'I'll see you soon.'

'You will,' I murmured, only just managing to stop myself from doing some lecherous eyebrow waggling.

Luca leant in and kissed me again. The ensuing zinger was so stratospheric I was amazed it didn't catapult me right up to the fourth floor without the need of the stairs.

Grinning stupidly at each other, we pulled away. Once again, I watched Luca turn on his heel and head towards staff quarters. However, unlike last night, this time I was high on happiness.

I floated up the four flights without even pausing to catch my breath. What was it about romance that made the world such a fabulous place? My rose-tinted specs were firmly in place, perched over the bridge of my nose. Everything was wonderful. Glorious. Abso-flipping-lutely fantastic.

As I fished in my pocket for the key to the room, I gazed

fondly at the door's scruffy paintwork. Yes, even *that* was picture perfect.

Smiling to myself, I went in and flipped on the light. But as the door slammed shut behind me, I ground to an abrupt halt. My eyes widened in horror as a scream died in my throat. My larynx made a peculiar, strangled noise as shock whooshed through me. For there, perched on the end of the bed, was George.

Chapter Fifty-Four

'Hello, Sophie,' said George calmly.

I opened my mouth to speak, but no words were forthcoming.

'Cat got your tongue?'

He nodded at the patio door, and I spotted Bella's nose pressed up against the glass. She was waiting for me to feed her, but now wasn't a great moment.

I put out a hand to steady myself.

'What the hell are you doing here?' I croaked.

'Isn't it obvious?' George raised his eyebrows quizzically. 'I'm on my honeymoon.'

I stared at him incredulously, trying to make sense of his presence in this room. Was I was hallucinating? George would have needed a passport for international travel. However, that document was safely locked away in my bedroom at Catkin Cottage.

'How did you get here?' I gasped.

'The same way as you,' he said simply. 'By plane.'

His facetious coolness was starting to get to me. This could not be happening.

'That's not what I meant,' I snapped, recovering slightly.

'Keep your voice down, Sophie,' said George mildly. 'If

you're going to lose your temper, it's best other residents don't hear.'

'Lose my temper?' I repeated, gaping at him. 'Sorry, George, can we just rewind for a moment? I asked you a question which you still haven't answered. *How* did you get here?'

'I've already told you–'

'Yes, I heard the bit about modern aircraft,' I said impatiently. 'Forgive me if I'm wrong, but I thought a passport was required to take a flight. Your passport is at my house.'

'Was.'

'Was what?' I asked, brow furrowing in confusion.

'Has the Italian sunshine messed with your head?' asked George, frowning theatrically. It was obvious he was enjoying my reaction to his unexpected presence. 'I know you can be a little fluffy at times. A tad ditzy. However, you're not usually this dense. My passport *was* locked away at Catkin Cottage – until I gained access.'

'You broke into my home?' I cried.

'Of course not. Breaking and entering isn't my style. I used the spare key.'

'But you don't have a spare key.' I shook my head. None of this was making any sense. 'We never gave each other keys to our respective homes.'

George smiled indulgently.

'One doesn't have to be intellectually gifted to know that most people leave a spare somewhere – for emergency purposes, obviously. I popped over to your mate's house, assuming she'd be a keyholder.'

'Yes, Sue told me you'd turned up. She also said she'd sent you packing.'

'She did. Quite a feisty gal pal, your Sue. Clearly the one who wears the trousers in her marriage to the hapless Charlie. Anyway, I drove home. Scratched my head. Pondered for a bit. *Slept on it*, as one might say. And then it came to me. I was quite cross with myself for not realising it earlier.'

'Realising what?'

'That most people leave spare keys under plant pots.'

My hand flew to my mouth.

'Bingo!' said George happily. 'I headed over to Catkin Cottage but was intercepted by an interfering Little Waterlow resident who'd been visiting your immediate neighbour. The battle-axe in question must be distantly related to your bestie, because she said' – he posted quotation marks in the air – '"If yer don't sling yer 'ook, I'll get our Fred on yer." I deduced that Fred wasn't a German Shepherd. Rather, the old bag's long-suffering husband.'

I silently sent up a prayer of thanks for busybodies like Mabel Plaistow. The octogenarian might sometimes be a pain in the tubes, but she'd had my back.

'So' – George continued – 'rather than create a scene, I drove off, and returned when the nosy parker wasn't around, and your immediate neighbour had gone to bed.'

'You had no right to do that,' I scowled.

'I must admit, sweetheart, I did curse you several times as I stumbled around in the dark. I upended twenty-something pots looking for that elusive key. Eventually I found it and let

303

myself into the house. After poking around in various cupboards and drawers, I discovered what I was looking for in your bedroom. After that it was simply a case of booking the next available flight. At such short notice, there was a bit of a delay. Evidently Naples is a popular destination. You gave me quite the runaround, darling.'

'I'm not your darling,' I growled. 'As far as I'm concerned, George, you broke into Catkin Cottage. I think the police might take a dim view of your actions.'

George stood up. Suddenly the room seemed to shrink.

'And as far as *I'm* concerned' – he hissed, moving towards me – 'you *stole* my passport. What do you think the police would have to say about that, hm?'

Intimidated, I took a step back.

'How did you get into this room?' I demanded, but a wobble had crept into my voice.

'Dear oh dear,' he tutted, taking another step towards me. 'You really are even more stupid than I thought. How do you think I got in?' He gave me a ghastly smile before producing a key identical to the one in my hand. 'The guy on reception checked me in.'

'Luigi?' I took another step backwards. 'B–But…'

Surely Luigi knew about my wedding fiasco? That I was here on my own? That I'd run away from my cheating new husband? Luca had said that his staff were aware of my sudden singledom. Was it possible that Luigi, the night receptionist, who worked alone, was the one person oblivious of my situation?'

George moved closer.

'I presented myself at reception, explained that I'd missed my flight due to a family emergency, but was now joining my wife, Mrs Sophie Baker. Luigi sat down at his computer, checked my name was on the system, then asked to see my passport. Satisfied, he gave me a key to our room.'

The hairs on the back of my neck began to prickle. I didn't like those last two words. *Our room.* As far as I was concerned, this was a totally unacceptable situation, and no way was this man sharing my sleeping space.

'There's just one problem,' I ventured.

'What's that?' asked George, taking yet another step towards me.

'We're finished.'

'Now, now, Sophie. Let's not start mudslinging. Not on our honeymoon.'

My heart was starting to pump unpleasantly. I took another two steps backwards... and felt the solid wooden panels of the main door against my back. Suddenly George was towering over me. I stared up at him.

'Our marriage was over before it even began,' I quavered. 'And we're most definitely *not* on our honeymoon.'

George's face twisted.

'Oh, but I think you'll find that we are.'

Chapter Fifty-Five

'Move away from me, George,' I cringed. He was now so close to me his paunch was nudging my stomach. 'I said–'

'I heard you the first time, darling.'

His breath was warm on my face and sour from airline coffee and plastic-wrapped sandwiches. I turned my head away.

'I'm warning you,' I quailed.

'Oooh, I'm scared,' he mocked.

'I mean it, George. I won't be responsible for my actions.'

'My goodness, I had no idea my meek little Sophie was so full of gung-ho. It's quite exciting. In fact, you're starting to give me a reaction.'

Suddenly it wasn't just his belly jabbing me. Horrified, I raised my arms and pushed hard against his chest. I was still holding the key to the room and despite it digging into George's skin, he didn't seem to notice. Nor did he budge. It was like trying to move a mountain.

'That's it,' he breathed, as we tussled. 'Fight me. I like it. That's why I had a thing about Jackie. She used to like games. The teasing little bitch. Go on, Sophie. You'll have to push harder than that. Jackie and I did role play.' George's breathing was becoming ragged. 'She'd dress up as a cop. We'd play act. She'd arrest me for speeding and tell me she'd fine me on the spot if I didn't spank her arse.'

Oh, dear God. This could not be happening.

'Then go to Jackie,' I puffed, shoving with all my might.

George took an involuntary step backwards, but there wasn't enough room for me to duck under his arm and break free.

That said, where could I escape to? Out to the balcony garden? The fence dividers were too high to clamber over. That left the possibility of hitching up my hemline and hopping over the wrought iron rail. But then what? Fly through the air? Arms and legs windmilling before landing on the road below, hoping that my bones didn't break as my body went *splat* on the tarmac? Or maybe, if I put my all into it, I could clear the road and instead crash, like the waves, against those vicious rocks.

George grabbed my wrists, yanked my arms upwards and slammed me against the door. The key I'd been holding clattered to the floor.

'I can't go to Jackie,' he panted. 'She wants Graham back. But never mind her. It's you I now want. Especially when you're behaving like this.'

Having ensured I was well and truly pinned against the door, he lowered his lips to mine. I instantly whipped my head sideways.

'Get off me, George, or I'll scream so loudly everyone on this floor will come to see what's going on and–'

George released one of my wrists and clamped a hand

over my mouth. My head banged painfully against the door.

'Scream, Sophie?' he murmured. 'I don't think so, darling. The only screaming you're going to do is when you cry out with pleasure.'

He released my other wrist and began pawing at my top. Omigod, no-no-no-no-*noooo*.

Breathing was becoming an issue. The palm of his hand wasn't just covering my mouth, it was over my nose too. George might think we were acting out some aggressive roleplaying, but I knew otherwise. He needed stopping. Immediately. And to hell with the consequences.

Both my hands were now free, and I didn't waste a moment. I stomped hard on his feet, grabbed his testicles, then gave them a sharp twist. In the next moment I'd dealt his windpipe a blow.

George's initial bellow of agony was cut off by the impact of my hand on his Adam's apple. His eyes bulged as he wheezed. His reaction was an open book to read, the changing expressions rolling swiftly into one another. Surprise. Pain. Anger.

As he lurched backwards clutching both his crotch and neck, I stamped on his feet again, then pushed my thumbs into his eyeballs for good measure.

Temporarily blinded, he staggered sideways, then crashed into the wall, all the while groaning loudly. Seizing my chance, I went to flee but realised I had nowhere to go.

George was now bent double and blocking the door to the corridor. Panicking and terrified, I started to run aimlessly backwards and forwards.

Scream, Sophie, SCREAM!

Good idea.

Well, go on then, what are you waiting for?

'ARGH,' I screeched. 'ARGHHH.'

Get outside. To the balcony.

I scampered to the patio door. Outside it was dark, but in the glow of a single courtesy light, I could make out Bella. She was still hanging around, waiting to be fed, but her eyes were now wide with alarm.

As I catapulted into the garden, shrieking like a World War Two siren, Bella instantly fluffed up. Terrified by the noise, she scrambled over the fence leaving me running uselessly around in circles, going nowhere.

'ARGHHHHHHHHH,' I shrieked again.

'I say,' said a camp voice. 'Are you okay?'

A perma-tanned face appeared over the fence that divided our two gardens.

'Help,' I bleated. 'HELPPPPP.'

George chose that moment to lumber through the patio door.

'Sorry, matey,' he puffed. 'It's just a lover's tiff.'

'GET AWAY FROM ME,' I hollered. 'CALL THE POLICE,' I shouted to my neighbour.

Would this man believe that I was a woman in need, or take George's word and believe we were having a noisy *domestic*? Was there someone else who could help? Someone who did your bidding before calling in a favour. According to Luca, there was.

'CALL DON CORLEONE,' I bellowed.

'I don't think I know him. Do you have his number?' asked my neighbour.

'Tell Luca,' I wheezed. 'He's the manager. Please... get him.' I couldn't keep this up. My legs were turning to jelly. 'Hurry,' I gasped, as I collapsed down on the grass and mud. The puddles hadn't fully dried out from the earlier cloudburst. 'He's on... the roof terrace... tell him... Sophie... urgent.'

I was panting like a distressed dog in a vet's waiting room. Even worse, George was now standing over me.

'Come on, darling,' he said, pussycat smile back in place. 'Let's not disturb this nice gentleman any further. Come back inside. Just look at your legs! Let's get this mud off you and then we can kiss and make up.'

'Oh, I remember you now,' said the neighbour, peering more closely at me. 'Yes, it's coming back to me. Last Sunday.'

I gazed up at him in horror. Last Sunday was when George had telephoned, demanding that the holiday spending money be returned to our joint account. Afterwards I'd had a mini meltdown and let rip with a few choice words. Luca had assured me that nobody had heard my rant on account of everyone being at the beach. Evidently this gentleman had been around and caught every word.

'Let me see,' said the stranger, stroking his chin thoughtfully. 'You were very upset and screeched something about stinky bum holes, hairy bollocks and fuckity-fuckity–'

'You must forgive my wife,' George cut in smoothly. 'She's very highly strung.'

310

'Couldn't matter less,' said the neighbour.

He put up a hand in farewell, then retreated. And as he disappeared from sight, so did all my hope.

Chapter Fifty-Six

'Come on, sweetheart,' said George, hauling me to my feet.

I was like a rag doll, hardly able to stand, and trembling violently.

'Lean on me,' he instructed. 'That's it. Let's get you back inside. I'll make you a nice cup of tea, hmm? And then we can carry on where we left off.'

I groaned but was unable to resist. My body seemed to have lost all power and I felt exhausted.

It's the fight or flight thing, my inner voice piped up. *Your adrenals have produced a hormonal cascade.*

Why do I have no energy?

Oxygen. Lower oxygen levels contribute to the fatigue you're feeling.

What am I going to do if I need to struggle against George again? Right now, I couldn't do battle with a mouse.

You need to trigger a relaxation response.

How the heck can I achieve that when I feel like I'm in the company of a lion that might pounce at any moment?

Let him make you that cup of tea. Drink it slowly. Try and string it out so you can give your body a chance to return to normal. Then, and only then, will you be fit to make a second dash for it.

'That's it,' said George encouragingly. 'One foot forward. Now the other. Good girl. Left. Right. Left again.'

I was now vibrating from head to toe and as feeble as a newborn. George half carried and half dragged me back inside. As we stumbled over the patio door's ledge, he reached for the chair at the dressing table. Pulling it out, he gave me a little prod.

'Sit,' he instructed.

I collapsed down on it in a heap.

'Now then,' he said chummily. 'In a minute I'll make you that tea. First, I must shut the patio door. Wherever I go there seems to be a nosy neighbour, and we don't want Mister Meddlesome asking any more questions.'

George closed the door and, to my dismay, not only locked it but pocketed the key. It jingled as it landed in his pocket. He caught my expression.

'Yes, there are two keys in my pocket. Both doors to this room are now fully secured.'

My stomach lurched with fear as I looked at him dully.

'You can't run away,' he said, wagging a finger playfully. 'Meanwhile, sit there quietly. You need to recover. In a little while we'll carry on where we left off, okay? However, if you wouldn't mind toning down the roughness. That testicle twist did rather make my eyes water. It's a good thing I'm a forgiving soul, darling. Many husbands would have been unimpressed with such aggression. No matter. I shall look forward to taming my little tiger and making her purr.'

I didn't answer and instead remained slumped on the chair. My body might have been motionless, but my brain was whirring.

'Where were we?' he chirped. 'Oh, yes. Tea. Let me grab some water.' Now that George was in control again, he was all smiles. 'Won't be a mo.'

He lifted the kettle from its base and made off to the bathroom. My eyes followed him as he momentarily disappeared. It was then that I spotted my key. It was by the door. I'd dropped it when George had grabbed my wrists. Thankfully, he hadn't noticed. Could I somehow grab it when he wasn't looking? Now was an ideal opportunity, what with him busy elsewhere.

Shuffling my bottom to the edge of the seat, I tried to stand up, but my legs refused to comply. I gave a low moan of despair.

'Don't fret,' George called. 'I'm coming back.'

He reappeared, the kettle in his hands. Resting it back on its base, he flicked the switch.

'These silly little kettles take so long to boil. Meanwhile, you'd probably benefit from some sugar. Let me check out the biscuit supply.'

He returned to the kitchenette, humming away to himself as he clattered about. Gingerly, I tested out my legs for a second time. This time they obliged.

Cautiously, quietly, I took a step forward. Then another.

'Oooh,' I heard George exclaim. 'Chocolate chip cookies *and* custard creams. Lovely.'

I edged past the kitchenette and was relieved to see George had his back to me. Silently, I stooped down and scooped up the key. George's humming turned into cheerful whistling, as he ripped apart the packet of chocolate chip cookies, plastic wrapping noisily crumpling under his fingers. Hardly daring to breathe, I pointed the key at the lock, steadying my hand. I needed to get it into its slot first time, without stabbing about, otherwise the noise would forewarn George, and the last thing I wanted was him turning round and seeing me poised for escape.

Taking a deep breath, I silently darted forward. The key slid into the slot, and I quickly twisted it sideways. My heart soared as the locking mechanism gave way, clicking loudly.

Alerted, George spun round just as I leant down on the handle. Adrenalin was once again whooshing round my body, and it put wings on my heels.

I was through the door in a jiffy, racing up those stairs to the sixth floor like an Olympic sprinter. Behind me I heard George bellow with rage. He gave chase but wasn't as nimble or fast as me.

I duly charged through the double doors to the roof terrace, startling a handful of couples who were sitting under the stars enjoying a quiet drink.

Glancing frantically about, I spotted Luca perched on one of the tall stools at the bar. As he spotted me, his face momentarily lit up, but changed to concern when he noted my distress and appearance – mussed -up hair… mud all over my legs and clothes.

'Sophie,' he said, leaping to his feet and grabbing hold of me.

The short burst of adrenalin I'd managed to summon up, instantly sputtered out. I collapsed against him, breathless, my

315

chest heaving.

'Whatever's happened?' he said urgently, just as George erupted onto the roof terrace.

The double doors flew back on their hinges startling hotel guests for a second time. One or two made chuntering noises. It hadn't been part of their peaceful evening plans to witness a wild-eyed woman hotfooting it across the roof terrace, closely followed by a furious man.

George took one look at Luca with his arms around me, and his face contorted with rage.

'I don't know who the hell you are, but get your hands off my wife.'

Chapter Fifty-Seven

For a moment, the two men simply stared at each other – one in surprise, the other in fury. Terrified, I darted behind Luca, using him as a shield.

'Who are you?' George growled.

Luca was unfazed by George's aggression.

'I'm the owner of this hotel.'

That rocked George. He immediately dropped the belligerence and made a stab at geniality.

'Ah, right. Good to know,' he said, realising that it might not do to upset the proprietor of the place he was booked to stay at. He stuck out a hand. 'I'm George Baker, Sophie's hubby.'

Luca looked at George's hand but didn't shake it.

'I don't think so,' he said quietly.

George's mouth fell open.

'I beg your pardon?' he spluttered, withdrawing his hand. 'I most certainly *am* Sophie's husband and have the marriage certificate to prove it. It's in my suitcase – not that it's any of your business.' He was getting narky again. 'Anyway, I don't have to explain myself to you, even if you *are* the owner of this crummy joint. Are you aware the lift isn't working? Utterly disgraceful. Now if you don't mind, I'd like to spend what's left of the evening with my wife.'

He attempted sidestepping Luca and grabbing my hand.

'Get away from me,' I hissed, jumping out the way.

Some of the hotel guests, annoyed at having their starry-night cocktails disturbed, had initially stood up to leave. However, upon catching the gist of the conversation between the proprietor, the irate man and the dishevelled woman, bottoms were once again settling back down on chairs. Everyone wanted to know what was going on, and several pairs of eyes were on stalks.

Aware of the audience, George changed tack.

'Sophie, darling. Stop acting as if you're afraid of me,' he wheedled. 'You're behaving like a right old silly billy. Let's go back to our room and get changed for dinner.'

'Mr Baker,' said Luca. 'I'm going to have to ask you to leave.'

'Leave?' George gave a bark of incredulous laughter. 'I don't think so. I'm on my honeymoon.'

'I know all about what happened. That's right' – Luca gave George a meaningful look – 'I'm talking about your farce of a wedding, and please don't attempt to contradict me. You married Sophie while secretly conducting an affair with your best man's wife. Then, not content with wrecking your bride's life, you attempted to leave her stranded in a strange country with no money or even a roof over her head. That is despicable behaviour.'

'How *dare* you speak to me like that,' George hissed, his face suffused with anger. 'I'll have you know I'm a respectable businessman.'

'I don't care if you're the King of England,' said Luca. 'You have no moral compass whatsoever. What sort of man plans a wedding with one woman while cheating with another? You're disgraceful.'

George's chin jutted.

'There are two sides to every story. Sophie ran out on me. I've come here to sort things out.'

I peered at George over Luca's shoulder.

'That's not happening. Not now. Not ever.'

'Sophie, please, don't do this to me. Okay, hands up' – George stuck his arms in the air – 'I made a huge mistake. Yes, I was a naughty boy. But I'm not the first man in the world to be distracted by a bit of skirt and I won't be the last. I told you before, we can get through this. We certainly don't need this interfering busybody' – he jabbed his forefinger at Luca – 'adding his tuppence worth. Darling' – George put his hands together, as if in prayer – 'can we *please* go back to our room?'

'No,' I said. My voice was low but firm.

'Right, I've had enough,' George snarled, completely losing his temper. 'I know what's going on here.' He glared at Luca. 'You've got the hots for my wife, haven't you? In fact, I suspect there's already something going on between the two of you.' His eyes flicked to me. 'That explains, Sophie, why you came scampering up here instead of running out to the street. You knew this chap was going to be here. You made a beeline for him. I suspect you both had a prearrangement to meet on this roof terrace. I'm right, aren't I? I can tell by your respective expressions. You,

Sophie, look like Miss Gormless with your mouth hanging open, and as for *you*' – George glowered at Luca – 'don't you *dare* preach to me about cheating on my wife when she's now cheating on *me* with *you*.'

'Is this true?' said a voice.

There was a stunned silence while the three of us tried to figure out who'd asked that question. Not George. Not Luca. And most certainly not me.

'Answer me,' demanded the voice.

George took a sideways step, and in so doing revealed a striking looking female. My brain scrambled to make sense of who she was. It came to me in the same moment that Luca said her name.

'Ariana. Whatever are you doing here?'

Chapter Fifty-Eight

'Why do you think I'm here?' Ariana's eyes flashed. Her English, whilst accented, was flawless. 'To give you another document to sign? To discuss inheritance tax? Or even to advise you about the possible sale of *Il Castello*?'

'Er… you tell me.'

'In the last few days, I've not been able to go anywhere – not even to my local supermarket – without people coming over and extending their condolences on you and I no longer being together.'

'Oh, come on, Ariana, you know fully well–'

'Yes.' She instantly cut him off. 'I'm aware of the small-town mentality of this place, and that we aren't an official couple. But I thought we might become one. We've been out and about together. You even took me to dinner.'

'Look, I'm sorry,' said Luca, holding up his hands. 'You *offered* to show me around, for which I was grateful, and I believed the dinner was nothing more than a solicitor talking with her client. If you thought otherwise, then I apologise. I don't know what else to say.' He let his hands fall back to his sides. 'I never led you on. Never gave you any encouragement other than being friendly which, it transpires, you and half the folks around here have badly misconstrued.'

'Evidently,' she conceded. Her beautiful eyes narrowed, and her expression darkened. 'However, it's hard to admit defeat to someone who' – she jerked her head at me – 'is quite ordinary by comparison.'

Well, really! Talk about a public putdown.

'Yes' – Ariana spat at me – 'I've heard everything about you. The Englishwoman whose husband went off with someone else, on their wedding day no less.'

'I didn't go off with another woman,' George protested.

'Not for the want of trying,' I chimed in.

'Actually, I'm not interested in your story,' said Ariana haughtily. 'I have my own heartache to deal with.' She arranged her features to match the inner drama queen she was intent on channelling. 'Never have I been left so broken or humiliated.'

Is this woman for real? asked the little voice in my head.

Apparently so.

'Meanwhile, Luca' – Ariana continued – 'I think it best that another solicitor handles your future legal matters.'

'That might be wise,' he conceded.

Ariana gave Luca one last lingering look. Her eyes were bright and shiny, but not one tear dared to wreck her immaculate makeup. She then spun on her heel with George staring after her. There was a strange look on his face, and one could almost see the little cogs whirring in his thought processes.

'Wait,' he called.

Ariana paused, then turned back to regard him.

'What?'

'Well, I, um, don't appear to be married anymore. I mean… I am, but not for much longer. Would you… care to go for a drink? Or have dinner with me – if you haven't already eaten?'

My mouth dropped open as I stared at George incredulously. Flipping heck. From raving loony in our hotel room, to Prince Charming with a total stranger. Quick worker, or what?

Ariana gave George a cool once over. He must have passed muster because her reply swiftly followed.

'That would be… most acceptable.'

'Excellent,' George smiled.

He briefly turned back to me.

'No hard feelings, eh, Sophie? After all, you've made it clear you don't want me, so…' he trailed off.

'Go for it,' I shrugged.

Personally, I couldn't believe my luck at this unexpected turn of events.

'I'll be gone tomorrow,' George assured. 'Perhaps in due course we can civilly sort things out. And, er, regarding the holiday money that was in the joint account. You keep it. Think of it as, um, compensation for everything that's happened.'

'Oh, that's *awfully* good of you,' I said, trying and failing to keep the sarcasm out of my voice. It was lost on George. His mind was already elsewhere.

Deeming it now safe to step out from behind Luca, I watched my husband-that-never-was walk off with Ariana to the accompaniment of booing from a couple of guests.

'Good riddance,' one shouted.

Privately, I was thinking the same, for there went two individuals who had behaviour patterns that conflicted with the social norm. I didn't know if there was a label for such people, nor did I care. As far as I was concerned, the pair of them were welcome to each other.

Chapter Fifty-Nine

Much later, I crawled into bed and briefly reflected.

It now seemed a lifetime ago since Luca had taken me in his arms by the marina, whirled me around under the stars and then kissed me. And it seemed like a century ago that I'd floated up the stairs to my room all the while deliciously anticipating a romantic rendezvous on the roof terrace with the very handsome *Signor Lamagna*. I'd been in no doubt that, eventually, Luca would have led me by the hand to his private quarters where I'd have ended up in his bed.

And right now, I *was* in Luca's bed. But alone.

My eyes shuttered down as I rehashed the remainder of the evening.

After Ariana and George had left, Luca had accompanied me back to my room. I'd quickly showered, changed into a clean outfit, then grabbed my night clothes and washbag.

We'd finally shared a drink together, but not upstairs overlooking Maiori's inky black skyline. Guests had still been lingering, no doubt wanting to gossip about what they'd witnessed between the handsome proprietor, the fiery Italian lady, the pale Englishwoman, and the irate man dressed from head to toe in grey.

Instead, we'd headed down the stairs to Luca's rooms.

We'd then sat, side by side on his sofa, drinking hot chocolates as we'd chatted.

'George didn't hurt you, did he?' Luca had asked.

'He... scared me a bit.'

I hadn't wanted to dwell on *what might have been.* Nor had I told Luca everything that had happened in Room 410. That said, he'd had his suspicions. After all, I'd burst onto the roof terrace seeking him out while covered in mud and out of breath.

I now gave an involuntary shudder. I'd seen a side to George Baker that had rocked the socks off me. Perhaps some women liked that trait in a man. The assertion. Some would call it *masterfulness.* I preferred to call it *control* – and in the most unpleasant of ways.

I snuggled further under Luca's bedcovers, hugely relieved that it was all over. George was currently out with Ariana, and I was safe.

Meanwhile, Luca had opted to sleep on the sofa.

'I'm not sharing a bed with you while your husband is around,' he'd gently said.

'But he's not my husband,' I'd protested. 'Only in name. You heard him. He's even spending the evening with another woman.'

'I know, but I don't feel comfortable knowing George is under the same roof as us. Let's press the pause button. Just for now. When he's checked out, I'll be the first to sigh with relief.'

'Closely followed by me,' I'd declared.

'Tomorrow is a new day. A new beginning. Agreed?'

'Agreed,' I'd smiled, feeling a slither of joy seeping back into my heart.

'I want to take you to Positano,' he'd murmured, stroking my hair. 'It's very romantic. And then, when we get back' – he'd given me such a blowtorch smile I'd squirmed with delight – 'we'll pick up from where we left off.'

'Dancing on the quay by the marina?'

'If you like,' he'd said, leaning forward and dropping a kiss on the end of my nose.

'I do like,' I'd nodded.

I now wiggled my toes under the duvet and sighed with contentment. After everything that had happened – the upset, the drama – thankfully all was well.

I was also now experiencing a strange sense of being in the right place, at the right time, and with the right person – and that my life was finally on the right track.

As I drifted off to sleep, I could have sworn a soundtrack began to gently play in the background of my mind. It was the same song I'd heard on the quayside when I'd danced with Luca. *Storia d'Amore.*

Behind my eyelids, a soft light filled the previously dark space. A hazy image began to form, and I strained to make it out. Three people came into view. I concentrated hard. Focussed on their faces. Suddenly my heart swelled with love. It was Mum, Dad and Carly. They were waving at me and giving me the thumbs up. Laughing, I waved frantically back just before the image faded.

And then I tumbled down, down, down. Down to that soothing place. Sweet sleep.

Chapter Sixty

I watched a seagull swoop down, land at my feet and then squawk shrilly. It was after a piece of my *Delizia al Limone* – Lemon Delight – a cake synonymous with the Amalfi Coast. The sponge was filled with lemon custard and was one of the Campania region's most popular desserts.

'Not a chance,' I told the bird.

It ruffled its feathers, gave a shriek of indignation, then strutted off to hassle someone else.

Luca and I were seated at a pavement café in Positano enjoying the late Wednesday afternoon sunshine as well as each other's company. For the moment, we were alternating between people-watching and chatting.

Earlier, Vittoria, the daytime receptionist, had confirmed that George had checked out. He'd returned to the hotel in last night's clothes, having stayed the night at Ariana's.

Indeed, when George had returned to the hotel, Ariana had been by his side. She'd gone up to Room 410 on the pretext of helping him pack. They'd left together half an hour later, with George loudly declaring that he would see her again very soon and couldn't wait to welcome her to the UK.

Evidently the pair of them weren't wasting a second in

moving on. Whether Ariana would stay with George for a holiday or eventually move in with him, I had no idea. All that mattered was that the pair of them would be leaving me and Luca alone.

'So, what do you think of Positano?' asked Luca, interrupting my thoughts.

'Stunning,' I said, licking lemon custard off my fingers. 'But hellishly busy.'

We'd arrived by water taxi hours ago.

As the boat had gone through its docking process and bobbed about on the waves, I'd once again marvelled at the stunning coastal scenery with its many houses painted in colours of pale pink, cream, lemon and tangerine, all seemingly stacked one on top of the other.

Luca had cautioned that the steps of the pedestrianised streets were challenging.

'If you thought the Lemon Walk was steep, then be prepared for scaling new heights in Positano.'

As we'd bounced over the boat's gangplank, we'd almost instantly been swallowed up by a heaving crowd of tourists.

There was an additional buzz in the air and, after Luca had eavesdropped on a conversation between two excited shopkeepers, it became apparent that this was due to some Hollywood celebrities being spotted in the area.

'The Amalfi Coast, and Positano in particular' – Luca had explained – 'are popular filming sites and attract a long list of celebrities. Last September, the locals went nuts after seeing Denzel Washington and Jeff Goldblum in town. Who knows' – he'd teased – 'at some point you might find yourself

329

sitting alongside Gwyneth Paltrow.'

Walking through Positano was like a stair-climber workout. The town was built on two steep hills, so every shop, café, bar, restaurant, and hotel were on sharp inclines overlooking *Marina Grande* – the harbour and ferry port.

Upon arrival, I'd hoped we'd do some sunbathing, but after seeing *Spiaggia Grande* heaving with shoulder-to-shoulder sunbathers and swimmers, we'd passed and opted to explore instead.

Hand in hand, we'd walked up hundreds and hundreds of steps, sometimes ducking inside one or two of the numerous shops. Embracing the interiors' inner coolness, we'd browsed clothing, perfume, sandals, ceramics and, of course, bottle upon bottle of the famous limoncello. Luca had insisted on buying me a large pink floppy sunhat, its brim prettily decorated with floral ribbon and silk flowers.

'A beautiful hat for my beautiful lady,' he'd declared.

'Compliments, compliments,' I'd answered, secretly delighted.

'Oh, yes, very flattering,' he'd said, dropping the hat on my head before giving me a cheeky wink. 'Especially as it matches the colour of your face.'

I'd made a playful swipe at him. What with the heat and the exertion of the climb, my complexion had made a beetroot look anaemic.

Eventually we'd found ourselves in a series of residential stepped streets. I'd privately wondered how old ladies managed to cope trying to get their shopping home. I'd had a sudden vision of myself clutching half a dozen weighty carrier bags, defeated after the first ninety-nine steps. Positano residents certainly had stamina.

We'd walked on, passing balconies full of flowering geraniums, rocks sprouting wild lilac blooms, front doors sporting all manner of ornate door knockers, houses edged with pots of cypress, olive, and lemon trees, then paused to share *acqua* with a friendly local who'd been sitting on the steps outside his house. Suitably refreshed, we'd wiped our brows and continued onward and upward.

Eventually, coming out on a main road, we'd stood on the dusty kerbside looking down on the nearly vertical town spread out below.

The church of *Santa Maria Assunta* had been plainly visible. Its colourful *majolica* tiled dome was one of the town's iconic symbols. The intricate pattern of yellow, green, and blue tiles had stood out against a forget-me-not blue sky and the Mediterranean Sea.

By this point, hat, or no hat, I was desperate for some proper shade. We'd bobbed under the low beam of a nearby restaurant whose window sign had promised air-conditioning and ice-cold wine. We'd then spent a couple of hours hungrily consuming a late lunch of pasta and seafood salad.

'The walk back will be much easier,' Luca had assured. 'Downhill all the way. We can stop at the bottom for coffee and dessert.' He'd looked a little furtive too. 'Also, there's something I want to talk to you about.'

'Okay,' I'd said, my curiosity piqued.

And now, here we were, sitting under a late sun which was making the sea sparkle like spilt glitter under spotlights. It was that magical time of day where the last light bathed everything in an almost ethereal golden glow.

Greedily, I ran my forefinger around the plate before me, licking up the last of the lemon custard.

'That was delicious.'

'You have some sugar around your mouth.'

I licked my lips.

'Gone?'

'Yes,' Luca grinned, but almost immediately the smile faded. Suddenly he seemed sombre.

'What's up?' I asked, leaning in.

He took my hand across the table.

'George has gone.'

'Thank God,' I said, trying not to shudder.

'And this Saturday, you'll be gone too.'

'That's three days away,' I said lightly, my tone belying a sudden pang of deep sadness.

I didn't want to think about leaving this place. Along with Bella the kitten, it had claimed a piece of my heart, not to mention the man sitting opposite me who had stolen an even bigger slice.

'I don't want you to go,' he said quietly.

'I don't want to go either, but I have to.'

'Why?'

'Why?' I repeated, not really understanding the question. 'Because… well, my home is in Little Waterlow. My work, too.'

'How do you feel' – Luca hesitated before taking a deep breath – 'about making your home here? With me?'

332

For a moment, I stared at him, open-mouthed.

'This isn't madness speaking,' he quickly added. 'Last night, I lay awake for hours, thinking it all through. You see, I have an idea.'

'W-What's the idea?' I stuttered.

'I've wrestled repeatedly with the decision of selling *Il Castello*. Whether to stay on the Amalfi Coast or go home to England. But' – he paused, struggling to find the right words – 'Maiori has crept into my very bones, so much so that I can't imagine not waking up by the sea under an Italian sun. I guess the place is in my DNA,' he shrugged. 'But the thing is, Sophie, I feel it with you, too. Whenever I have sat down to seriously think about making a long-term go of the hotel, in the back of my mind… somehow… I saw the project being in tandem with someone. A woman. And I don't mean Ariana,' he hastily added. 'Instead, a woman who was also my partner. When you first walked into the hotel foyer, greeting me in your terrible mispronounced Italian, you touched something deep within me. I don't know how to describe it. A feeling. Some sort of recognition. A *connection*.' He touched his heart. 'Right here. And that feeling won't go away. So – at the risk of you thinking this is lunacy talking – I wondered…'

'Yes?' I prompted, my voice little more than a whisper.

He dithered, unsure how to spit out what he was trying to say. Instead, I sensed him changing tack.

'I would like to stay in Maiori and continue revamping the hotel. Renovations would include a hair salon and spa. So' – he took another deep breath – 'how do you feel about setting up that side of business with me? I'm not asking you to invest. Well, not for the moment. But, maybe in time, you'd like to?'

I stared at Luca, my mouth still attractively hanging open, knowing that every word he'd said about a feeling... recognition... a *connection*... that it was all true. Because I'd felt it too. I still did. But to move here? To invest with someone who, while so familiar, was still someone I'd only recently met? It was a monumental decision. One that required a huge leap of faith.

For a moment, my thoughts tumbled over and over. Suddenly I was back on Brighton Pier, with Teddy quizzing me about a seaside fortune teller's prediction. Madam Rosa had categorically told me that George Baker was not the man for me. Instead, she'd talked about someone who lived where the sun was hot and had a passion for fine wine and good food. She'd even described him. This man had dark hair, eyes that twinkled with mischief, danced with merriment, and smouldered with love.

I looked at Luca. That description fitted him perfectly, and right now I couldn't doubt the love shining out of his eyes.

'This man is your future,' Madam Rosa had asserted. *'You will live and work side by side and be incredibly happy.'* Her certainty had been unwavering.

Omigod. Were her words simply a coincidence?

Hot on the heels of that thought came another memory. Last night's vivid dream with Mum, Dad, and Carly. They'd been waving at me, even giving me the thumbs up. Had that been a message from *the other side* or simply another coincidence?

Suddenly my mind detached, zoomed out of Positano, flew under the low sun, and landed in Little Waterlow. What did I have in this village to keep me here? Certainly, no family. I felt my heart momentarily squeeze. That said, there was my cherished bestie, Sue, and her kind hubby, Charlie. Then there was Teddy, of course. He'd been a hopeless husband but remained a dear friend. And then there was sweet Ruby who'd given me a job in her little salon. But employees always came and went. Ruby would find another stylist. And as for Sue, Charlie, and Teddy. Well, I would only be a short flight away. One could get around the world in a matter of hours. Friendships didn't have to end. Italy was only a hop, skip and a jump from Blighty.

What about Catkin Cottage? prompted my inner voice.

I could rent it out.

True. You could do a six-month letting while you trialled things with Luca.

That's a brilliant idea!

So, what are you going to tell him? The man in question is patiently sitting opposite, waiting for an answer. Don't keep the poor chap in suspense.

'Sophie?' Luca prompted. Dusk was settling, and Luca's face was now partly in shadow. 'I can't work out whether you're speechless with horror or dumbstruck with joy. Please put me out of my misery.'

His hands were still holding mine and I squeezed them. I'd only known this man for a handful of days but, somehow,

I'd known him for a lifetime too.

'The answer is' – I leant in closer, a smile on my lips – 'Yes. Or maybe I should say *si.*'

Luca's face lit up.

'Do you mean it?' he whispered, his eyes suddenly shiny.

'I do,' I answered.

At that moment a waiter came over, looking to see if our cups needed refills or whether we'd prefer an early evening spritzer.

'*Buona sera,*' he said.

'Bonner Sarah,' I replied.

Luca gave a guffaw of laughter.

'In which case, I guess it's time to brush up on your Italian pronunciation.'

THE END

A Letter from Debbie

The idea for this book came to me when Mr V and I spent a fortnight on the Amalfi Coast in Italy enjoying a second honeymoon and celebrating our twentieth wedding anniversary. The scenery was breathtakingly beautiful and the setting so romantic. We explored many more places beyond the ones that Sophie visited, but I didn't wax lyrical about all of them because, at the end of the day, this is a romance novel, not a tourist's guide!

Sophie's feline visitor, Bella, is based on the kitten that visited us several times way up on the fourth floor of our hotel. She had the tiniest squeaky miaow, and her pink nose complimented her black, white and marmalade colouring. I would have loved to have brought her home, but HRH Dolly would have had a nervous breakdown. She has never quite forgiven me for bringing a puppy back from Crete, never mind a kitty from Maiori. The Italians do look after their strays though and we would often see restaurant proprietors putting out platefuls of leftovers for the local moggies.

Il Castello is fictional but based loosely on the hotel we stayed at – and yes, the lift did work! The hotel really did have a balcony garden and a stunning roof terrace which was perfect for watching spectacular sunsets or sitting together quietly chatting under a canopy of stars.

In the part of Italy that Sophie explored, the language is *Neopolitan* (or *Napolitano*) and is a dialect common to the area. This explains why nobody understood me when I tried out my pidgin Italian! However, for the purposes of this book and to make my writing life easier, the characters within these pages speak traditional Italian.

Madam Rosa, Brighton Pier's amazing fortune teller, features in my novel *The Woman Who Knew Everything*. Despite her unexpectedly poking her nose into Sophie's life, it was nice to touch base with her again. If you want to know more about her, I've inserted the first three chapters of that book at the end of this one.

I started writing this novel in November 2022, happy that I had a plenty of time to finish before the deadline. Things went awry when Mr V twice suffered a prolapsed disc and his spine turned into the shape of an S. The first attempt to rectify it went well, but five weeks later he was back to square one. As I write this letter, he is recovering from surgery, walking about on crutches, but his back is far from straight. Fingers crossed he will be back to normal one day very soon.

Sophie's Summer Kiss is my eighteenth novel and the final in the *Four Seasons* series. It sees a return to the fictional village of Little Waterlow, a small Kent village not dissimilar to my own stomping ground.

I love to write books that provide escapism and make a reader occasionally giggle. You will also find some drama and sometimes that can be uncomfortable. Trying to once please a critical reader who said I only wrote *froth* and *fluff,* the next book saw me responding with a *take this* chapter which – yes! – horrified another reader who complained about having all her trigger buttons pressed. Can't win! So now I let my characters decide how the story is going to go. Best to buckle up, because sometimes there will be tense moments!

There are several people involved in getting a book "out there" and I want to thank them from the bottom of my heart.

First, the brilliant Rebecca Emin of *Gingersnap Books,* who knows exactly what to do with machine code and is a formatting genius.

Second, the fabulous Cathy Helms of *Avalon Graphics* for working her magic in transforming a rough sketch to a gorgeous book cover. Cathy always delivers exactly what I want and is a joy to work with.

Third, the amazing Rachel Gilbey of *Rachel's Random Resources,* blog tour organiser extraordinaire. Immense gratitude also goes to each of the fantastic bloggers who took the time to read and review *Sophie's Summer Kiss.* They are:

Eatwell 2015; Tizi's Book Review; C L Tustin – Author; Being Anne; Captured on Film; Pickled Thoughts and Pinot; School_librarian_loves_books; Books, Life and Everything; Inspiredbypmdd; Bookshelves and Teacups; Theloopyknot; Tealeavesandbookleaves; Autumnal_reading; Ginger Book Geek; Bookworm86; Splashes Into Books; Beauty Addict; calmstitchread; @nicraigwrites; htdk2002.reads; and last but not least *jen_loves_reading.*

Fourth, the lovely Jo Fleming for her sharp eyes when it comes to typos, missing words, and the like.

Finally, I want to thank you, my reader. Without you, there is no book. If you enjoyed reading *Sophie's Summer Kiss,* I'd be over the moon if you wrote a review – just a quick one liner – on Amazon. It makes such a difference helping new readers discover one of my books for the first time.

Love Debbie xx

Enjoyed *Sophie's Summer Kiss*?

Then you might also like *The Woman Who Knew Everything*.

Check out the first three chapters on the next page!

Chapter One

'Well, I don't know about your Christmas,' huffed Amber, thumping her handbag down on her desk, 'but mine was decidedly second-rate.' She shrugged off her coat and slung it over the back of her typing chair. With little enthusiasm, she leant forward and flicked on her dusty monitor. 'Please tell me that one of us had a marriage proposal before Big Ben bonged the midnight hour?' Amber raised her eyebrows at work colleagues Chrissie and Dee.

Chrissie, sitting at the desk opposite Amber's, shook her head. 'There was definitely no engagement ring in any of the Christmas crackers I pulled.'

Dee, sitting side-on to Amber and Chrissie, waved her ring-less fingers in the air. 'I'm still a single lady.'

'Never mind,' said Chrissie sympathetically. 'Perhaps the three of us will have Valentine proposals instead. The fourteenth of February is only six weeks away.'

'Girls,' said Amber, 'the three of us have been living with our men for ages. If they haven't proposed by now, maybe they never will.'

'Perhaps *we* should propose to *them*?' Chrissie suggested.

'That's a good idea,' said Dee. 'Is it a leap year?' For her, the idea of going down on one knee to her boyfriend seemed full of possibility. Although Dee could imagine Josh looking faintly horrified as he pointed out that weddings cost money. A *lot* of money. Dee had secretly been squirrelling away some of her wages every month for the last three years, in case Josh ever had a funny turn and suddenly wanted her to be Mrs Dee Coventry. Her savings wouldn't pay for anything lavish, but she'd happily settle for a second-hand gown off e-Bay, and say "I do" in the local registry office with only immediate family and close friends. Afterwards they could all go to the local pub's function room for a slap-up meal. A wedding didn't have to cost thousands of pounds. The important thing was *who* you married, not *how* you married.

'Well I'm not proposing,' said Amber grumpily. Her fingers tapped on the keyboard as she logged in. 'It's a man's job. I want Matthew whisking me off for a weekend somewhere staggeringly beautiful, preferably where it's warm and sunny.' A misty picture formed in her mind. There would be emerald-green fields carpeted with golden buttercups. Overhead a lemon sun would beam down as she and Matthew walked – naturally in slow motion – their hands linked as they laughed at some private joke. Then Matthew would pull her towards him, tenderly cup her face with his hands, all the while admiring the way golden sunlight haloed his girlfriend's fair hair. He would lower his head to her upturned cherry lips, and kiss her lovingly. Then, like the ultimate conjurer, Matthew would produce a Tiffany ring from thin air – ta da! In a sexy, husky voice he would declare his undying love, and beg Amber to be his lawfully wedded wife.

The picture faded and Amber grimaced. Tiffany rings might not be on the agenda if Matthew's Christmas present had been anything to go by. She'd been stunned for all the wrong reasons when he'd presented her with a tantalising little box. Her heart rate had tripled as she'd taken the proffered gift, checking Matthew's expression for clues. He'd been smiling. Good sign. With increasing excitement, she'd tugged off the ribbon and gift wrap. Her hands had trembled as, giddy with anticipation, she'd opened the box...to find a £9.99 pair of hoop earrings from Argos. She knew the price because she'd checked their website. After that Amber's Christmas had contained no more sparkle than a can of flat cola. Hell, she'd be thirty next birthday. Chrissie and Dee, both two years younger than herself, had the luxury of time on their side. If Matthew didn't hurry up and get on with it, she'd be creaking up the aisle on a walking stick.

Chrissie was inclined to agree with Amber when it came to proposals. At heart she was an old-fashioned girl and wanted an old-fashioned proposal. She and Andrew had been together for five-and-a-half years. In the beginning their relationship had been full of passion, laughter, and impulsive romantic gestures. Granted, things changed when you got down to the nuts and bolts of living together. She couldn't remember the last time they'd stared at each other with dewy eyes over the cornflakes, or when they'd last tumbled into bed and bonked like spring bunnies, but they loved each other. Didn't they? Although these days the dewy eyes seemed to have turned into scowling on Andrew's part, and the bunny rabbit bonking had become an infrequent coupling that was more perfunctory than passionate. On the rare occasion anything happened, it left Chrissie totally unsatisfied. She pushed those thoughts away. She didn't like to admit it to herself, never mind to Dee and Amber, but her relationship with Andrew was in the doldrums.

'So what's wrong with us, girls?' Amber demanded. 'Why haven't our men proposed?'

'I suspect,' said Dee, 'they're perfectly happy in their current comfort zones. Anyway, you know how that saying goes. "If it ain't broke, don't fix it." Look at Angelina Jolie and Brad Pitt. Lived together for eons, but were barely married for five minutes. Some wedding rings become a circle of doom.'

'Rubbish!' Amber scoffed.

'Talking of wedding rings,' said Dee conspiratorially, 'over the Christmas break I spotted a certain person at Bluewater shopping mall peering into the window of a wedding ring shop. She was on the arm of a much younger man.'

'Are you by any chance talking about Cougar Kate?' asked Chrissie.

'The very one and same,' said Dee, with a nod.

Cougar Kate, whose real name was Katherine Colgan, was the office siren at Hood, Mann & Derek Solicitors. Amber, Chrissie, and Dee had worked for the Gravesend law firm ever since leaving college with their secretarial qualifications. They'd seen staff come and go. They'd also witnessed Katherine Colgan's arrival after she'd sailed through the interview with the senior partner, Clive Derek. Nobody had been surprised at Katherine being a hit with the smarmy Clive. He was the office wolf. He was such a Lothario that if someone had draped a short skirt around his executive chair, he'd have waggled his eyebrows at its metal legs. Katherine Colgan had wowed Clive with her low-cut blouse, brightly lipsticked mouth, and enormous false eyelashes that she'd fluttered so quickly Amber had made a snide comment about tipping Katherine upside-down and using her to sweep the floor. Rumours were always circulating about Katherine. There were tales of her having had an affair with Clive Derek. The gossip was further fuelled by whispers that his wife had caught Katherine in a restaurant with Clive and made free with several glasses of wine. Katherine always defended herself insisting men misread the signals she gave off.

'What did the guy on her arm look like?' asked Amber curiously.

'Not sure,' said Dee. 'I only saw the back of him.'

'Then how do you know he was younger than her?' asked Chrissie.

Dee tilted her head in the manner of one considering. 'Well, for starters he wasn't bald. In fact, he had a lovely head of thick hair. It reminded me of your Matthew,' Dee said to Amber. 'And he was slim – no love handles like most middle-aged men. Oh, and he had a very pert bum,' she added.

'Perhaps,' said Chrissie, 'Katherine has finally found the man of her dreams.'

'Yeah,' said Amber cynically, 'but we all know that

where Cougar Kate is concerned, her boyfriend usually belongs to another woman.'

'Or,' added Dee, 'another woman's fiancé…or even another woman's husband.'

'As long as she keeps her cougar paws off my Matthew,' said Amber with a sniff, 'peace shall remain within the walls of this building.'

The three women briefly fell silent as they cast their minds back to the Christmas before last. Hood, Mann & Derek had announced there would be an office party and that members of staff were welcome to bring their other halves. Everybody had piled into the boardroom at half past five on the dot, devouring the buffet and hoovering up champagne. Then somebody had produced speakers and suddenly there was music. Everybody, partners included, had danced around the boardroom wearing paper crowns and singing off-key. It had descended into a massive piss-up with the young office clerk drunkenly jumping on the photocopier. He'd printed off two-hundred copies of his bare bum captioned with "World's Biggest Arsehole" before stapling them all over Clive Derek's office walls. And young Jessica, from Accounts, had grabbed nerdy junior partner Alan Mann by the tie and pulled him into the stationery cupboard, just as someone else was vomiting into Reception's feature potted plant. To top it all off, Katherine Colgan had undone another two buttons on her blouse and made a direct play for Amber's boyfriend. When Matthew had protested that he wasn't into "older women", Katherine had turned an unfetching shade of magenta and spat, 'I'm a cougar, *darling*,' thus coining her nickname.

Amber had been incensed and shoved the remains of a salmon quiche into Katherine's face whereupon Amber's boss, Steve Hood – who'd been the least drunk of them all – had flicked on the overhead fluorescent lights and called time.

'At least Katherine apologised to you the following morning,' said Chrissie.

'Damn right too,' Amber growled.

There had been no Christmas party this year on the grounds of cutbacks and a need to tighten financial belts. In reality, the partners had decided to boycott it. There had been a nasty episode on the morning after the party with an elderly female client. Mrs Fosberry had arrived early at Hood, Mann & Derek for an appointment with Clive Derek. She'd been directed to Clive's office to wait. Upon seeing the clerk's captioned backside plastered all over the walls, Mrs Fosberry had suffered a mild coronary. The paramedics had barely finished strapping the pensioner on a stretcher, when the junior partner's wife had turned up in a rage. Mrs Mann had cannoned into a paramedic, tripped over the stretcher, and landed on the gasping Mrs Fosberry. Hauling herself up, Mrs Mann had demanded to know who *sodding Jessica* was and why *sodding Jessica's* telephone number had been tucked into her *sodding husband's* jacket that she was taking to the dry cleaner. Fortunately, the client had lived and Alan Mann's marriage had survived. However, the partners had mutually agreed the rumpus hadn't been good publicity for the firm. There would be no more Christmas parties.

At that moment the door to the girls' shared office

opened and Cougar Kate walked in.

'Morning,' trilled Katherine. 'Happy New Year to you all! I trust everyone had a good Christmas?' She beamed at them one by one. 'Just thought I'd pop by while things are relatively quiet and invite you all to my birthday celebration this Saturday evening.'

Three sets of eyebrows shot up into three hairlines. Since when had Cougar Kate ever been Kate the Mate?

'Oh, er, I'm not sure if I'm already doing someth–' began Chrissie.

'Cancel it,' Katherine ordered. 'I won't hear any of you say no. Firstly, it's my fortieth. Secondly, instead of having a big bash, I'm doing something really alternative. I'm having a psychic evening!'

'A what?' asked Dee.

'You know... a fortune teller... a clairvoyant,' Katherine explained. '*Madam Rosa* will be reading auras, palms, and tarot cards in my very own front room. One-hundred-percent accuracy guaranteed.'

The girls exchanged looks before Amber answered for them all. 'Count us in. We want to know if our other halves will ever propose.'

'Don't we all, sweetie,' said Katherine with a big smile. She had large teeth that reminded Amber of Bruce the shark in *Finding Nemo*. Hungry. Predatory. 'Good, that's settled then. I'll ping you all an email with my home address. See you!' And with that she turned on her heel, shutting the door quietly after her.

'Did you hear that?' asked Dee. '*She* wants to know if

she's going to get proposed to as well. So that guy I saw on her arm outside the wedding ring shop must be her beau after all.'

'Bully for her,' said Amber sourly. 'On the plus side, if Cougar Kate is loved-up that means she'll leave our men alone.'

'Surely you don't believe all that clairvoyant nonsense.' Chrissie rolled her eyes.

'Who knows,' said Dee, wistfully thinking of her secret wedding savings. 'But I would certainly like to believe it. Roll on Saturday night.'

Chapter Two

Amber slotted her key into the front door of her terraced house. The place was in darkness. Matthew wasn't home. Again. He seemed to be coming in later and later. Not that it was *late* late, but at quarter-past six in the evening he used to beat Amber home by half an hour. Up until a few months ago she'd come home to a smiling boyfriend who'd already started cooking their dinner. They would eat together whilst snuggled up in front of the telly. Afterwards, Amber would make her contribution by clearing up the kitchen and doing some ironing. Then she would go upstairs and run a deep bubble bath which they'd share together. Matthew's long legs would stick out at right-angles to her shoulders. She'd always been given the luxury of lying back, because Matthew had insisted on taking the end with the taps.

Amber wondered how late Matthew would be tonight. Unlike her employers, who always closed from Christmas Eve right the way through to the third day of January, Matthew had returned to work the day after Boxing Day. Between then and New Year's Eve he'd arrived home at eight, half past eight, nine o'clock, half past nine, and then not at all. Amber hadn't told a soul that she'd spent the last night of the year on her own. She'd hugged Mr Tomkin, her cat, and sobbed into his ginger fur. Matthew's excuses were always the same. Work, work, work. Busy, busy, busy.

Like Amber, Matthew worked locally. His career in digital marketing had its moments of stress, as did all jobs. But Amber wasn't sure if she believed Matthew's recent excuses. There was the one about Matthew's boss demanding the team stay longer at the office to reach their end-of-year targets. Okay, that sounded plausible. But then there had been the rather far-fetched one about going for a few drinks with workmates on New Year's Eve, completely forgetting what day it was, accidentally getting blotto, and crashing on a mate's couch. Matthew's justification had been fluently delivered, and Amber had desperately wanted to believe it, even though she suspected Matthew was lying. On New Year's Eve, she'd rung his mobile more than thirty times. At first her calls had been hesitant and apologetic. But, as worry kicked in, her voicemails had become tearful and frantic.

Stifling a yawn, she walked into the kitchen and rummaged through the freezer. Thanks to the Christmas break and bank holidays, the first week of the New Year at Hood, Mann & Derek had been only three days. It had felt like three months. And now, on the cusp of the weekend, Amber couldn't wait to have a long luxurious sleep-in. Her fingers hovered over a couple of steak-and-kidney pies. Should she cook one or two? Matthew used to order a takeaway for them both on a Friday night. Recently he'd stopped doing that. Amber was instantly reminded of another reason Matthew had given for lateness. On the Friday before Christmas, he'd arrived home with his breath reeking of onion bhajis. He'd blamed his boss yet again for making him and the team work late. Matthew had explained away the smell of spices by saying a colleague had volunteered to get a take-out from the Star of India. The restaurant was right next to their offices. Matthew said he'd been grateful to his colleague because no-one had gone hungry whilst toiling away at their desk. Amber had made suitable noises about being glad Matthew wasn't famished, and how thoughtful Matthew's colleague was, and how awful his boss was starting to be. Matthew had arranged his features into one of weary acceptance and said, 'It will all be worth it in the long run. The next promotion is bound to be mine.'

Amber's thoughts fragmented as Mr Tomkin shot through the cat flap. He yowled a greeting, then began to weave around her ankles, head-butting her legs.

'Hello,' she cooed, stooping to stroke his soft head. 'At least one of the men in my life has turned up for some dinner.'

She removed two steak-and-kidney pies from the freezer. She'd cook both anyway. So what if one wasn't eaten? Matthew could always re-heat it tomorrow when she went out with Chrissie and Dee to Cougar Kate's psychic evening. Amber peered in the cupboard under the sink where Mr Tomkin's cat food was kept. She withdrew a sachet of rather stinky flaked fish.

'Someone's a lucky boy having a trout treat this evening,' she said to the purring cat, and set the dish down for him. Her mind wandered to another trout, and most definitely an old one. Cougar Kate. Amber couldn't stand her. From the moment Katherine Colgan had arrived at Hood, Mann & Derek, Amber's "people radar" had gone haywire. Amber was someone who could suss a person in five seconds flat, but she'd figured out Katherine Colgan in half a heartbeat. The woman had *devious* stamped all over her, from her heavily made-up face to her pumped-up silicon breasts. When Katherine Colgan had arrived for her interview with Clive Derek, Amber had been in Reception collecting a By Hand courier delivery. Amber had watched with interest as Clive had greeted Katherine, his eyes lighting up like Harrod's at Christmastime. Katherine had simpered a greeting and extended one hand. For one ridiculous moment Clive had looked like he was going to press Katherine's hand to his lips. The stupid idiot. Amber hadn't been remotely surprised at Katherine and Clive's rumoured fling, and Katherine had made no secret of the fact that she was looking for a hubby – even if he did belong to somebody else.

Amber turned the oven on and began chopping veg. Thankfully her own boss wasn't a letch. Her mind wandered to Steve Hood. He'd joined the firm a couple of years ago when Amber's old boss, Bernard Blake, had retired. Amber had heaved a sigh of relief when she'd been informed by Human Resources that her new boss would be Mr Stephen Hood. She'd been a bit twitchy about old Bernard going in case she'd been made redundant. Steve was everything dear old Bernard wasn't – thirty years younger, a whole foot taller, and extremely good-looking. Steve had opted to leave the rat-race of London and work closer to his home in the picturesque village of Culverstone Green. Within a year he'd been made a partner. Amber would not have passed a Jeremy Kyle lie-detector test if the presenter himself had stuck a microphone under her nose and asked whether she had a crush on Steve Hood. *All* the secretaries had a crush on Steve Hood. What was there not to like, especially as he was so eligible. Despite having now worked for Steve these last two years, she still didn't know much about him. She smiled as she remembered the last day of their first week working together.

'See you on Monday,' Amber had trilled, pulling on her coat.

'Sure. Have a nice weekend,' Steve had replied.

'Up to anything nice?'

'Yes, chilling out.'

'Doing what?'

'Absolutely nothing if I can help it.'

'Nice. But won't Mrs Hood expect you to mow the lawn and wash the cars?'

He'd grinned. 'No. There isn't a Mrs Hood, and I pay a man to mow the lawn, and I take my car to the car wash.'

Amber had secretly been thrilled to hear there was no Mrs Hood, although she didn't know why she'd felt that way. After all, she had her own boyfriend thank you very much, and one she was hoping to eventually marry. But she'd persisted in her nosiness with Steve Hood.

'So, doing anything nice with your girlfriend on Saturday night?'

'I have plans, but not with the girlfriend.'

Amber had pulled a face. 'Aw, that's not very nice. I

hope she's not annoyed that you're not spending time with her.'

'No,' he'd smiled at Amber's dogged questioning. 'The girlfriend definitely won't be put out because there is no girlfriend.'

'Oh, right,' Amber had said casually as she'd zipped up her coat. There had been something about Steve's tone that had been friendly but firmly polite in letting her know he wasn't answering any more questions. She'd deduced there and then that Steve Hood must be gay, which was probably just as well. Amber hadn't told anybody about how her heart had bounced about when Steve strode past her desk and said, 'Good morning, Amber,' in his deep sexy voice. She'd even been a little bit fanciful thinking that perhaps his accompanying smile had been just for her. It had certainly made her knees wobble when she'd gone off to the staff kitchen to make his morning coffee. She truly hadn't liked Steve playing havoc with her emotions. It had made her feel disloyal to Matthew. Since then, whenever she'd enquired on a Monday morning if Steve had had a nice weekend, she'd not been surprised to hear he'd had a great time cycling with a mate, or fishing *with a mate*, or hitting golf balls *with a mate*, or playing football *with a mate*. She'd heaved a sigh as she'd organised a Land Registry search, privately lamenting that it was always the good-looking guys who were gay. Two years later her heart still leapt with joy at the sight of Steve every morning, but knowing he was gay meant she no longer became flustered.

As she scraped carrots, the landline rang, bringing her

back to the present. She quickly wiped her hands before snatching up the phone.

'Hello?'

'It's me,' said Matthew.

'Hi.' Amber felt her tummy start to knot. Interesting. Since when had her boyfriend's lateness affected her so much that butterflies took off in her stomach for all the wrong reasons?

'Don't bother cooking for me. I have to work late.'

'Again?' Amber's shoulders sagged. She'd allowed herself to get carried away with the vegetable peeling. She'd never eat all this. 'Why?'

When Matthew spoke again he sounded impatient. 'Because I'm trying to further my career, Amber. Surely you realise that? I'm doing this for us. It would be helpful if you were supportive instead of sounding like a nag.'

Stunned, Amber opened her mouth to say something but then shut it again. The last thing she wanted was Matthew thinking she didn't support him. After all, if he achieved promotion he'd receive a salary increase. And hadn't he said he was "doing this for us"? A beam of hope flickered through her. If Matthew was promoted and received a salary increase, maybe he'd think about putting a ring on her finger – instead of two rings through her earlobes.

'Sorry,' Amber apologised. 'I didn't mean to sound annoyed, darling. I'm simply a little disappointed. I haven't spent a proper evening with you for, well, ages.'

'Sometimes these things can't be helped,' Matthew huffed. 'And before you ask, I'll be working tomorrow too.'

'But tomorrow is Saturday!'

'Yes, Amber, I do know what day comes after Friday, and there you go again. Whining.'

'N-no, I'm not,' said Amber quickly. 'I'm just surprised, sweetie.' Her voice was placating, and she hated herself for it. Shouldn't Matthew be the one placating her?

'There's a big account up for grabs. I want to make sure I'm the one who gets it. I probably won't be home until early evening. I know you like us to go out on a Saturday night, but I'll be too tired. Sorry.'

'That's fine,' said Amber, deciding to play it cool. 'I wouldn't have been able to go out with you anyway. I have my own arrangements.' Amber felt a smidgen of satisfaction that she was turning the tables for one night. This time it would be Matthew home alone with only Mr Tomkin for company.

'Oh?' Matthew sounded surprised. 'Where are you going?'

Amber felt a burst of happiness. *Matthew does care about what I'm up to after all!* 'I'm out with Chrissie and Dee. We're going to Cougar Kate's.'

From the other end of the phone came silence. When Matthew eventually spoke, he sounded puzzled. 'Who?'

'You must remember her! She was at the office party, last Christmas. Don't tell me you can't recall the woman. She launched herself at you.' When Matthew didn't speak, Amber prodded his memory. 'She had a trout pout, and plastic bosoms like a life-sized Barbie doll.' Amber couldn't help being derogatory where that woman was concerned. At the other end of the phone the silence continued. Clearly Matthew was having trouble recalling who Amber was sniping about. 'Her proper name is Katherine Col–'

'Yes, I remember now,' Matthew interrupted. 'What on earth are you doing spending time with her? I thought you couldn't stand her?'

'I can't,' Amber confessed. 'But she absolutely insisted we all attend her fortieth birthday celebration.'

'Fortieth?' Matthew made a harrumphing sound. 'Surely she means *fiftieth*.'

Amber grinned. 'I thought it was only women who had the monopoly on being bitchy!' This was more like it. The two of them were having a joke at Cougar Kate's expense.

'What exactly will you all be doing?' asked Matthew curiously.

'She's having a psychic evening. Some woman in a head-scarf and gypsy earrings is going to tell everyone their fortune. Cougar Kate has a secret lover. She made some comment about wanting to know if he was ever going to–' Amber ground to a halt. She didn't want to mention a marriage proposal. Otherwise, Matthew might put two and two together and realise that she, too, was hoping for a bit of information about whether or not her near future contained wedding bells. Getting your boyfriend to put a ring on your finger, especially a boyfriend like Matthew, required the softly-softly approach. 'Er, she wants to know if… her lover will leave his wife.'

Matthew snorted. 'What a load of tosh. You don't honestly believe all that twaddle, do you?'

'No, of course not,' said Amber hastily. Even if this Madam Rosa *did* tell Amber that Matthew would eventually whisk her down the aisle, the fact remained that Amber wouldn't really believe it until it had happened. She wasn't that gullible.

'Well have fun at your psychic evening tomorrow with... whatever–she's–called... Clapped Out Kate,' said Matthew, suddenly brisk. 'Meanwhile, I'll see you later.'

'Bye, darling,' said Amber. 'I love y–'

But she was talking to herself. Matthew had already rung off. Amber's buoyed–up emotions popped like a soap bubble. For a couple of minutes there she'd managed to kid herself that everything between them was okay.

Returning the handset to its cradle, she stared at the pile of veg on the chopping board. Since when had her relationship changed from love and fun to, well, indifference? She didn't know. These days Matthew was more like a brother, and an irritable one at that. It had happened so slowly she'd not even noticed. Never had she felt so miserable.

Filling the steamer with water, she tipped the vegetables into the top pan and put the lid on. Suddenly she was glad she was seeing this acclaimed psychic. Maybe, just maybe, Madam Rosa would be totally brilliant, read Amber's palm and say, 'Your boyfriend is a gem. He's hard–working and saving every penny for a secret wedding. One day soon you're going to get the surprise of your life. Hang in there!'

Amber didn't really believe in all that nonsense. However, she was so desperate for crumbs of information

360

about her relationship, she was prepared to give Madam Rosa the benefit of the doubt. Roll on tomorrow night.

Chapter Three

Chrissie slotted her key into the front door of the crumbling maisonette she shared with Andrew.

Their home was on a sprawling council estate on the outskirts of Gravesend. She was desperate to move. She'd love a house like Amber's – a dear little two-up-two-down in New Ash Green, complete with chocolate-box sized garden filled with flowering tubs. Amber's home was surrounded by woodland pathways and restful fields. By contrast, Chrissie's estate was bounded by a network of roads punctuated with industrial parks and chimneys that constantly belched smoke.

The estate, no matter what hour of the day or night, was never quiet. Many of its residents were unemployed. There was always somebody playing music at three in the morning, or hanging out on a street corner doing a dodgy deal, or having a domestic indoors, or screaming at their kids – like Fran on the other side of the maisonette's dividing wall. At least twice a week a police siren wailed through the roads that criss-crossed like scars on a convict's face. The Old Bill's flickering light would flash against Chrissie's bedroom curtains, like a blue spaceship coming in to land.

For Chrissie, the only advantage of living here was the

proximity of the bus stop. Monday to Friday the local transport service rumbled all the way into town dropping her outside the front door of Hood, Mann & Derek. Fortunately, the fares weren't too pricey. Which was just as well, because Andrew was always asking Chrissie to bail him out of financial trouble. He had a credit card that delivered a regular statement full of spiralling figures. He often couldn't meet the monthly minimum payment. Chrissie couldn't remember the last time Andrew had paid his share of the rent. His contribution to the grocery bill was getting smaller by the week. She couldn't understand what he did with his money. After all, he worked. He kept telling her that electricians didn't make very much, but she was sure they earnt a lot more than a secretary working for Gravesend solicitors. Sometimes Andrew did the odd private job but where the money went, she didn't know. Once she'd dared to ask, and Andrew had got very stroppy. He'd argued that he didn't ask how she spent her wages, so to quit nagging about how he spent his. She'd answered him back and said, 'It's quite obvious how I spend *my* wages – I pay for *your* share of things.' He'd punished her bluntness by ignoring her for an entire week. In the end Chrissie had been the one to deliver a grovelling apology to smooth things over.

Chrissie loved Amber and Dee like sisters. It went without saying they were both her best friends. However, she hadn't confided in them about how Andrew really was. Why? Because she was ashamed. Instead, she'd painted a picture of him being a hard-working guy, one who didn't take her out because he was always busy with private

363

weekend jobs to supplement their income. She'd also made out that they were saving up to get on the property ladder, which legitimately excused her from Amber and Dee's occasional trips to Bluewater shopping mall. Her besties thought nothing of blowing twenty quid on a lipstick they didn't need, but had to have because they liked the colour.

Chrissie spent her wages on essentials, never frivolity. Her wardrobe for work was a supermarket's clothing brand. Such clothes were more affordable than the garments hanging on the mannequins of Bluewater's brightly lit shops. To Chrissie, the enormous mall was a slice of heaven. She'd love nothing more than to join Amber and Dee as they went into shoe shop after shoe shop and deliberated whether to buy Ugg boots in tan or black. She couldn't imagine spending over a hundred pounds on footwear. Instead, Chrissie had bought some cheap imitations off e-Bay for ninety-nine pence.

As Chrissie entered the maisonette's narrow hallway, she heard the television blaring from the lounge. She stuck her head around the door. Andrew was sprawled in an armchair, a can of lager in one hand. On the floor, by his feet, were two empty tins.

'Hi,' she smiled.

'Hello,' he replied, before loudly belching. 'What's for dinner? I'm starving.'

Chrissie lived in hope that one day she'd walk in and find the table laid and a hot meal awaiting her. That was what Amber's boyfriend apparently did for her. Lucky Amber. How she'd love a boyfriend like Matthew. No wonder

Amber was desperate to wed him. He was so hard working. So caring. Chrissie wanted to get married simply because that was how she'd been brought up. Her parents had expounded the virtues of keeping her head down at school to bag a decent job. They'd also suggested it was through the workplace one met a like-minded person with similar values. Their lessons to Chrissie had been simple: study, date, become engaged, marry, have children, then bring your own children up to do exactly the same thing you'd done. But somehow the game plan with Andrew had gone wrong.

They'd met at college when he'd been studying to be a spark and she'd been on her secretarial course. Chrissie had instantly been attracted to the good-looking lad with the floppy fringe, and he'd made a beeline for her. So far, so good. They'd moved into the maisonette together not long after they'd both started work. Previously, Andrew's divorced aunt had lived in it, but she'd met and subsequently married a much older man with an enormous pension pot. She'd moved into her new husband's house but, rather than relinquish the maisonette, she'd opted to illegally sub-let the council property to Andrew and Chrissie at a discounted rate. The maisonette was meant to be a stop-gap home while they saved up for their own property. But somewhere along the way Andrew had settled into a routine of going to the pub for darts nights, or PlayStation games on a rota with other beer-swilling buddies.

Chrissie absolutely hated it when it was Andrew's turn to host a games evening. The lounge would be filled with burly men stabbing at consoles, carrying on like they were Darth

Vader taking over new universes. Invariably, on those nights, Chrissie would absent herself. She'd climb into bed with an old paperback that Dee had finished with, only to nod off, but then be awoken in the early hours by the stink of weed creeping through the gap under the bedroom door. Last time around she'd caused a bit of a rumpus. How dare Andrew let these men outstay their welcome *and* stink her home out with illegal substances!

Throwing back the thin duvet she'd marched, bug-eyed and sporting bed-hair, towards the lounge. The door had crashed back on its hinges startling everybody.

'That's IT!' she'd bellowed. 'Some of us have work in the morning. Get your feet off my chairs and shift your backsides out of my house, NOW. And take your funny fags with you – do you HEAR?'

Andrew had been appalled. He'd squinted at her through the fug, eyes glassy from dope. One of his mates had looked Chrissie up and down.

'Fuck me, Andy. Is this yer missus? I'd give 'er a right pasting for speaking to yer like that. It's fuckin' humiliating. What a cow.'

'GET OUT,' Chrissie had screamed. On the other side of the maisonette's wall, Fran's kids had woken up and started bawling. Seconds later Fran could be heard shrieking at them to shut up and get back to sleep.

After everyone had left, Andrew had been so disgusted he'd spat at her. Chrissie had been stunned. In the morning he'd grudgingly apologised but quietly seethed about her laying down the law in front of his mates. The ridiculous thing was, Chrissie had ended up feeling the guilty one. Just because she didn't do recreational drugs, did that make her a prude for not allowing Andrew and his mates to *relax* with a bit of wacky baccy? Had she really been bang out of order? Was she a harridan?

Occasionally, and it really was very occasionally, Chrissie would fantasise about being swept off her feet by some gorgeous hunk who didn't run up credit cards, didn't drink gallons of lager, didn't break wind to order, and gave her some attention. But another part of Chrissie pushed such thoughts away. She had no self-esteem or confidence. She didn't believe herself to be attractive, like Amber or Dee. Her long brown hair was never styled. She wore it every day in a ponytail that trailed the length of her back. She didn't have money to waste on hairdressers and highlights, and she rarely wore makeup.

'Any chance of egg and chips?' asked Andrew, jolting her back to the present. 'I'm off to the pub in half an hour with the boys and need something to mop up the booze.' He patted his stomach by way of explanation. 'Oh, and before I forget, the lads will be here tomorrow night. It's my turn to host, so no barging in and kicking off.'

'That's fine,' she said stiffly. 'I'll be out.'

Andrew's eyes widened with surprise. 'Oh? I was counting on you making us all chip butties.'

'Sorry,' she shrugged.

'Do you have to go?' asked Andrew irritably.

'Yes, it's a work thing,' said Chrissie, bending the truth. 'It would be bad form not to.'

'Right,' Andrew huffed. 'Well don't let me hold you up with the egg and chips.'

Chrissie shut the door. On her way to the kitchen, she hung her coat on one of the pegs in the hall. She was twenty-seven years old, but right now felt older than Cougar Kate, although nothing like as glamourous. Ha, and she was hoping some unknown clairvoyant would have her grinning with pleasure at news of Andrew proposing!

Chrissie sighed as she set about pulling the frying pan from the cupboard and shaking oven chips on to a baking tray. She couldn't leave Andrew unless she moved back home with her parents – and who wanted to go home to Mummy and Daddy at the age of twenty-seven?

This wasn't the life she wanted, but she didn't know how to extricate herself. Maybe Madam Rosa could give her a few pointers. Roll on tomorrow night.

Also by Debbie Viggiano

Wendy's Winter Gift
Sadie's Spring Surprise
Annie's Autumn Escape
Daisy's Dilemma
The Watchful Neighbour (debut psychological thriller)
Cappuccino and Chick-Chat (memoir)
Willow's Wedding Vows
Lucy's Last Straw
What Holly's Husband Did
Stockings and Cellulite
Lipstick and Lies
Flings and Arrows
The Perfect Marriage
Secrets
The Corner Shop of Whispers
The Woman Who Knew Everything
Mixed Emotions (short stories)
The Ex Factor (a family drama)
Lily's Pink Cloud ~ a child's fairytale
100 ~ the Author's experience of Chronic Myeloid Leukaemia

Printed in Great Britain
by Amazon